Someone to Remember

WILD WIDOWS SERIES, BOOK 5

MARIE FORCE

Someone to Remember
Wild Widows Series, Book 5
By: Marie Force

Published by HTJB, Inc.
Copyright 2025. HTJB, Inc.
Cover Design by Kristina Brinton
Print Layout: E-book Formatting Fairies
ISBN: 978-1966871231

HTJB, Inc.
PO Box 370
Portsmouth, RI 02871 USA
marie@marieforce.com

The Wild Widows Series

Book 1: Someone Like You *(Roni & Derek)*
Book 2: Someone to Hold *(Iris & Gage)*
Book 3: Someone to Love *(Wynter & Adrian)*
Book 4: Someone to Watch Over Me *(Lexi & Tom)*
Book 5: Someone to Remember *(All Cast)*
Book 6: Someone to Save *(2027)*

"But little by little,
as you left their voices behind,
the stars began to burn
through the sheets of clouds,
and there was a new voice
which you slowly
recognized as your own,
that kept you company
as you strode deeper and deeper
into the world,
determined to do
the only thing you could do
determined to save
the only life you could save."
—Mary Oliver

The Wild Widows Characters

UPDATED THROUGH
SOMEONE TO WATCH OVER ME

Adrian Parker – lost wife Sadie after she gave birth to their son Xavier, in a relationship with Wynter Hartley

Angela Radcliffe—lost husband Spencer to accidental fentanyl overdose. Mother of Jack, Ella and new baby, Joshua, sister to First Lady Sam Cappuano.

Aurora – husband convicted of rape

Brad Albright – DC Firefighter/paramedic, lost wife Mary Alice in same fentanyl poisoning ring as Spencer Radcliffe. Kids Daphne and Drake.

Brielle – lost husband Mark in a skiing accident. Had their son Charlie after Mark died

Carter – son of Iris's late husband Mike and Eleanor

Christy – husband, Wes, suffered an aortic dissection, mother of teenagers Shawn and Josie

Darren Tabor – Roni's friend and former colleague at the Star

Darryl – Iris's biological father

Derek Kavanaugh – wife Victoria was murdered, daughter Maeve

Dylan Connolly – Roni's son

Eleanor – woman with whom Mike had Carter

Gage Collier – lost wife Natasha and eight-year-old twin daughters, Ivy and Hazel, in a drunk driving accident

Gwen – Hallie's late wife who died by suicide.

Hallie – lost wife Gwen to suicide; seeing Robin, who has stage-four breast cancer

Iris Levington – husband Mike was killed in a plane crash, children are Tyler, Sophia, Laney

Jim – Lexi's late husband who died of ALS

Joy – lost husband Craig to natural causes

Justine – Roni's mother

Kinsley Davis – husband, Rory died from pancreatic cancer, kids are Christian and Maisy

Lexi Nelson – lost husband, Jim, to ALS after a four-year battle, lives with Tom Hammett, her high school crush

Luke Freeman—a doctor who lost wife to colon cancer a year before he joins the group. Has four children, the eldest is Beckham, who is friends with Iris's son, Tyler. Other kids are Nolan, Clarissa and Phoebe.

Mimi and Stan – Gage's MIL and FIL, Natasha's parents

Naomi – lost fiancé David to lymphoma

Nia – Adrian's sister, married to Mick, their kids are Chantelle and Malik

Patrick Connolly – Roni's husband killed by a stray bullet on 12th Street in the District

Robin – love interest of Hallie. Has two children, Elias and River.

Taylor Cummings-Lonergan – founded the group with Iris and Christy, has since moved on with second husband, Will Lonergan. Children are Eliza and Miles Cummings.

Tom Hammett – Lexi's love interest/roommate

Trey – love interest of Christy

Veronica/Roni Connolly – husband Patrick was killed by stray bullet, parents are Justine and Roy, sisters are Rebecca and Penelope

Victoria – Derek's deceased wife

Wynter Hartley – husband, Jaden Hartley, died of bone cancer. Wynter's new daughter is named Willow Jaden Hartley. In a relationship with Adrian Parker.

Xavier Smith Parker – Adrian's son with Sadie

Prologue

A year has passed since we last caught up with our Wild Widows—and it's been a busy year, indeed. While Iris and Gage planned a Thanksgiving weekend wedding, Roni and Derek moved into their new house and decided to push their wedding to next summer to give them more time to plan their big day and get settled in their new home. Wynter and Adrian eloped on April Fool's Day and had a party to celebrate with all their closest friends.

Angela's third child, born three weeks after Dylan Connolly, and who wasn't named in SOMEONE TO WATCH OVER ME, is introduced in this new book.

Lexi and Tom have been enjoying their relationship as well as his return to full health and have begun making some plans for the future. Many of the other Wild Widows have been making their own plans.

As always a reminder that the timeline of this series is way ahead of the First Family, which is why Angela and Roni are just now having their babies in that series. Bear with me on the timing. I have to move the Widows ahead at bigger leaps to ensure they're ready for their new beginnings.

Now that we're all caught up on the latest news, here's SOMEONE TO REMEMBER...

One

Taylor

From the second I got the call from Will's foreman telling me there was an accident on the job site and Will was taken by ambulance to Inova Fairfax Hospital, I'm locked in an unimaginable nightmare. My brain nearly stops functioning. The one thought that registers in the chaos is that if they're taking him to Inova, that means he's hurt badly, or they would've gone somewhere closer to where he was working.

I must've texted my neighbor to come stay with the kids, but I don't recall doing that. One minute, Kate wasn't there, and the next, she was. She summoned an Uber for me and told the driver to hurry, to get me to my husband at the Inova ER as quickly as possible.

Will was working an overnight shift supervising workers on a building that's way behind schedule, so they made the decision to go to twenty-four-hour shifts to catch up.

Thank God my kids are already asleep and won't know anything about this until the morning.

On the way to Inova, I think about the people I should notify. His parents and mine, siblings, friends. But I don't tell anyone yet because fear grips every part of me and has made it so I can't move or think or do anything other than pray. I'm sick to my stomach with dread, déjà vu and disbelief.

Will promised he'd never leave me or my kids. He's been our port in the storm as we learned to live without Greg, my first husband and my children's father, who died at twenty-nine from brain cancer seven years ago when I was just twenty-seven.

The driver gets me there quickly, but I'm so not ready to face whatever is waiting for me inside. When he pulls up to the emergency entrance, he turns toward the back seat. "I hope everything is okay."

"Thank you." It takes two tries to get the door open, and when I get out, I feel unsteady on my feet. For a second, I fear I might topple over onto my pregnant belly.

Until I see Will's smiling, handsome face, and he tells me not to worry about anything because he's fine and he'll take care of me and the kids the way he always has, nothing will be okay. I've come to rely on him, which is entirely his fault. He's made himself essential to me and my children, and the thought of even a day without him at the center of our lives is unfathomable. I rush toward the reception desk in the crowded emergency department.

"Be right with you."

It takes all the self-control I can find not to start shrieking for someone to tell me where my husband is.

After several tense minutes pass, I say, "Please... My husband was brought in by ambulance. William Lonergan. I need to know... to see him. Please."

"Taylor!"

I spin around to see Will's foreman and friend, Bryan, coming toward me. "Come with me. The doctor promised an update as soon as possible."

Bryan puts his arm around me and leads me to a room where two of Will's employees are waiting. Their pale, shocked expressions add to my anxiety.

"Wh-what happened?"

"He fell off scaffolding."

Bryan helps me into a chair when the legs under me would've collapsed.

"How far?"

"About fifty feet."

"Oh my God." I want to ask why he wasn't attached to safety gear, but I can't get the question past my fear.

"Taylor..."

I look up at him, terrified by the way he says my name. The single word is laced with agony.

"Sweetheart... I don't think he's going to make it. It's possible... Well, I think he broke his neck."

"No." I can't. *Please, God. No.*

I'm not sure what happened after that, but when I come to, I'm in a bed connected to monitors with an IV in my hand. The echo of the baby's heartbeat is a steady cadence.

I have no idea what's going on until I see Bryan pacing at the foot of my bed, his face wet with tears. And then I remember. Will. Fell fifty feet off scaffolding. Might've broken his neck. Is probably dead.

My Will. The man who stepped into my life—and my kids' lives—after we lost Greg and made everything better for us... Oh my God, the baby. Our little boy is due in a month.

"Bryan."

He stops pacing and turns to me. His devastated expression says everything I don't want to hear.

I dissolve into heartbroken sobs. "No."

Bryan comes to my bedside and takes my hand. "I'm so sorry, Taylor. They think he died on impact and didn't suffer."

I shake my head as tears spill down my cheeks. *This cannot be happening.* How will I ever tell my kids? They barely remember the man who fathered them, and they adore Will. He became their daddy one skinned knee and tea party at a time.

"Is there someone I can call for you?"

If I tell people, then it becomes real.

My beautiful Will is dead.

"I want to see him."

"I don't think that's a good idea."

"I need it. Please. Will you take me to him?"

"Let me see what I can do," he says reluctantly.

After he leaves the room, I stare at the dry-erase board that bears my name and my nurse's name, wondering how this nightmare can be happening again. How am I supposed to go on without the man who put me back together with his love and devotion to me and my kids?

He was so perfect from the beginning that I didn't agonize over whether I should be with him, the way most widows do with new relationships after a terrible loss. Falling in love with Will was the easiest, most natural thing to ever happen, and I didn't stop for one second to ask for anyone's permission to be happy. I left my widowhood behind, became a wife again and never looked back, except to honor Greg's life at every birthday, anniversary and sometimes just because I was thinking of him on a random Friday. I've never stopped thinking of him even as I built a happy new life with Will. Keeping Greg alive in the memories of our children has been one of my primary goals since we lost him.

"They said you can see him shortly," Bryan says when he returns.

"I need my friend Iris." She's the only one I want. She'll know what to do. "Do you have my phone?"

When he hands it to me, the first thing I see is a message from my neighbor Kate asking how Will is doing.

I'm also shocked to see it's now after midnight. What the hell? "Did I pass out?"

"Yeah, you were out of it for a long time. You scared us."

I'm so blinded by tears I can hardly see the screen as I find Iris's number and make the call that'll make it official.

I'm a widow.

Again.

Iris

A MIDNIGHT PHONE call is never a good thing. That's my first thought as I turn over in bed to grab my phone off the bedside table, hoping to quiet it before the ringing wakes Gage. I see the name TAYLOR on the screen and am immediately wide awake as I take the phone into the bathroom and close the door. I haven't spoken to my friend and cofounder of the Wild Widows in a few weeks, and she's never called this late.

"Hey."

"Iris."

"What's wrong?"

All I can hear are deep, wrenching sobs that fill me with anxiety over what she's going to tell me.

"Taylor, honey..."

"It's Will."

After being widowed for more than five years, she remarried two years ago and is expecting her first child with her second husband.

"What about him?"

"He... he was killed in an accident at work."

"Oh God, no."

"Iris..." A world of need is conveyed in the way she says my name.

"I'm coming."

"I... I'm at Inova. I passed out..."

"Are you okay? Is the baby?"

"I..."

"I'll be there in thirty minutes."

"I can't do this again. I just can't."

"I'm on my way. Do you want to stay on the phone?"

"I, um, I don't think so."

"I'll be right there, honey."

"Thank you."

Gage comes into the bathroom as I throw on clothes. "What's wrong?"

"Taylor's husband, Will, was killed in an accident at work."

I catch his expression as the news registers like a gut punch and worst-case scenario for a widow—hearing it can happen again.

"I'll come with you."

"You don't have to. You barely know her."

"But I know all too well what she's going through. Or I should say… I know what it's like to have it happen once. This…"

"I know. It's unbelievable, and their baby is due in a month."

"Good God."

"Hurry. I have to get to her."

My mom slept over last night so we could go out with our Wild Widows friends. Thankfully, I can leave the kids with her because I really want Gage with me. I text her to let her know we have to leave.

While he goes into our walk-in closet to get dressed, I brush my teeth and put my hair up with hands that refuse to follow basic commands because they're trembling so hard. Any time something like this happens to someone I know, it takes me right back to getting the phone call about my husband, Mike, being killed in a plane crash while I was at home with three little kids, including an infant.

I'm sure Gage feels the same sickening sense of déjà vu over the loss of his wife and eight-year-old twin daughters in a drunk-driving accident.

Tragedy of any kind resurrects feelings and memories we'd much rather forget than relive, but we put ourselves out there to support others in the same situation. That's the mission of the group Taylor and I cofounded with our friend Christy in the early days of our widowhoods.

Now Taylor has been widowed again.

It defies belief, and it's yet another reminder that we're never safe from catastrophe, even after walking through the fire to survive a monumental loss.

Gage's hands on my shoulders startle me even though I'm staring at the mirror and should've seen him coming. I can't focus through the haze of disbelief and unbearable grief for my sweet friend.

"Are you ready?"

"I... I don't know. This is just..."

"It's unbelievable and terribly unfair. She'll need us—and the rest of the group."

"Yes, she will." I place my hand over my aching gut. "I've never, for one second, considered that it could happen twice, even though, I mean... I know it can, it's just..."

"It's shocking and so very sad. And it's a reminder that we can't take anything for granted."

"I was just thinking the same thing. I couldn't go through that nightmare a second time."

"You could and you would. The same way you did the last time, because you have children and you wouldn't have a choice, but we don't need to worry about that now. We need to get to Taylor."

Thank goodness for him. I've had that thought so often since he moved in with us. He's an amazing source of support any time I need it, never more so than during my treatment for stage-zero breast cancer. This must be how he'd felt when I was first diagnosed, and he was forced to face the possibility that he could lose me, too.

I've gotten good at supporting young widows over the years, which is a skill I never imagined I'd have when I was still happily married to Mike. But in the years since I lost him so suddenly, I've learned a lot about grief and the unique challenges faced by younger widows who still have most of their lives ahead of them.

Topics such as dating and sex—and judgment from those who think it's too soon or whatever stupid thing they might say —as well as blending families and dealing with two sets of in-laws have become routine to me, but this... Being widowed a second time before the age of thirty-five... I have zero experience with that one and would've preferred to keep it that way.

When we're on the road to Inova in his Range Rover, Gage reaches over to take my hand.

"You're freezing."

"It's shock. My hands always get cold when something terrible happens."

"How do I not know that about you?"

"Thankfully, there hasn't been this kind of shock in a while." I glance over at his strong profile as he keeps his gaze pinned to the dark road. "How will I get her through this? I don't have the tools..."

"You do. You have everything you need."

"I don't know. This is next-level, Gage. And what will it do to everyone in the group to hear about this?"

"It'll be a kick in the teeth for everyone, but it's not like we didn't already know it was possible."

"Knowing it and having it actually happen to a friend are two very different things."

"You're right, but the process will be the same for her—and for us as her supporters—only this time, she's better equipped to handle it."

"No one should have to go through this twice."

"That's for sure."

"We're going to have to tell the others..." I absolutely dread the thought of sharing this with our widow friends.

"Not yet. Let's see Taylor and figure out what she needs first. We'll tell them later."

I'm relieved to take his advice, which is always spot-on. He's been at this longer than me and most of the others, and his insight is invaluable to us.

"Gage..."

"What, honey?"

"We need to get with Joy and make your adoption of the kids final so if anything ever happens to me..."

"It won't."

"If it does, I want them with you, and we need to make that official."

"Before the wedding?" We're getting married the Saturday after Thanksgiving, which is less than two weeks from now.

"Right freaking now. I don't want to leave anything to chance."

"I hope you know what it means to me that you'd want them with me."

"Of course I do. You're their Daddy Gage, and it's what they'd want, too."

"We'll get that done, but first we have to take care of Taylor."

We also have to take care of the other Wild Widows, who'll be rocked to the core by Taylor's tragedy.

We'll get them through it. Somehow.

$$Two$$

Taylor

While I wait for Iris to arrive, I stare up at the ceiling, blinded by tears, thinking about Will and reliving our story, from the day he came to give me an estimate on damage to my roof after a storm. Our connection was immediate. He emailed me the estimate along with a note that said, *Whether I get to fix your roof or not, maybe you'd have dinner with me?*

I sob as I recall receiving that message after telling Kate that the cutest guy came to give me an estimate on the roof. Kate said it was the first time she'd seen my old sparkle since Greg died.

After getting Will's note, I texted Kate to come for wine and news.

She was at my back door five minutes later. When I told her the cute roof guy asked me out, she screamed so loud, she scared my daughter, Eliza, who came rushing into the kitchen to find out what was wrong.

"It's okay, honey," I told Eliza. "Auntie Kate is screaming because she's happy."

"You guys are weird," she said with six-year-old disdain

before returning to the show she'd been watching in the family room.

"Tell me everything," Kate said. "Leave nothing out."

My whole body is convulsed with sobs.

A female doctor comes in to check on me. "Mrs. Lonergan, I'm Dr. Goodwin. I'm so very sorry for your loss."

"Th-thank you. The baby..."

"He's doing just fine. Your blood pressure is a little high, though, so I want to keep you overnight."

"I... I have to go home. My kids. I need to be with them."

"It's safer for you and the baby to be here right now. Do you have someone you can ask to stay with them?"

"Yeah. I'll call her."

I don't want to call Kate, who loves Will almost as much as I do, and tell her he's dead.

"I want to see my husband. They said I could..."

"Your friend Bryan said you have a friend coming to be with you. Do you want to wait?"

"Yes, Iris is coming. I need her." I look up at the kind young doctor. "What am I supposed to do? How can Will be dead? I lost my first husband..."

Her kind face softens with compassion. "Oh no. I'm so sorry."

"I can't go through this again," I say through sobs. "My kids... The baby... How will I do this?"

She takes my hand. "I can't possibly know what you're going through, but your baby needs you, and your older children do, too."

"I... I know... I just don't know how..."

"I'm here," Iris says as she rushes into the room.

The doctor steps aside to let her in.

She hugs me tightly as I sob. Despite the despair and overwhelming grief, I'm comforted by her presence. We hug for a long time before she pulls back to look at me, her face awash in tears. "What do you need?"

I appreciate that she knows the drill and doesn't start with platitudes such as "at least he didn't suffer," or any of the other stupid things people say when they've never been where we are.

"They're keeping me for observation because my blood pressure is high."

"Then you're in the right place for yourself and the baby."

"I was waiting for you before they take me to see him."

"I'll be right by your side for whatever you need."

"I have to tell people."

"I'll do that for you."

"I can't ask you to call his parents. I have to do that."

"Then I'll sit right here with you while you do."

"How do I tell them this? He's their pride and joy."

"You just say the words. It's all you can do."

I stare at my phone for a long time before I pick it up to make a call that'll forever change the lives of people I love. They've fully embraced me and my children and made us part of the Lonergan family. What'll happen now that we've lost our connection to them?

I'm sick to my stomach as I look for my mother-in-law's number. My thumb hovers over her name for a long moment until I press the button to make a call that'll devastate them.

Claire has been a wonderful friend to me and grandmother to my kids. My heart is shattered as she picks up the call, her voice hoarse from sleep.

"Taylor... Honey... Are you all right?"

"I... It's Will."

"What? What's wrong?"

"He had an acc-accident at work and..."

She screams so loudly that I have to hold the phone away from my ear.

"Please don't tell me..."

In the background, I hear my father-in-law, Frank, asking what the hell is happening.

"Will. Something happened to him at work."

"The thing on the news," Frank says. "Was that him?"

"I... I don't know about the news, but he fell from scaffolding. They... they said... he probably died on impact."

Claire's wails shatter me. Will was her favorite—according to his older sisters—and their favorite, too.

Frank takes the phone. "Where are you, honey?"

"Inova ER."

"We're coming."

The call ends abruptly. What else is there to say?

"They'll call his sisters, right?" Iris asks, looking as gutted as I feel.

"Yes."

That's when I notice Gage by the door. "Come in," I say to him. I've met him only a couple of times, but his presence is comforting because he, too, gets it. I still read his inspiring Instagram posts every day.

"I'm so sorry, Taylor."

"Thank you for coming." He's a widower, so I wouldn't have blamed him for sitting out my catastrophe. I appreciate that he came.

"We're here for the long haul," Gage says. "Whatever you need, whenever you need it."

His sweet words bring fresh tears to my eyes. Who could've imagined when I cofounded the Wild Widows with Iris and Christy that I'd need the group twice in one lifetime? Not me. That's for sure.

"I want to see Will."

"Let me go find out about that," Gage says.

"His foreman, Bryan, was here and asked about it earlier, but I haven't heard anything more."

"I'll be right back."

"It's good of Gage to be here," I tell Iris. "He barely knows me."

"But he knows what you're going through, and he wants to help. We both do."

"Other friends would've tried to talk me out of seeing Will. You guys know not to do that, which is what I need right now."

"You're in charge."

"I have to call my parents and ask them to stay with the kids." I make yet another excruciating call to my parents, who adored Will and were so thankful for the happiness he brought back to my life.

"What's wrong?" my mother asks.

"Will is dead."

"*What?*"

Her cry wakes my dad, who takes the phone from her. "What happened?"

I have to say it again, through tears and despair so deep, it's all I feel. "Will died in an accident at work."

"Oh God, Taylor. I don't know what to say, honey."

"Can you and Mom relieve Kate with the kids? She's been there for hours."

"Of course. What about you? And the baby?"

"My friends Iris and Gage are here with me. The baby is fine, but the doctor is keeping me for observation. My blood pressure is up, but I'm okay... Or, well, not at all okay, but you know..."

They've been through this with me before. The last time, however, we had plenty of warning that Greg's valiant battle was coming to an end. The shock of this loss will take months, if not years, to fully process.

"Tell Kate we're on our way," Dad says. "And, honey, we're so, so sorry." His voice catches on a sob. "We loved Will like a son."

"I know, Daddy. He loved you, too."

"What should we say to the kids when they wake up?"

"Tell them I'll be home soon." My kids are intuitive, wise beyond their years. They'll take one look at the grandparents they know as well as they know anyone and realize something terrible has happened.

"Okay, honey. Keep us posted on how you're doing. I wish there was something more we could do."

"Knowing you're with my babies is what I need right now."

"We love you. We're so sorry."

"I love you, too."

I no sooner end that call than the phone rings with a call from Kate.

"That's my neighbor. She's with the kids. I... I need to tell her..." I'm so drained after telling our parents that I can't imagine going through it all again, even for one of my best friends.

"Do you want me to do it?"

"Would you?"

"Of course." Iris takes the call. "Hi, Kate, this is Taylor's friend Iris. She... she asked me to tell you that Will..." Her eyes fill. "He died from his injuries."

I can hear Kate's wail despite the call not being on speaker.

"They're keeping her for observation since her blood pressure is elevated. Can you stay with her kids until her parents get there?" After a pause, she says, "Thank you, Kate." Another pause. "I will."

She hands me the phone. "She's heartbroken."

"She adored him from the start. She was the first to know he'd asked me out." Thinking about the beginning of our romance has me smiling until I remember it's over now, and then I'm sobbing again in Iris's arms. "How?" I ask her. "How will I ever do this again? And my kids... They love him so much."

"I wish I had the words you need right now, but there're simply none that would be adequate. This is grossly unfair."

"I don't know what to do. What do I do, Iris?"

"You take it one minute at a time, and you keep breathing. That's all you can do."

"My Will. My sweet, precious Will..."

I'm crying so hard, I can barely breathe. How can he be

gone? He was twirling me around the kitchen—slowly due to my late pregnancy—this afternoon before he left for work. Or was that yesterday afternoon now? I don't know… I've lost track of time and everything else in the last few horrific hours.

Gage returns with a nurse pushing a wheelchair. "We can take you to him, Taylor."

Iris and the nurse help me out of bed and into the chair.

I'm shocked by how weak and feeble I feel when I did a maternity exercise class yesterday morning with no problem. Shock has sucked the marrow from my bones and left my muscles quivering as if I've run a marathon.

I didn't experience those physical effects when Greg died because I had months to prepare for that loss. As much as I dreaded his death, I also welcomed it by the time it happened as it also ended his terrible suffering. There was a comfort in knowing he was free of the disease that took so much from him —and us. There's no such comfort in losing my perfectly healthy second husband.

The nurse disconnects me from the baby monitor and asks Iris to push the IV pole as we roll down a long hallway. Every health care worker we pass along the way looks at me with sympathy that makes me want to scream. I've already done this once. I want to tell them I don't want their goddamned sympathy. I want my husband.

I want my Will.

I'm weeping silently as we come to a stop outside a closed door. "Iris."

"I'm here, Tay. I'm right here."

I reach for her cold hand and hold on tight as we enter the room where the lights have been dimmed.

Will looks like he's sleeping on the bed. Someone covered him with a light blanket that I grasp as I stand for a closer look. His skin is already different, waxy, and his head is at an awkward angle, which I realize is from the broken neck. His gorgeous dark hair that gets curly when he needs a haircut is matted with blood from a cut on his forehead.

I drop my head to his chest and wail as the reality becomes impossible to deny now that I've seen him with my own eyes. The familiar scent of our laundry detergent clinging to his light blue denim shirt is like salt in an open wound.

Iris is there, holding me as I'm overcome with unbearable grief for myself, my kids and our unborn child who'll never know his father.

I can't do this without him. I simply can't.

I'm not sure how long we're there in that oddly lit room with the body of the man who was my whole life a few short hours ago and is now gone forever. I raise my head to look at his face, to kiss his cold lips that used to kiss me back with so much heat and desire. There's nothing now but despair as I run my fingers through his soft, dark hair, which is the one thing that feels the way it should.

"I love you so much. I always will."

Iris must've helped me back into the chair. I'm so undone I can barely function as she pushes me back to my hospital room. When I arrive, Will's parents are there, and their faces tell the story of complete devastation.

They bend down to hug me and ask where he is.

Gage takes over, offering to show them to their son.

I'm thankful for him because I simply cannot.

Iris and the nurse help me back into bed, and the nurse reconnects me to the monitor.

The echo of the baby's heartbeat is a reminder that I'll soon be a single parent to an infant and two other children who've already endured enough grief in their young lives. Even years after losing their dad, they still occasionally cry themselves to sleep. They lead happy, joyful lives but are always aware that someone important is missing. Now there'll be two people missing.

I've always known life isn't fair, but this is just too much.

"What can I do for you?" Iris asks.

"I don't know." I stare at the far wall, focusing on a black dot that gets my full attention. As long as I'm staring at that dot, I don't have to think about the monumental task that lies before me. I don't have to think about how I'll tell my kids this devastating news, or how I'll have a new baby on my own, without the daddy who couldn't wait to meet him. There'll never be a photo of Will with his son, a thought that sends me into new sobs right when I thought I'd run out of tears.

Iris crawls into bed with me and wraps her arms around me. She says nothing, which I appreciate. What is there to say that would help me right now? Not one damned thing, which she knows.

We're still wrapped up in each other when Will's parents return to my room, their expressions haunted and devastated. They look to me for something I don't have to give—an understanding of how such a thing could've happened to this man we love with all our hearts. But I have no answers.

If my love could've saved him, he would've lived forever.

Three

Iris

I've been through some rough shit in my life, but this is one of the most excruciating things I've ever experienced. My heart is shattered for Taylor, her children, Will's parents and everyone who loved him. I hold her through that long, awful night. I'm there every time she wakes with a start to remember once again that Will has died, and the life she carefully rebuilt for herself and her children has died with him.

Gage stays, too, sleeping fitfully in the recliner chair next to the bed, there for us if we need him.

It means so much to me that he stays when he certainly doesn't have to. I try to put myself in Taylor's position, and I simply can't let my mind go to a place where I've lost him, too.

When we were first widowed and coming to terms with our new realities, Taylor and I were introduced by mutual friends who thought we might take comfort in each other. They were right. She and I made a pact. We swore to each other that we'd survive our losses, and we'd embrace optimism and hope as we guided our fatherless children through an uncertain future. We vowed that we didn't need a man to make us whole, but that we'd embrace and welcome a new love if it came our way. Those were the central tenets upon which we founded the Wild Widows with Christy.

After Taylor married Will, she chose to move on from her active involvement in the Wild Widows, which I certainly understood. Dwelling in that place of deep grief, reaching out to others in need of what we had to offer and guiding them through their widow journeys takes courage and fortitude. Every time we encounter a new widow, we're forced to relive the worst day of our own lives as we help them navigate their loss.

At times, I think about stepping back from active involvement in the group, as does Gage. Then we consider the enormous amount of good we've done through the Wild Widows, not to mention the found family of fellow travelers who've become our closest friends, and we keep showing up for those who need us.

It's almost like a calling at this point, and Gage feels the same way.

But this... How do I encourage Taylor to retain optimism and hope after tragically losing *two* husbands? Where will she find the strength to go on, to rebuild yet another new life from the ashes of a life she loved with a man she adored? Of course, like so many of us, she'll have no choice but to go on for the sake of her soon-to-be three children.

And how will I support my other widow friends through the secondary trauma of realizing this terrible thing can happen again? So many of them have moved into new relationships with open and hopeful hearts that'll be broken by Taylor's unspeakable loss.

These are the thoughts that keep me awake for most of that long night, holding my sweet friend through the worst grief either of us has ever known.

When the sun comes peeking through the blinds, I'm no closer to answers to my most pressing questions.

A young female doctor comes by on rounds and notes that

Taylor's blood pressure has stabilized. She unhooks the fetal monitor and puts on gloves to remove the IV, jobs normally done by the nurses, but I appreciate that she does them herself to expedite things for Taylor.

"I'll sign the discharge paperwork for you, but make sure you follow up this week with your OB."

"She will," I reply for her.

"I'm very sorry for your loss."

"Thank you," I say.

The doctor places a business card on the tray next to Taylor's bed. "If there's anything I can do for you, don't hesitate to call. My cell number is on the back."

"That's very kind of you."

She nods and turns to leave the room.

I rub Taylor's arm. "Tay? She said you can go home. The kids will be looking for you."

"I don't want to go home."

What can I say to that? I wouldn't want to go home if I were her either. When she gets there, she'll confront the fact that the man she made that home with will never come walking through the door again. She'll have to tell her children that the daddy who helped to heal their broken hearts is gone forever, like their first dad.

It's unfathomable.

We lie there for a long time without moving. I'm not sure if she's asleep or awake until she suddenly gets up, moving slowly but steadily as she goes to the bathroom and shuts the door.

I turn toward Gage.

He reaches a hand out to me.

I curl my fingers around his and keep my gaze fixed on his, drawing strength from him the way I do so often these days.

When the bathroom door opens, I release his hand and sit up to figure out what Taylor needs.

"You guys should get home to your kids," she says in a dull and flat tone. Her eyes are red, raw and swollen.

She opens the closet door to find her clothes.

"We'll take you home," Gage says.

"You don't have to do that."

"We know," he says. "We don't mind."

Taylor returns to the bathroom to get dressed.

When she's done, Gage and I each take a turn in the bathroom before we walk her to the nurse's station to pick up her discharge paperwork.

They insist on giving her a ride to the exit.

Taylor takes a seat in the wheelchair and looks straight ahead, not seeing the sympathetic looks she receives from various staff members on the way to the main doors. By now, everyone has heard about the expectant mother who's been widowed for the second time.

My heart is heavy as I walk beside her while Gage goes to get the car.

I can't help but think of the first day after learning Mike was killed in the plane crash, and how surreal it was to have to deal with people and life things and hungry children as if my whole world hadn't imploded. That day, I had no idea how my widow journey would unfold. Hell, I hadn't even realized yet that my widowhood would be a "journey."

All I knew then was that my heart was shattered, my children were devastated, and I had no idea what I was supposed to do without the man I loved with all my heart. I needed him to show me the way through, only he wasn't there anymore, and I had to find my own way.

This time, Taylor knows what's ahead for her and her children. She must feel like she's standing at the base of Mount Everest, looking up at an impossible challenge, trying to once again find a way to the top.

When I offer her the front seat of Gage's Range Rover, she declines, opting for the back seat as I direct Gage to her home in Falls Church.

For the first time all day, I check my phone and see a text

from my mother, expressing heartbreak for Taylor and her kids. *Don't worry about a thing here. I can stay as long as you need me.*

My eyes fill with tears as I'm overcome with gratitude for her and my stepdad, who've held me up through all the good times and bad. They're always there for me and my kids—and now Gage, too—and I couldn't do life without them.

Thank you, I respond to her. *Not sure what Taylor needs today, but we're taking her home now. Will keep you posted.*

Give her our love.

I will.

At some point, I have to tell our Wild Widows about this, but I'll take care of that dreaded task later.

Speak of the devil... I receive a text from my friend Roni, who asks what Gage and I are up to today, as we often spend time together with our kids on the weekends.

I leave the text unanswered for now.

Roni and Derek, two of our Wild Widows, are due to be married in the spring. We've been looking forward to celebrating two people who've been to hell and back after losing their spouses, as they step boldly into their chapter two, creating a new family with the children they had with their late spouses.

Gage and I are getting married later this month.

Adrian and Wynter quietly tied the knot back in April and told us afterward when they hosted a party to celebrate.

Life is marching forward for the rest of us as Taylor's falls apart once again.

Gage reaches across the center console for my hand. His warmth makes me realize how cold I am.

Thinking of Taylor's sweet kids and the news she's bringing home to them makes me sick to my stomach. I turn to her and see that she's staring out the window. "Tay."

"Yeah?"

"How can we help when we get you home? What do you need?"

"I have to tell the kids."

"We'll be with you for that and anything else that has to be done."

"You should go home to your family. You guys don't need to go through this with me. You've already suffered enough."

"Unless you tell us to get lost, we're not going anywhere for as long as you need us."

"Don't put yourself through it, Iris. I appreciate you being with me overnight, but you don't need to walk this path with me again. You two are on your way to happily ever after, and that's what you should focus on."

"What would you do? If this had happened to me, what would you do?"

She has no answer for that.

"You'd come running, and you'd stay for as long as I needed you, regardless of how painful it was for you to relive it."

A sob erupts from her chest. "No one should have to do this twice."

"You're absolutely right, but no one should ever have to do it alone. We're here for you and the kids for the long haul."

"I want you to promise me..."

"Anything."

"If it's too much for you, go home. I'll understand better than anyone ever could. Promise me."

"I promise."

When Gage squeezes my hand, that small show of support is everything to me. I spoke for both of us, but I knew he'd understand. We don't agree on everything, but in our interactions with other young widows, we're usually in lockstep.

Several cars are parked outside Taylor's home.

"Oh God, my sister's here, too."

"Do you want me to ask her to give you some space?"

"That's okay. She wants to help."

"Remember how this goes, Tay. You say what, how, when, who... You're the boss."

She nods and takes a deep breath before she gets out of the car.

Her kids must've been watching for her, because they come bursting out of the house in a flurry of arms, legs, light blond hair and freckled faces.

They both look just like their father.

Before disaster struck, Taylor had joked that she hoped there'd be a smidge of her in the new baby.

Her parents stand in the doorway, looking like survivors of the apocalypse, which is how this must feel to them.

"Mommy, is the baby okay?" Eliza asks.

"We're both doing great," Taylor replies with forced enthusiasm.

Miles holds up a blue balloon animal. "Look what Grandpa made for me. It's an elephant. Can you tell?"

"I see it," Taylor said.

"Grandpa is *so* silly." Miles sees us there and smiles. "Are the kids here, too?"

"Not this time, buddy," I tell him, trying to hold back tears.

"Where's Daddy?" Eliza asks when she realizes Will isn't with us.

Taylor puts a hand on each of them, directing them toward the door. "Let's go inside to have a talk."

Eliza glances up at her, taking a closer look at her mother and not liking what she sees. "What's wrong?"

Her concern goes right over Miles's sweet little head as he charges on ahead of them into the house.

"Mommy," Eliza says.

"Did you say hi to Auntie Iris and Uncle Gage?" Taylor asks.

"Oh, sorry," Eliza says with a small smile. "Hi."

"Hi, honey." I hug the child I've known since she was a baby. We've celebrated every one of her birthdays together and had more playdates than I can count over the years. They've been less frequent since Taylor and Will got married and life marched on for both of us, but Eliza knows I'm one of her mom's special friends. Our kids adore one another and are always happy to get together.

Miles is friendly and sweet to Gage and me as he shows Gage his trucks and the race car Daddy got him for his birthday.

Knowing what's ahead for these precious kids, I'm gutted. Devastated. Wrecked.

I'd give anything to spare them from the pain that's coming.

Four

Taylor

This is the most excruciating thing I've ever had to do. My precious babies. They love Will so much, and he's the only daddy they've ever really known.

From the first time Will met them, he gave them one hundred percent of his time and attention every chance he got. Nothing mattered to him more than we did, and he made us feel that every day of the three beautiful years we spent with him.

"Mommy," Eliza says, "what's wrong?"

Hearing that, Miles stops what he's doing with his new race car to study me the way his father used to do when he sensed I was upset about something. Greg would stare me down until I spilled whatever was troubling me. Miles is similarly gifted in getting me to tell him things I'd rather keep to myself. I don't mind, though, because I love seeing Greg in him.

Miles comes over to sit on my right side.

Eliza is on my left.

My parents hover close by, their devastation obvious to me

but not the kids. How hard it must've been to hold it together for them until I got home.

Iris and Gage take seats across the room, giving me space but fortifying me with their presence.

I hug my babies close to me as tears slide down my cheeks. Our gorgeous wedding photo sits on a table, Will and I gazing at each other, each of us holding one of the kids, all of us smiling and happy and excited to start our new adventure.

We got only two years of marriage, three years together. Nowhere near enough.

"Mommy..." Eliza's little voice wavers as if she already knows what I'm going to say.

"Last night, there was an accident at Daddy's work."

Miles goes stiff in my arms, trying to break free.

I hold on tighter because he has to hear this, even if he doesn't want to.

"Daddy took a very bad fall off a high place, and he died."

Eliza's wail of agony will play on repeat in my mind forever.

"No," Miles says. "Daddy's fine. We're supposed to play catch this afternoon. He promised we would."

"I'm so, so sorry, sweetheart. There's nothing Daddy wanted more than to play catch with you today."

Miles begins to sob, and when he pulls away from me, I let him go because my dad is right there to pick him up and hold him while I focus on Eliza.

"I don't want Daddy to go to heaven." It breaks my heart that she's already fluent in the terms of grief and grieving at such a young age. "I need him here."

"I know, sweetheart. I do, too, and he wants to be here with us."

"Does this mean we won't have the baby now?" she asks.

Her little face is wet with tears as a new heartache sets in.

"No, not at all. We'll still have the baby, and we'll love him with all our hearts, and we'll talk about Daddy so the baby will know him, too."

"It's not fair," Eliza says as sobs rock her tiny body.

"It's not at all fair."

"Did it hurt?" she asks. "Daddy's accident?"

"I don't think so. They said he died right away."

My mother wipes her face with a tissue and then hands some to me. I wipe my face and Eliza's while keeping an eye on my dad and Miles. Thank God for them, I think for the millionth time since Greg was diagnosed.

My sister, Amanda, comes in from the backyard and stops short when she sees me talking to the kids.

Normally, she'd come charging in and take over, but for once, she holds back and gives us the space we need.

"What do we do, Mommy?" Eliza asks. "What should we do?"

I glance at Iris, who's also dealing with tears.

She gets up and comes over to sit on the floor in front of us. She reaches for Eliza's hand and kisses the back of it. "You're going to keep doing all the things you love—going to school and seeing your friends and playing softball and lacrosse. That's what Daddy would want you to do. He'd want you to do the things that make you happy with the people you love."

"Is he with my other daddy?"

"I'm sure they've found each other in heaven, and they're talking about how much they love you and Miles and your mommy."

Her chin quivers as she tries to contain her sadness. "You really think so?"

"I'm sure of it."

My phone is buzzing with texts and calls, so I punch in my code and hand it to Iris.

"I'll take care of responding to everyone for you."

"Thank you. I can't handle that right now."

"I know."

I remember being inundated after Greg died and not having

the bandwidth to reply to anyone, even our closest friends and family.

Amanda comes to sit with me, putting her arm around my shoulders. "I'm so, so sorry, Tay."

I lean my head on my big sister's shoulder as my parents snuggle the kids. "Thanks for coming." She stayed with me for a month after Greg died, many nights sleeping in my bed so I wouldn't be alone. I love her dearly, but sometimes she's overly opinionated about things that're none of her business, such as when I started dating Will and she thought it was too soon, even though it'd been five years. It took me a long time to forgive her for saying that out loud.

"Of course. What can I do?"

"I have to get with his parents about what they want for services."

"Do you want me to handle that?"

"That's okay. I'll do it."

Once, when I was very young, I got sucked into a riptide at the beach in Ocean City in Maryland when we were there for a family vacation. I can still vividly remember struggling against the current that was determined to sweep me out to sea, before a lifeguard saved me.

From the moment I woke up today, I've had that same sense of struggling against a current that's intent on sweeping me into the unknown once again. I wish the feeling wasn't familiar, but it's just like it was after Greg died. Only this time, it's colored by shock. Widows debate which is worse—seeing a spouse through a dreaded illness or losing them suddenly. I used to say the illness was worse, the prolonged suffering, the doctors' appointments in which there's never any good news...

But this is worse. A regular day in a regular life in which lightning strikes out of nowhere and takes the one person you need the most. It'll take me months, if not years, to wrap my head around the fact that Will is never coming home again.

He'll never come through the door bringing the scent of fresh air and hard work.

He'll never wrap his arms around me from behind when I'm at the sink or the stove and kiss my neck and tell me how much he missed me while he was gone.

He'll never cuddle me in bed or make sweet love to me or talk to our baby about all the things they'll do together.

He'll never wrestle with Miles or let Eliza paint his nails.

He'll never meet the baby he wanted so badly that I agreed to have one more just for him.

As if he knows I'm thinking of him, the baby checks in with a hearty kick to my ribs.

Will loved feeling the baby move inside me. He was endlessly fascinated with everything about his child and was counting down the days until the due date, which is now just over a month away. I'm absolutely devastated that he won't get to meet the little boy he wanted so much.

"I need a shower."

"Do you want help?" Amanda asks.

"That's okay. Stay with the kids, will you?"

"I'll be right here for as long as you need me."

I squeeze her arm and stand on legs that're unsteady beneath me.

"Where're you going, Mommy?" Eliza asks.

"To take a shower. I'll be right back. Auntie Amanda, Grandma and Grandpa are here if you need them."

"I want to come with you," Eliza says.

"Give Mommy a minute to shower," my mom says. "She'll be right back."

Eliza isn't happy with that, but she doesn't say anything else as I walk upstairs to the bedroom Will and I fully renovated together to make it ours after we decided to stay in the house Greg and I had bought because it was best for the kids. Our bedroom is painted in a shade of navy blue that I thought would be too dark, but Will insisted it would be awesome, and he was right, as usual.

Our bathroom wallpaper is a navy-and-white stripe over beadboard trim that Will installed himself. I run a hand over the glossy white paint on the trim and recall the weekend we spent working on the bathroom while my parents had the kids. He made everything fun, even tasks I usually hated, such as painting.

After he installed the tile I'd chosen, we made love right on the floor.

I drop to my knees on the navy area rug and sob as it becomes clear to me that I can't stay in this house that tragedy has now visited twice.

I'm going to have to move.

Iris

I'VE RESPONDED to the inquiries from Taylor's friends and extended family. Everyone is shocked for her and the kids and asking what they can do to help. I promise someone will get back to them when we have more information. One of her friends from the kids' school offers to start a meal train, and I tell her I'm sure that Taylor would appreciate it.

I hope that's the case. As long as her parents will be here to receive any drop-offs, that is. I don't want her having to interact with people until she's ready to.

"Do you think you should go home to see the kids?" I ask Gage.

"I was going to suggest that, if you're okay with it."

"I'm okay, and my mom is probably ready for a break. Will you tell them what happened?"

"You don't want me to wait for you?"

"What do you think we should do?" I love having someone to ask again, not to mention someone who always knows the right way to proceed. Gage is truly one of the wisest people I know, even if much of that wisdom is hard-won through terrible loss.

"I think it would be okay coming from me. They don't know Will that well, but they'll feel for Eliza and Miles."

"Yes, they will. Tell them they'll see the kids soon. Maybe they can make some cards for them or something."

"That's a good idea. I'll suggest that. What should we do about the Wild Widows?"

"I dread having to tell them this."

"I know. Me, too."

"But I can't let them hear it from someone else."

"Maybe you should call Christy and talk to her about the best way to handle it."

"That's a good idea. I'll do that."

He gets up and then bends to kiss me. "You'll call me if you need me?"

I take his hand. "Always."

We gaze at each other for a long moment as a million thoughts go through my mind about life and love and loss and the precarious nature of it all.

"Please be careful driving," I tell him, almost afraid to allow him out of my sight.

"I will."

"I love you."

"I love you, too."

I don't want to let him go, but the kids need one of us, and Taylor needs me. I release him reluctantly so he can go to my babies. They love their Daddy Gage so much and will be happy to see him.

After he leaves, I call Christy.

"Hey, I was going to call you today. You won't believe what happened."

"Christy."

"What? Iris, what's wrong?"

"Taylor's husband, Will, was killed in an accident."

She lets out a sound of agony that's all too familiar to me. "No."

"He fell from scaffolding at work last night."

"Oh my God, I saw something about that on the news. And she's about to have the baby..."

"It's horrible."

"Iris... How in the world can this happen to her again?"

"We've been asking that all night. It's unreal."

"What does she need? What do you need?"

"I have to tell the others, and I'm worried about that. All we talk about is hope and optimism. Hearing about this could destroy their faith in such things. I'm barely hanging on to my faith, even with Gage by my side all night."

"I feel sick for her."

"Me, too. What do I say to the others?"

"You tell them, just like you told me, and you remind them that Will had a freak accident, and despite how it seems, this is no time to give up on hope or optimism for the future."

"That sounds like bullshit."

"It did to me, too, as I was saying it, but it's what they need to hear."

"My faith is rocked. To the core."

"I'm sure, but, Iris... You're our true north, our fearless leader, our first call in good times and in bad... As hard as it is for you as the person who's known Taylor the longest, you have to be strong for the others. You have to show them you're not letting it knock the legs out from under you, even if it has."

She's right. "I'll do my best."

"You always do. And I'm sorry you're the one who bears these burdens. It's just the reality of it."

"I know."

"Do you want me to help you make the calls?"

"Do you have time for that?"

"I'll make time."

We divide the list by the people we're closest to. I end up with Roni and Derek, Wynter and Adrian and Lexi, while Christy takes Joy, Brielle, Hallie, Kinsley and Naomi.

"I suppose I should text Aurora, too." She became part of our group after her husband was charged with rape, but she hasn't been to a gathering in a while. "She knew Taylor well back in the day."

"Yeah, good idea. Let me know if you need anything after you make the calls."

"You do the same."

"Tell Taylor... Tell her I love her, and I'll be there for her."

"I will. It'll mean a lot to her."

"Goddamn it, Iris. Just God fucking damn it."

"Yeah, for sure."

We agree to talk later and end the call so we can notify the others of this tragic news. I'm dreading every one of those calls.

Christy

"WHO WAS THAT?" my partner, Trey, asks after I put down the phone. "And what's wrong?"

"That was Iris. Our Wild Widows friend Taylor, who founded the group with us, lost her second husband in an accident."

His handsome face goes flat with shock. "Oh my God. No way."

My hands are shaking, and I feel sick to my stomach.

He comes to me, puts his hands on my shoulders and looks me square in the eyes. "What do you need?"

"I... I don't know." For some strange reason, I want him to leave me alone, which is a first since I gave myself permission to fall in love with him. Normally, I can't get enough of him. We have a rare Saturday without my kids because they're at sleepovers. "We had plans... I just... I don't know."

"Don't worry about anything. I'll call to cancel the reservations. We can do it another time."

"I'm sorry."

"No need to apologize. I totally understand."

He can't possibly understand how this feels, but I love him for trying as he bends at the waist to hug me. I let him even as everything in me wants to scream at him not to touch me, to quit making himself so necessary to me now that I know how easily I could lose him, too.

"Christy…"

"Yes?" I'm stiff as a board and cold all over, as if Taylor's tragedy has happened to me or some such ridiculous thing.

"Look at me."

I force my muscles to move as I lift my chin to meet his intense gaze.

"You're scaring me. Are you okay?"

"I… I don't know." I'm shivering so hard, my teeth are chattering. This whole thing reminds me of that awful day when Wes came into the house clutching his chest with a bewildered expression on his face in the seconds before he dropped dead at my feet from an aortic dissection. As always, I recoil from those memories.

"Babe… Talk to me."

"I… It's got me triggered." I swallow hard against the huge lump in my throat. "I'll be okay."

"What can I do?"

It's been so long since I felt this way that I don't remember what it takes to get to the other side of it. After you survive something like that, you don't want to think about *how* you did it. You just want to be removed from ever experiencing that kind of trauma, shock and grief again. And now my sweet friend has been thrust into that nightmare again after already having lost her first husband. It's unfathomable.

I realize Trey is waiting for me to answer his question. "There's nothing to be done other than calling our mutual friends to give them the news. I'll want to see Taylor later, if she's up for it."

"Whatever you need, honey. I'm here."

"Thank you."

I can't tell him I want to curl up in a ball in bed, pull the covers over my head and tune out everything and everyone forever. That way, nothing can ever hurt me again the way it did to lose Wes so suddenly and traumatically. It's a blessing of sorts that my kids didn't know Will that well, having met him only a handful of times. Taylor's kids are quite a bit younger than mine, so we don't hang out with them very often. At least Will's death won't be another big loss for them.

But Taylor's kids... They loved Will so much, and he was so great with them. Those poor babies—and the new baby, too. My God, what a fucking tragedy any way you look at it.

My head feels too heavy to hold up as I'm swamped with exhaustion that reminds me of my early grief after losing Wes, when I'd suddenly hit a wall. That's another thing that hasn't happened in a very long time. Moving like a zombie, I get up and walk to the stairs.

I'm aware of Trey following me, but I'm detached from him, as if he's become a stranger in the last few minutes, or something equally dramatic. An hour ago, feeling like that toward him would've freaked me out. Now I can't be bothered to care about trivial things such as messing up my second chance at true love.

I hear Trey talking to someone, but I don't know who.

What does it matter?

What does anything matter?

Roni

MAEVE AND DYLAN are on the playroom floor in our new home in Alexandria, surrounded by toys. They're endlessly delighted with each other, and I'm thankful to her for all the attention she gives to him. At four, she's the most delightful little girl, and I'm so lucky to have a hand in raising her, and Dylan is running around at eighteen months. It's a big deal to take on someone else's child, but Derek and I are committed to each other—and each other's children—and it's a relief to finally be settled in a home we chose together.

We found a gorgeous old Craftsman-style house that was fully renovated by the previous owner with choices I would've made myself in every room. Derek and I are madly in love with our new place, and we've enjoyed hosting friends and family here.

I have to be honest, though. Leaving the home I created with my late husband, Patrick, was much harder than I expected it to be, even almost two years later. The transitions, from then to now, from first love to new love, from my home with him to my new home with Derek... Each of them is an important part of my widow journey, but the mixed emotions that come with each stage can be overwhelming at times.

Making space for a future with Derek while honoring my past with Patrick can be a tricky balancing act, especially since I was leaving such an important part of my story with Patrick. We loved our place in the District and spent most weekends looking for antiques and other treasures to decorate our home, much of which has now been sold or rehomed.

"Heartbreak on top of heartbreak" is how Derek described it as we shed possessions from our first marriages so we could move forward in our new lives together. Those months were full of brutal decisions and lots of tears as we chased the joy of our new happily ever after.

I kept a few things I can't bear to part with such as some of our most-listened-to records, his favorite baseball caps, his signed photo of Cal Ripken and some of the awards he won for his work and have given them special placement in the room I'm using as my home office. Derek has a similar collection of

Victoria's special things in his office. We've also put framed photos of Patrick in Dylan's room and Victoria in Maeve's.

Every day, we talk about both of them with the kids, trying to keep them present in their lives even as I become Maeve's mother more every day, while Derek is the only father Dylan will ever know. Life is so strange and painful and wonderful— often at the same time, which can make for a tilt-a-whirl existence at times.

Derek strolls into the room, shirtless, unshaven, hair standing on end, and my heart gives a happy lift at the sight of him. I love what he calls his weekend slob look, which is a huge departure from his polished weekday appearance as deputy chief of staff to President Cappuano. As one of Nick's top advisers, he works a lot of weekends, so I'm always thankful for the ones we get to spend together.

He plops down on the sofa next to me. "Good morning. Kiss me."

"You're bossy today," I say, smiling as I press my lips to his.

"Thanks for letting me sleep in. I can't remember the last time I did that."

"It's been a minute."

"Your turn tomorrow."

"I won't say no to that."

Maeve rolls onto her back. "Daddy, Dylan and I are having a staring contest, and he keeps winning."

"His eyes are younger than yours. That's why you always beat me."

"So he'll *always* win?"

"Possibly, but you'll be better than him at other things, and he'll be your best buddy."

"He already is." Maeve turns back to Dylan, pushing his toys into his reach. She's such a helper, and we love to say we couldn't handle Dylan without her.

I put my hand on my chest. "My heart."

Derek smiles a lot these days, a vast difference from when I first met him. Then he was overwhelmed by the responsibility of caring for Maeve as a single dad while holding down a huge job and managing the lingering grief of losing his wife to murder. After she died, he learned that his marriage had started as a scheme to get a plant close to then-President Nelson's team.

Thank God for the letter Victoria left for him, professing her love and devotion, despite how things had begun. She was murdered because she refused to cooperate with the men who forced her to deceive him. Her murderers, including former presidential candidate Arnie Patterson and his sons, Christian and Colton, will finally stand trial in the new year. I'm dreading that and hoping it doesn't cause a huge setback for Derek.

I'll be right there with him through it all as he fights for justice for his late wife, but I hate that he has to reopen that wound once again. Eventually, I'll do the same when the man who accidentally shot Patrick goes to trial. Like Derek, I've attended every pretrial hearing and will continue to show up for as long as it takes to make sure the man who took my precious husband from me pays for his crime.

As hard as it was, I've forgiven him, though. His life was also destroyed by the events of that day. A while ago, he wrote me a letter expressing his profound sorrow over Patrick's senseless death, a gesture I truly appreciated. He's been held without bail and is separated from his girlfriend and young children while he awaits trial. I don't want to feel for him, but I do. One moment of madness ruined a lot of lives.

Derek is down on the floor with the kids, and I'm filled with contentment in this new family we've built for ourselves out of the ashes of our former lives. I was "lucky." I found my chapter two soon after Patrick died, not that I was looking for it. But there he was at my favorite coffee shop—and then at my workplace after I started as the first lady's communications director. He understood what I was going through in a way no one else I knew ever could've. In many ways, his friendship—

and that of our Wild Widows friends—helped me to survive losing Patrick.

My phone rings with a call from Iris, which has me smiling as I answer. She's one of the best things to come out of my widowhood. I love her like a sister. "Hey, how's it going over there?"

"I've had better days."

The way she says that sends a shaft of fear through me. "What's wrong?"

"Taylor lost her husband, Will, in an accident at work last night."

"No." I've met Taylor and Will twice at Iris's home, and I'm immediately heartbroken for them and their children. Oh God, she's due soon with the baby...

Derek looks up at me, his brows furrowed, tuned in to unfolding disaster.

"Wh-what does she need?"

"I don't know yet."

"If there's anything we can do..."

"I'll keep you posted."

"What do you need?"

"Could you take my kids for the night? My parents have a wedding tonight for their close friends, and I—"

"Of course we can take them. Do you want me to come get them?"

"I'll drop them on the way back to Taylor's, if that's okay."

"We'll be here all day."

"Thanks, Roni. I really appreciate it."

"I want you to tell me what you need because I know you'll go all out to support her. Let me take care of you."

"Thanks. That means a lot to me."

"Love you."

"Love you, too. I'll text when we're on the way."

"Sounds good."

I press the red button to end the call.

"What happened?" Derek asks, his expression guarded.

"Taylor's husband, Will, was killed in an accident at work last night."

"Oh no. The thing we saw on the news last night... That was him."

We saw coverage of an unnamed construction company owner falling more than fifty feet to his death.

"Isn't she having a baby soon?"

"She's due next month."

"My God."

Maeve tugs at Derek's arm. "Daddy, keep playing."

"In a minute, pumpkin."

When she goes back to her toys, Derek reaches up for my hand.

This news has landed like a punch to the gut. Even though I don't know Taylor very well, I sure as hell understand what it's like to suddenly lose a husband. *Widowed a second time.* Most of us in the group live under the assumption that we've had our great heartbreak, paid our debt to the Grim Reaper and can relax going forward, confident in the universe's unspoken assurances that we're safe from here on out.

This news is proof that it's simply not true. None of us are immune from anything, especially tragedy.

"Roni."

I realize Derek has been talking to me. "I'm sorry. What did you say?"

"Are you all right? You kind of checked out on me for a second there."

"I can't believe this. Like, how is it possible?"

He moves from the floor to the sofa and puts his arms around me.

I breathe in the scent that's become synonymous with home and family and love and safety... The idea that he, too, could be ripped out of my life... He works for the president, for God's sake... A random shot could take him out any time.

"*Roni.*"

I'm so deep in the rabbit hole of doom that it takes a shake from Derek to rouse me out of the spiral.

And then I'm crying in deep, gut-wrenching sobs that scare the kids.

Derek retrieves Dylan, and Maeve climbs into my lab, wrapping her pudgy arms around my neck and whispering to me the way I do to her when she's upset.

"It's okay, Mommy," she whispers. "Everything will be okay."

She's only recently started calling me that, and it tugs at my heart every time she does. I cling to her and the assurances I need so badly right now. "Thank you, baby. I'm okay."

It's a huge shock to learn that this new life I've carefully built for myself could easily become another house of cards.

Dylan is crying, so I exchange children with Derek, my partner in all things in this new life, and cuddle my son. Tears roll silently down my face as I gaze down at him, my late husband's twin.

It's all so fucking unfair.

I want to scream on Taylor's behalf. How in the world could this have happened? That she has to undertake *another* journey as a widow—and with *three* children this time? She was so happy with Will. I saw that for myself, and it gave me hope when I was first understanding that my friendship with Derek could turn into something more, something like what Taylor had with Will.

Her kids adored him, too. Those poor babies, losing two daddies in one childhood, and the baby who'll never know his father.

Dylan falls asleep in my arms.

Derek takes him from me and puts him down for his nap and gets Maeve settled for "quiet time" in her room. That often leads to a nap, but we can't count on that anymore.

Then he comes back to help me up.

I let him lead the way to our room, where he settles me in our bed and then crawls in next to me, wrapping his arms around me.

"Whatever you're thinking, stop it. Just stop. I'm fine, you're fine, the kids are fine, and we're going to stay that way."

"What she must be going through…"

"We'll be there for her. Every step of the way."

I nod because that's all I'm capable of right now. I ache for Taylor, knowing all too well what's ahead in the days, weeks, months and years to come.

Five

Iris

At home, I go through the motions of packing up the kids for a night with Aunt Roni, Uncle Derek and the kids, whom they love. I hated to ask them so last minute, but I knew the kids would be excited about going there, and I want them to be happy so I can focus on whatever Taylor needs.

I'm in Sophia and Laney's room, trying to pack for them while my mind races with a million other thoughts. Having to tell our friends this news is killing me, but I can't let them hear about it from others. Will's accident has been all over the news, and it wouldn't take much to draw a line from that story to Taylor.

Wynter returns my call as I'm zipping the girls' bag shut. She's laughing when I take the call. "Xavier just said fuck, and Adrian is *losing* it."

Under normal circumstances, I'd be laughing right along with her. She's one of our biggest success stories among the Wild Widows. But right now, I'm barely holding it together.

"What's wrong, Iris?"

"I'm afraid I have some upsetting news about a widow

friend. Do you remember meeting Taylor and Will at my cookout last summer?"

"Of course. She's having another baby soon, right?"

"Yes, she is." God, this sucks. It took forever for Wynter to buy in to the hope and optimism we sell and to believe she could rebuild her life after losing her young husband, Jaden, to cancer. Now she's happily married to Adrian, his son, Xavier, and her and Jaden's daughter, Willow.

"Is the baby okay?"

"Yeah, all is well there, but, honey... Will was killed in an accident at work last night."

"*What?*" The word comes out as one long exhale. "Is she... Her kids... *Fuck.*"

"Yeah, it's a nightmare. I didn't want you to hear it on the news."

"A guy Adrian knows played basketball with him. He said his friend was killed on the job and had a baby on the way. I didn't connect him to Taylor... God, Iris."

"I know."

"What should we do?"

"She'll need us when she's ready."

"She won't want us and our toxic positivity."

"I think she will eventually."

"I don't know... What reason would she have to believe in our bullshit anymore? Why would any of us believe in it if something like this can happen?"

"As Gage said, we have more of a chance of being struck by lightning or winning Powerball than being widowed twice in a lifetime."

"I don't know... This is like the last fucking thing I needed to hear. Right when I'm starting to have some faith in the future again."

"I know, honey. I'm sorry to have to tell you this news. I wanted you to hear it from me, and I want you to hear this, too... When Taylor and I talk about the Wild Widows, which we do once in a while, even though she isn't active anymore, we always say you're our proudest success story."

"What? *Me?* Why me? She barely knows me!"

"Oh, Wynter," I say on a sigh. "I wish I had video of who you were when you first joined us so I could show you how far you've come. You were so angry and bitter and entertaining suicidal ideation and generally convinced your life was over because Jaden died."

She has nothing to say to that, so I continue. "And now… you've found the courage to have Willow and to love Adrian and Xavier and to build a whole new life for yourself."

"For all the good it'll do me if they can end up dead, too."

"Wynter… Come on. Don't think that way. We have to hold on to hope, even at times like this when it might seem pointless. Please don't let this send you spiraling back to where you were when you've come so far from that starting point."

"I'll try not to, but it won't be easy. I already hold my breath any time Adrian takes the kids somewhere without me."

"I understand that, believe me. Gage has said the same thing to me about when the kids and I are out without him and how worried he is, even though he knows we're fine."

"How are we supposed to live like this, Iris? I mean, seriously… *How?*"

"One minute at a time, my friend. We hope for the best and try not to constantly anticipate the worst. That's all we can do, because so much of it is out of our hands."

"That's the part I can't handle."

"Yes, you can. You're doing a beautiful job of handling it, and we're so very proud of you."

When she sniffles, I realize she's crying. "None of this would be possible without you and the group you founded with Taylor and Christy. You guys literally saved my life. Please tell me what I can do to help her."

"I'll let you know."

"Please do. Adrian will want to help, too."

"As we all know, she's got a long road ahead of her and will need all the help she can get for quite some time. There'll be lots of chances to help. I know she'll appreciate your kindness."

"Tell her... Tell her we love her, even though I barely know her. That doesn't matter. I love her, and I'll be there for her. So will Adrian."

"I'll pass that on. It'll mean a lot to her. I'll let you guys know about this week's meeting and if anything changes."

"Hey... Iris... Are you okay in all this? You step up for everyone when shit goes sideways. Sometimes I worry about the toll that takes on you."

The Wynter I first knew never would've asked that question, which is just another reason I'm so proud of her. "I'm okay, honey. Gut-punched like everyone else but doing whatever I can for Taylor and her kids, which is the only thing that matters right now."

"You matter tremendously to all of us. Take care of you while you're taking care of everyone else, okay?"

"I will. I promise. Talk soon. Love you."

"Love you, too."

I'm wiping tears off my face when Gage comes into the room, looking for me.

"What now?"

"Nothing new. Just filling Wynter in on what happened."

"How'd she take it?"

"Hard, but she wants to help Taylor, even though she barely knows her."

"She's come a long way, our Wynter."

"That's what made me teary."

"Tyler is all packed up and can't wait to get to Derek's so they can play video games."

"Thanks for helping him." I grab the suitcase along with essential blankets and stuffed animals. "Let's get going."

Gage puts his hands on my shoulders. "You're running on

adrenaline, babe. Should you get some sleep before we go back?"

He was up all night, too, but all his concern is for me, as always. "I'd like to go back to Taylor's to help out where I can. I can grab a nap at some point. You don't have to come if you're tired."

"If you're going, I'm going."

I'm relieved to have him by my side every day, but especially on days like this. "Thanks."

He hugs me. "Hang on to me when it gets to be too much, okay?"

And he always knows just what I need, which is such a gift to me in this new life we've built for ourselves. "So very thankful for you always, but more so than ever when the shit hits the fan."

"I'm right here. Forever and ever."

"Thank God for that."

Wynter

I DON'T KNOW what to do with myself after the call from Iris. I planned to clean out Xavier's clothes today to pack up the things he's outgrown and put them in the attic in case Adrian and I decide to have a baby together someday. We have no plans for that now, but you never know what might happen, especially now that we're married. Everything feels possible after we exchanged vows.

But after talking to Iris, I'm still sitting in the middle of Xavier's room while he and Willow nap in her room, staring at the wall as I think about what Taylor must be going through.

I fall into a deep rabbit hole of what it would feel like to lose Adrian, after everything we both went through to find each other and to build this new life together with our children. Despite his intense fear of childbirth after losing his wife, Sadie, when she gave birth to Xavier, he stood faithfully by my side when I decided to have Jaden's baby after I learned he'd frozen sperm before his cancer treatments.

While I loved Jaden with every fiber of my being, my relationship with Adrian is different. Jaden and I fell in love when we were kids, before life kicked us in the teeth with his cancer diagnosis. It's different with Adrian, more mature, grounded in grief and focused on our children, who forced us to grow up and deal with our shit so we can be the best possible parents to them.

I try to imagine what it would be like to raise Xavier and Willow without Adrian, and I can't. I simply cannot. The very thought of it makes me feel nauseated and cold all over.

I'm still sitting on the floor in Xavier's room when Adrian returns from a run and comes to find me. "There you are."

He's dripping with sweat and smiling the way he always does when he sees me after even the shortest time apart. He takes a closer look at me. "What's wrong? Why are you pale as a ghost?"

I don't want to tell him, because then he'll know, too, that it's possible for a widow to lose their chapter two. I don't want him to hear that, but of course I can't keep it from him forever. He'll hear about it eventually.

"So, um, Iris called while you were out."

He uses the hem of his tank top to dry the sweat on his face, exposing the defined abs I'm obsessed with. "Is everything okay?"

"She told me that Taylor's husband, Will, was killed in an accident at work."

I'm watching him so closely that I witness the exact second when my words—and the implications behind them—register with him.

"No way. No. Wait. They have a baby due soon, don't they?"

I nod. "Next month."

Adrian drops to his knees next to me. "This is devastating."

"Beyond."

For a long time, we sit next to each other, not touching but connected in our shared grief for Taylor—and ourselves. Having this happen to someone we know is unthinkable, especially when she's expecting a child with Will soon. It's heartbreak on top of heartbreak.

"Did Iris say how she is? Taylor, that is…"

"Not good at all. I told her we'll want to help…"

"Anything we can do."

"I wonder if she'll come back to the group."

"I don't even know what to say to this. It's got me speechless."

"I get it. My brain shut down after Iris called."

"Brings it all back, doesn't it?"

"Yeah. For sure. Knocked the wind out of me."

"Me, too."

I have no idea how long we're there, on the floor of Xavier's room, processing this news and battling utter despair for someone we barely know. We've both met Taylor—and Will—a few times at Iris's house, but we don't know her like we do the other widows in our close-knit group. It doesn't matter, though. We understand what she's going through… Well, sort of… We can't know what it's like to have it happen *twice* in one lifetime.

"I'll… I'll make some food for them," I finally say after a long silence.

"That'd be good."

"It feels insignificant."

"What else can we do but show up and offer as much support as we can?"

"True. I just feel so…"

"Devastated."

"Yeah, me, too." He reaches over to take my hand. "It's not going to happen to us."

"Right."

"No, really, Wynter. It won't."

My throat is so tight from the effort not to bawl my head off that all I can do is nod. I want so badly to believe he's right, but we know better than most people that there're simply no such guarantees.

I clear my throat. "What should I make for them?"

"Don't her kids love that mac 'n' cheese Iris makes?"

"They do. I'll make that."

"Save some for our boy. It's his favorite, too."

"I will."

He stands and helps me up. "It always makes us feel better when we do something to help."

I wrap my arms around him, which I never do when he's sweaty, but what do I care about such things at a time like this?

He holds me close and kisses the top of my head. "We're okay, baby. I swear. Everything is fine. Our friend is suffering, and we'll be there for her, but we're going to be all right."

I cling to his assurances, because what else can I do? I don't tell him that Jaden once said those very words to me and look at how that turned out.

Six

Lexi

Tom has planned a romantic day for us that began with breakfast at our favorite diner, followed by a long, leisurely drive into the mountains for a hike at Skyline Drive, which was one of my favorite places to go with my late husband, Jim. Tom knows that and has helped me to reclaim a spot I used to love by going there together to make new memories.

He's thoughtful that way, incorporating Jim into the life we're building together because he understands that Jim will always be part of us. That makes him the perfect partner for me, despite my lingering concerns about his heart condition.

I still can't think about the evening I returned to the home we shared, at that time as platonic roommates in deep flirtation, to find him passed out on the floor of the living room in cardiac arrest, without wanting to run screaming from him.

But... since the incident, he's changed everything, from his diet to his exercise program. He's all but stopped drinking alcohol and is fanatical about watching his cholesterol and other risk factors.

There's nothing he could do that he's not doing, which

gives me comfort despite the anxiety that lingers long after something like that happens—especially after losing my first husband to ALS.

We've scored a beautiful late autumn day and other than some traffic due to others having the same idea Tom had, we have an enjoyable ride through still-colorful foliage. We've had an unusually chilly autumn this year, which has kept the leaves colorful longer than usual.

He has his music app set to a classic rock playlist and sings along to Foreigner as we get closer to the parking area for the hiking trail.

The first few times we came here together, I experienced memories of Jim that left me feeling triggered for a few days afterward. Tom encouraged me to talk about it rather than trying to bury the pain, and I was surprised to find that it helped to share my grief with him. It was as if he relieved some of the burden simply by listening to me talk about the things I remembered and how I still ache for Jim. I appreciate that Tom is never threatened by the fact that I'm still in love with the man I lost so tragically.

After we park, we don waistbands that hold water bottles and basic first aid supplies. We sun-screened before we left the house and have more with us to reapply later.

Tom tugs my Capitals ballcap down to shade my eyes. "Ready?"

"Let's go."

He takes my hand to lead the way to the trailhead and holds on most of the way up, except for when we pass others on the trail and drop to single file, after which he immediately reaches for my hand again.

His love, and that of my close friends and family, has made me happy to be alive again, which wasn't the case after I first lost Jim. For a long time, I didn't think I'd be able to go on. The ordeal of his illness, followed by the trauma of his death, sucked the life out of me. When I look back at that time now, it exists in this odd, cloudy place in my mind. I can't quite make out the details, but I vividly remember the raw, unrelenting pain that came with thinking my life was over because his ended.

In many ways, Tom is the best thing to ever happen to me because he's shown me that's simply not true, as much as it might've once seemed like it.

As the trail gets steeper, we double down on making the climb to the summit, where the spectacular view of the Blue Ridge Mountains and the Shenandoah Valley makes it worth the effort.

"Ah, look at that. So, so beautiful."

Tom kisses me. "Yes, you are."

"Sure I am, in all my sweaty, red-faced glory."

"If I say you're beautiful, you aren't allowed to argue with me."

"Is that another new rule?"

He's always making funny rules for us, such as never go to bed without kissing him three times—at least—and morning sex before coffee on the weekends.

"I believe I'll be adding that one to the list."

I'm gazing at the gorgeous scenery, and when I glance at him, my witty retort dies on my lips when I see that he's dropped to one knee. *What is happening?*

He takes my hand and gazes up at me with all the love he's shown me every day since we first reconnected, years after high school, where we first became aware of each other.

My eyes are full of tears as I notice we've attracted a crowd of other hikers who are watching us. "Tom..."

"My sweet Lexi, I love you so much, and I love the life we've created for ourselves. You saved me in every possible way, and I want to spend the rest of my days with you. Will you marry me?"

After Jim died, I said I'd never get married again, but Tom has changed my mind about a lot of things, including remarriage.

"Yes," I say in a whisper as I fall to my knees to kiss him. "Yes, I'll marry you."

A cheer goes up from the onlookers.

"I got it on video for ya," one of them says.

Tom gathers me into a tight hug. "Thanks for saying yes."

I laugh even as tears spill down my cheeks. "Thanks for asking."

"I wasn't sure if I should, but I figured it was worth a shot."

"It was perfect and thank you for doing it here."

"I had a little talk with Jim before I asked you. I told him I'd try to take care of you like he did, and I'd love you enough for both of us."

This man... This dear, sweet, sexy, funny, adorable man.

"Thank you for that. For getting it. For making him part of this and us and, well, all of it."

"He's always with us, Lex. I never forget that you had to lose him to get to me, and I promise I never will."

We hold each other for a long time, until the guy who took the video runs out of patience waiting for us.

"You want the video or what?"

I wipe my face and laugh. "We want it. We definitely want it."

Angela

SATURDAYS ARE different now that Spencer is gone. What used to be family time is now just another survival day for me, with my eldest out of school, my middle one out of sorts and a baby getting molars who can't be pacified no matter what I do for him.

Being stuck at home with two kids who desperately miss their dad, the "fun" parent, and a seventeen-month-old who refuses to nap is my idea of hell. And yes, I love my children with my whole heart, the way I did before their dad died suddenly from an accidental fentanyl overdose.

But like everything since Spence died, I feel differently toward them—and everything—than I did before. The weight of being fully responsible for three small beings sits on my shoulders like a thousand-pound boulder that I won't get out from under for almost twenty years, if then. That thought keeps me awake at night, even when the baby is finally sleeping and giving me an opportunity to do the same.

I'm attempting to feed Joshua when I get a text from my friend Brad Albright, who lost his wife, Mary Alice, to the same toxic fentanyl that killed Spencer. After being introduced by my sister Sam at one of the court hearings for the perpetrators, we've bonded over our common loss and become buddies as we adjust to single parenthood with five children between us.

My kids are driving me batshit crazy. You want to meet at the park?

I juggle my phone around feeding the baby to reply, *God yes. We'll be there. What time?*

Two?

See you then.

This'll be the third time in recent weeks that we've met Brad and his kids at the park. Last weekend, we took the kids for pizza afterward, which sparked a lot of questions from my intelligent, intuitive son Jack, who's eight and still grieving his father hard.

"Is Mr. Brad your new boyfriend?"

"Are you going to marry him?"

"Will he be our new daddy?"

I answered no to each of his questions. "Mr. Brad lost his wife the same way we lost Daddy, and he's become a friend who understands what we're going through. That's all it is."

"Are you going to get married again?"

"I'm in no way ready to even think about something like that. Right now, I'm focused on you and Ella and baby Josh and working on the foundation we started to help other people who struggle with opioid addiction like Daddy did. That's all I'm thinking about."

"If you get a boyfriend, will you tell me?"

"When the time is right, I'd tell you, but that's not going to happen any time soon, if ever."

"You shouldn't be alone forever. Daddy wouldn't want that."

"How do you know that?"

"He told me."

"What? When?"

"When we went fishing last summer, or I guess it was the summer before last now. He said if anything ever happened to him, he hoped that we'd be happy."

I've been thinking about that for days now as I become more furious with my late husband with every day that goes by without him. That he could've burdened Jack with such a thing, as well as giving him reason to worry that something might happen to his father long before it actually did... It's unbelievable and further proof that Spencer hadn't been in his right mind for quite some time before his death.

All because of a back injury sustained during a football game with his college friends that I told him not to participate in, fearing he'd get hurt. I never could've imagined the chain of events that would result from that decision to revisit his misspent youth. If only he'd listened to me... He'd still be here with us and would've had no reason to tell Jack what he wanted for his family if he died.

The revelation from Jack has been so shocking that I haven't told anyone about it yet. Rather, I've sat on it for days, processing the many implications. I'll make sure Jack's therapist knows about it before they meet next week.

Intense anger at the man I loved more than life makes everything else more difficult. From helping my kids to bathe, dress, eat, play, go to the bathroom, get to sleep or whatever it is they need, I'm dragging all that anger along with me. It becomes harder all the time to keep it hidden from them. Lately, I find myself talking to one person about the anger—the only person who truly understands what I'm going through.

Brad Albright.

He's furious with his late spouse, too.

We're aware that addiction is an *illness* and should be treated as such, but he didn't even know his wife, Mary Alice, was addicted until it was too late. In my case, we did everything we could to get help for Spencer, including mortgaging our home and our future to pay for multiple trips to rehab that didn't work. Because of my sister, the first lady, and brother-in-law, the president, I received millions in donations after Spencer died, which gives me financial security that many widows, like Brad, don't have.

He won't hear of me helping him financially, but I'll keep offering until he lets me. I plan to use most of the money to fund the foundation I've started in Spencer's memory to help people like Brad, whose lives have been ruined by opioid addiction.

Joshua Charles, whose middle name is in honor of my late father, has fallen asleep while feeding, so I put him down to nap while I feed Jack and Ella some lunch.

"Mr. Brad invited us to meet them at the park today," I tell the kids as I cut PB&Js into squares and serve them with apple slices. "Doesn't that sound fun?"

"I love the park," Ella says.

"I don't want to go," Jack says. "Let's just stay home."

Before he suddenly lost his father, who was also his favorite person and playmate, Jack never would've turned down a trip to the park.

"It'll be fun," I tell him, "and it'll get us out of the house for some fresh air."

"I don't want fresh air."

He's gearing up for a serious tantrum, so I do what his therapist suggested and disengage for now as I prepare to leave the house with two young children and a baby. I pack one bag for the older kids and another for Josh. I toss in drinks, snacks and changes of clothes in case the kids get wet or muddy, one of which happens just about every time we go anywhere.

When I'm ready to go, I load Josh into the baby car seat and help Ella into her jacket. "You don't have to play at the park, Jack, but you do have to come so the rest of us can go."

He doesn't care for that news, but he grabs his sweatshirt and heads for the car. He's outraged by everything lately, not that I blame him. He's got good reason, and I'm trying to respect his feelings while walking the fine line of keeping our lives moving forward. It's a delicate balancing act on the best of days and a much more trying task on the weekends when his dad's glaring absence is that much more pronounced.

I ache for all of us, but mostly for him.

While Ella is sad that her daddy has died, she's almost too young at three and a half to fully process the implications of someone being gone forever. Jack, on the other hand, is all too aware of what *forever* means, and his little heart is shattered.

Brad and I have talked a lot about how difficult it's been to parent our kids through this loss. His seven-year-old daughter, Daphne, is unusually perceptive for such a young child and is having an awful time coping with her mother's absence. His four-year-old son, Drake, is sad and moody and having temper tantrums for the first time but doesn't seem to fully grasp what happened to his mother. He cries for her at bedtime every night, and Brad is left feeling helpless to mend their broken hearts while managing his own debilitating grief.

Nothing in either of our lives prepared us for these challenges, so we rely on each other as we navigate our way through them.

As I drive to the park, I glance in the mirror to check on Jack, who's staring out the passenger side window, his expression unreadable.

"Mommy, let's sing," Ella says.

"No singing," Jack says in the testy tone that's new since disaster struck.

"Why no singing?" Ella asks.

I can almost hear her chin wobbling as she fights tears. She's still not accustomed to Jack being mean to her when he never was before their father died. He used to dote on her and indulge her every whim. Now, he has no patience for her, which is another loss for my sweet baby girl.

"I vote for singing." I put on Ella's favorite soundtrack, *Moana*, and turn up the volume, delighting in the joyful sound of her voice. She sings at the top of her lungs, which used to make Jack laugh.

Not anymore.

The next time I look in the mirror, I notice that Jack's face is red from the outrage of it all.

I wish I knew what to do for him.

Seven

Brad

The kids are excited to see their new friends. If there's one blessing to come from the sudden, shocking loss of their mother, it's been the outpouring of love and support we've received from everyone in our lives. As hard as they try, however, none of them can understand the hell we're in better than Angela and her kids, who are right there with us on this journey none of us asked to be on.

We meet at Stead Park near Dupont Circle. Parking can be a problem, but we luck out with a spot on the street about three blocks away. Not too bad, given that it's a sunny autumn Saturday.

I have to jog to keep up with the kids as they race toward the playground. It's nice to see them excited about something and to know that not only will they be occupied for the next hour or two, but they'll also be tired later from the activity. That'll make for an easier-than-usual bedtime.

As I watch them play and keep an eye out for Angela and her kids, it occurs to me once again that I often took my wife for granted. She handled most of the bedtimes—and everything else with the kids, for that matter—while I picked up extra shifts at the firehouse whenever I could get them, to pay the bills. I was so focused on providing for my family that I sacrificed precious time with my wife and kids that I can never get back.

The guilt eats at me. I knew her bad knee was still giving her trouble almost a year after surgery, but it never occurred to me that she'd become addicted to the pain meds—or that she'd seek them out on the street after her doctor refused to prescribe any more. To be honest, I'd gotten sick of hearing about her freaking knee. I thought she was using it as an excuse to do less around the house. The guilt has been heavy since I realized how bad it had to have been to drive my rule-following wife to seek out illegal drugs to combat the pain.

I let her down by not taking her pain seriously enough. If only I had listened to her when she told me it was so bad, it made her almost delirious. I thought she was being dramatic, as she was known to be from time to time. I dismissed her claims and went on with my life, oblivious to the private war she was forced to wage when even the person closest to her didn't acknowledge the gravity of her situation.

Thinking about that keeps me awake at night, long after my grief-stricken children are asleep. The thing I can't get past is that, as a highly trained paramedic, I should've seen the signs that she was fighting addiction, but I never noticed a thing. Truth be told, I wasn't looking close enough because I had enough to deal with at work without taking the time to figure out what the hell was going on with her.

I chalked up her changes in behavior to the stress of caring for two young children and all their needs while managing a tight household budget and a bad knee. That would've been enough to make anyone a little crazy, or so I thought. Now I know it was much more than that, and I never put two and two together until disaster struck.

I have nightmares about how she looked that morning

when I went to check on her and found her dead in our bed. I knew right away that she was dead, but I still tried to bring her back. That's what I'm trained to do, after all. But nothing I did could change the reality. She was dead, and she had been for a few hours by the time I found her.

So, in addition to the grief over losing the woman I loved and the mother of my children, I feel incredibly guilty for not realizing much sooner that she was dealing with a monster that'd overtaken our lives without me even knowing it. And I feel guilty for being furious with her for allowing that to happen.

And yes, I know she didn't "allow" anything, but I can't help how I feel about it. Why didn't she sound the alarm from the rooftops that she had a huge problem and had resorted to breaking the fucking law to feed it? Why didn't she tell me she was in trouble? I'll never understand why she didn't do that—and it's why I'm still so fucking angry with her, even as I miss her, sometimes so much I think I'll die from it.

Angela is the only person in my life who understands what it's like to walk around gripped by love, grief and anger for the person we've lost. Some days, the anger is so big, I forget what it was like to love her. Then I'll remember something from the past, and the love comes rushing back to remind me that before the grief and anger arrived, the love was there, it was real and it changed my life in so many ways.

Before Mary Alice, I was a selfish asshole, focused on work, playing basketball and softball, partying with my boys, sleeping with random women and staying far away from anything that smacked of commitment. She was the first woman I'd ever met who made me want to be a better man. I wanted to be better for *her*. I was in love with her by our second date and was willing to change my whole life to accommodate her and our relationship by our fourth date. We were engaged within six months of meeting and got married a year later.

I never had a single regret about changing everything to

bring her into my life, and things were great between us until she injured her knee running a 5K, and our lives spiraled out of control after surgery to correct a torn ACL went badly eighteen months before she died. She was in unbearable pain all the time, and every doctor we consulted said the same thing—she needed a knee replacement. But she was so afraid of another surgery that she held off on scheduling that procedure.

Then I noticed she seemed to be doing a little better, and I started to feel optimistic that maybe she'd turned a corner. Now I know it was because she was procuring drugs on the street to deal with the pain after her doctor refused to give her any more. In my wildest dreams, I can't imagine her going through the motions of figuring out how to find illicit drugs. I've been through her phone from top to bottom and found no sign of her outreach there, so there must've been a friend or acquaintance or someone who steered her in the right direction.

In the months since her death, no one has come forward to confess to being involved, nor do I expect them to. Whoever they are, I hope they're plagued with guilt over leading an innocent woman to her death.

Yeah, so... The anger extends far beyond Mary Alice to that nameless, faceless person who told her where to get the drugs that killed her. They couldn't have known they'd be laced with fentanyl but come on. The whole world knows that's the risk that comes with taking any medication that doesn't come from a pharmacy.

Drake comes running over to the bench where I'm sitting. "Daddy, here they come! Here comes Ella!"

He's crazy about Angela's daughter, who's only a few months younger than him. Her son, Jack, is more reserved and not as friendly to my kids as Ella is. Angela has told me that he's taken his father's death very hard, as they were super close. My heart goes out to him. He's a sweet kid from what I can tell, but he's obviously hurting. I wish there was something I could do for him, but for now, I let him take the lead, hoping we might eventually be friends like I am with his mom and Ella. Baby Joshua is adorable and always happy.

I get up to take the baby from Angela and settle Josh in a shady spot on the bench while Ella runs off to play with Daphne and Drake.

"No Jack today?" I ask when Angela sits next to me.

"He's in the car." She points to the red minivan that she can see from where we're sitting. "He said he might come out to play, but he's not sure he feels like it."

"Poor guy. I feel for him."

"I do, too," she says with a sigh. "I wish I knew what to say or do to make him feel better."

"I hate to rely on a tired old cliché, but in time, perhaps he'll start to gain some acceptance and be able to move on."

"Maybe, but I worry that he'll never again be the light-hearted, funny, sweet boy he was before he lost his dad."

"He might not be, but hopefully, he can find some peace with his loss and start to enjoy life again. I didn't know his dad, but I'm sure that's what he'd want for him."

"He definitely would. Spence and Jack were best friends. He'd want Jack to smile and laugh and enjoy the things he used to before disaster struck. I hope we'll get there eventually, but it's not going to happen today. He's in a real mood."

"Do you think it would help or hurt if I tried to talk to him? I could ask if he wants to play catch or something? I brought the football in case Drake wanted to play."

"I suppose it couldn't hurt anything. He's sick of me hovering over him. Are you sure you don't mind?"

"Not at all, if you can keep an eye on Daphne and Drake."

She hands me the keys to her car. "I've got them."

I grab the football. "Be right back."

"Hey, Brad?"

I turn back to her.

"I'm sorry in advance if he's rude to you."

"Don't be. He's grieving. He gets all the passes."

"For now. Not forever."

"Let's just deal with today. We can worry about forever another day."

I like to make her laugh. It changes her entire disposition, giving me a glimpse of what she might be like when she's not dealing with overwhelming sadness. We've both been surprised and disappointed to discover that year two is rougher than year one in many ways. The gritty early grief has given way to a reality that seems to get harder rather than easier.

I jog across the grass to where she parked.

Jack is sitting on the passenger side, looking out the window. The tablet on his lap has gone dark.

I tap lightly on the window, so I won't scare him.

He looks over at me.

I hold up the football and raise a brow. Tipping my head, I ask if he wants to come out and throw the ball.

For a long moment, he has no reaction.

As I wait for him to decide, I toss the ball from one hand to the other. When I miss and have to bend to retrieve it, I stand up to find him smiling. I unlock the car and pull the handle to open the sliding door. "Clearly, I could use some practice. What do you say?"

"Did my mom send you over?"

"Actually, I asked if I could come. Drake still can't throw a decent spiral. I bet you can, though, right?"

"Uh, yeah. I could do that when I was four."

"I don't believe it. Come show me."

His deep sigh breaks my heart. He doesn't want to throw the football with me. He wants his dad, and I'd do anything to be able to give him that. But since I'm all there is right now, I'm elated when he releases his seat belt and climbs across to get out of the other side of the car.

I toss him the football. "Show me what you've got, hot stuff."

"Go long."

As I jog across the open expanse of grass, I glance over to see Angela watching, hand on her heart, when Jack throws a perfect spiral my way.

Taylor

THE DAY IS an endless parade of people, food, sympathy and tears. My older sister, Laura, has driven up from North Carolina and takes command of grief central, recording each delivery and who brought it for the eventual thank-you notes we'll send. We've done this before. We know the drill all too well. Maybe I should start a business called Widows 'R' Us or something like that to help people through these first horrendous days after loss since I'm so good at it.

Flowers arrive along with fruit platters and more food than we can eat in a month. Thankfully, we're also overrun with friends and family, so I ask Laura and Amanda to put out the food for the visitors.

I'm on the sofa in the family room with my feet up, hoping to alleviate the swelling in my ankles. After hearing about Will's death on the news, my midwife made a house call to check on me. She expressed concern about my swollen ankles and plans to return tomorrow to see if it's gotten any better. If not, we may be looking at an earlier-than-planned delivery for the baby. I really hope that doesn't happen. I'm not sure I can deal with a new baby right now on top of everything else, but of course, I want to keep myself and the baby healthy, so I'll do what I have to.

My kids slept on either side of me last night, their little bodies trembling with sobs long after they were asleep. I was awake most of the night, my brain racing with a million thoughts and my heart aching with intense sadness for my sweet Will. I miss him so much. I want to turn to him and ask him what I should do, but he's not there, and he never will be again.

I simply can't believe he's gone. He was just here the other day, kissing me—and then my baby bump—goodbye before he left for a double shift. He's been working a lot lately, as they tried to make up time lost during an unusually rainy autumn that put them behind schedule.

It's impossible to believe I'll never again see his handsome, smiling face. I've grown accustomed to living without Greg, as hard as that's been, but this time... Will was supposed to be my happily ever after, my reward for surviving the loss of my first love and the father of my children. We were supposed to last forever.

Now what am I supposed to do?

First chance I get, I want to move out of this house where I've lived with two husbands who died. This place is cursed, and you'll never convince me otherwise. I want to get myself and my kids out of here, but of course that won't be simple with a new baby due imminently, not to mention it's the only home Eliza and Miles have ever known. Leaving here will be another loss on top of the others.

But I can't stay here. It was hard enough to stay after Greg died in this house. It'll be even harder this time around, as the kids are old enough to have loved Will with their full hearts. Losing him is devastating for them. They've been very quiet today, accepting the outpouring of love from the people in our lives while coming to check on me every few minutes, as if they need to see with their own eyes that I'm still here.

My poor, poor babies.

Iris comes into the room, carrying a steaming mug of the decaf tea I drink while pregnant. It's no substitute for coffee, but it's better than nothing.

She sits on the coffee table and hands the mug to me. "I put some honey in it to sweeten it up."

"Bless you."

She glances toward my feet. "How are the cankles?"

"Still cankling, but maybe a little less than they were."

"Can I get you something to eat?"

"I don't think I could."

"I hate to say that you have to, but..."

"Maybe some soup or something like that. There's this lump in my throat..." I stroke the spot. "I can't get anything past it."

"I remember that lump and how hard it was to eat."

"I didn't have it when Greg died. I had it when he was first diagnosed, and it showed up often throughout his illness, but it wasn't there when he died." I glance at her. "As awful as it sounds, I was relieved after because he was free—and so was I. It sounds terrible to say that out loud..."

"I get it. I've heard other widows say the same thing after nursing a spouse through a terrible illness. Lexi talks a lot about the relief—and the associated guilt—after Jim died from ALS."

"That's another thing I wouldn't wish on anyone."

"For sure." She reaches for my free hand. "I wouldn't wish any of this on you. None of us would."

"Thank you for being here. What'd you do with your kids?"

"Roni and Derek have them for a sleepover."

"That's good of them."

"They send their love and said to tell you they're here for you and the kids. Whatever you need. All the Wild Widows I've spoken to have said the same thing."

"That's nice of them. Most of them barely know me. I went running off into my happily ever after without so much as a glance back at the group."

"No one blames you for that, Taylor. We're all about doing whatever it takes to survive."

"Still... I could've continued to give back a little here and there like you have."

"There was no need. We're good—or I should say as good as a merry band of widows can be."

I give her a small smile. "I'm a widow again. I have to keep saying it out loud because it's unbelievable that this can happen to the same person twice."

"It's incredibly unfair."

"What am I going to do, Iris? All I can think about is how I want to move out of here as soon as possible. This place is cursed or something. But that'll just upset the kids even more than they already are."

"Remember what we always preach... No big decisions the first year."

"How do I stay here after losing *two husbands* who lived here with me?"

"Why don't we cross that bridge in a week or two?"

"Yeah, I guess."

When Will's younger brother, Matt, comes into the room, Iris stands. "I'll see about that soup."

"Thanks."

Eight

Taylor

Matt takes Iris's place on the coffee table. Whereas Will had dark hair and brown eyes, Matt favors their mother, with reddish-brown hair and blue eyes. "Do you need anything?"

"I'm okay. Thanks."

His jaw clenches as he seems to struggle with his emotions.

Will always said Matt has no emotions and for most of his life didn't care about anyone but himself, so it's somewhat shocking to see tears in his eyes. "I can't believe he's gone."

"I know. It's a terrible shock to all of us."

"He was so, so excited about the baby. It was all he talked about."

"Yes, it was." The baby chooses that moment to deliver a swift kick to my ribs.

"Oh, wow. I saw that. It must feel so weird."

"I'm used to it by now. This is my third time."

"Right. So, I wanted to tell you... I... um... I want to be here for you and the kids. All of them, the way Will was. That's what he'd want me to do."

"I appreciate that, Matt, but we'll be okay. I mean, you're more than welcome to come see the baby any time you want."

"I want to see Eliza and Miles, too. They're part of our family after all this time. I don't want them to think we've forgotten about them. My parents feel the same way."

"It's very kind of you to think of them."

"Will was so happy with you and the kids."

"We were happy with him, too. I'm not sure how we'll go on without him. He was everything to us."

"I want you to call me. Any time you need anything. I'll be there for you. I mean it, Taylor. I know I haven't been the most reliable guy in the past, but I want to be there for you and the kids, the way Will would want me to be."

I'm not so sure Will would want that, but I don't have the heart to say such a thing to him. "Thank you, Matt. I appreciate it."

"You have my number, right?"

"I do." I also know he's the last person I'd call in a crisis. Or, I guess I should say, *another* crisis.

Iris returns with the soup she made for me, which gives Matt a reason to go back to wherever he was before he came in to talk to me. "Everything okay?"

"Yeah, just Will's fuck-up younger brother saying he's going to be there for anything I need."

"Ah, well, that's nice of him."

"What's funny is this time around, I recognize the gestures for what they are, whereas when Greg died, I thought everyone meant what they said. I know better now. I'm an *experienced* widow."

Iris's lips quiver with the start of a laugh.

"It's okay to laugh at the sheer madness of this whole situation."

"Except it's not funny."

"Remember what we always say—if we don't laugh, we'll never stop crying."

She hands me a mug with chicken noodle soup that smells so good, my stomach rumbles with interest.

"Thank you."

"Here are some crackers, too."

"You're the best." After I take a few delicious sips of the soup, I glance at her. "I'm sure you and Gage have stuff you need to be doing."

"We're where we need to be."

"Will's mom texted me about going to the funeral home..."

"Do you want us to go for you?"

"I can't ask you guys to do that."

"You didn't. I offered."

"It's too much, Iris. That's the last place you or Gage need to be."

"It's the last place *you* need to be. Stay home with your kids. We'll meet Will's parents there."

I don't feel right about asking two widows to go to a funeral home when it's not their family member who's died. "Are you sure? You should think about that. I don't want my tragedy to be a setback for you guys."

"We're okay, and we'll take care of anything you need. Do you have any idea what he would've wanted?"

Resigned and relieved to accept their kind offer, I say, "He said he didn't want to take up room by being buried, and I agreed with him, so we said we'd be cremated. His mom will want the big Catholic funeral, even though he was lapsed, so she can do what she wants as long as he's cremated after." I can't believe I'm talking about turning my sweet Will into ashes when he was just here.

Fucking tears. How do I have any left after losing *two* husbands? I dab at them with the napkin Iris hands me.

"How am I talking about funeral homes? *Again.* It's surreal."

"It's beyond surreal." She glances at the wedding photo of Will, me and the kids, the day we officially became a family. In many ways, that was the happiest day of my life because it was proof I'd survived losing Greg.

Hold my beer, said the universe. *Not so fast.*

"I must've really pissed someone off in a past life."

"No, you didn't."

"How else to explain the unexplainable?"

"I don't know, but it's nothing you did or didn't do—in any life. I refuse to believe that. Greg and Will wouldn't want you to think that way."

"How is this my life, Iris? *How?*"

"I don't know, sweetie, but I have to think that your story is still being written, and this is another chapter. Certainly not the end."

"It feels like the end of everything good."

"As you know, that particular feeling passes in time, even as the grief remains."

"All I see is a long, dark tunnel before me with no light at the end."

"The light will come back. I promise. And in the meantime, I'll be here for you, and the Wild Widows will be here for you, for as long as you need us."

"I wouldn't feel right going back to that group after leaving when I found my new happily ever after."

"Don't be silly. That group exists in large part because of you, and you'd be welcomed back with open arms by everyone."

"I don't know. I'll think about it."

"You don't have to decide anything today or tomorrow. Just focus on getting through each hour, and we'll talk about all that stuff later."

I hear the doorbell ring, and Christy comes in a few minutes later, walking right over to me and Iris to hug us both. It's clear to me that she's been crying.

"I'm so, so sorry, Tay."

"Thank you for coming."

"I brought some food. I didn't know what you might need."

"That's very nice of you."

She sits next to Iris on the coffee table and puts her arm around her. "What can I do?"

"I was just telling Taylor we'll be there for her for the long haul, regardless of her not staying active in the group."

"Of course we will. That's not even a question."

"Love you guys," I tell them with more damned tears filling my eyes.

"We love you, too."

Iris

TAYLOR IS RIGHT ABOUT one thing—a funeral home is the last place Gage or I want to be, but we do it for her so she can keep her feet up and hopefully alleviate the swelling that has her looking at a potential early delivery of the baby.

We bring the favorite shirt and jeans that Taylor chose for Will. Helping her make those decisions was brutal. Every piece of clothing brought back another memory of the man who's now gone forever.

Since we met Will's parents, Claire and Frank, last night, they thank us for coming and offer us seats at the conference room table, where the funeral director has set out refreshments that none of us want.

We go over the details of the service and let them know that Taylor intends to write the obituary but would appreciate their input.

Pallbearers are discussed, hymns and readings are chosen, and the program for the funeral begins to come together under the funeral director's gentle guidance.

"Taylor indicated that Will wished to be cremated."

"Oh," Claire says, her face flat with shock, "he never mentioned that to us. We assumed he'd be buried in the family plot."

"He told Taylor he didn't want to take up space on the earth and wished to be cremated."

"That... that's not what we want."

"It's what *he* wanted, Mrs. Lonergan, and it's what his wife wants."

She doesn't care for that, but I don't look away until she does. I hope she gets the message that Taylor's—and Will's—wishes take precedence over hers. Not that my heart doesn't ache for them both, because it does. Dear God, the thought of losing my adult child in the prime of his life is one of the worst things I can imagine. But Will was a grown man with a wife and family. If necessary, I'll remind them that his wife deferred to them on a Catholic service that Will wouldn't have wanted, but Taylor won't back down about the cremation.

Thankfully, Claire gives up without further argument on that point, and we conclude our business at the funeral home. The wake is set for Sunday, from four to eight p.m., and the service will be held the following morning at St. James Catholic Church in Falls Church.

Outside, I take deep breaths of chilly air as Gage holds the passenger door of his car for me. "Where to?"

"Back to Taylor's, I guess."

"I think we should go home and get some rest. You won't be any good to her if you get sick or run down."

He's aware that I get tired more easily than I did before I was treated for breast cancer and is vigilant about making sure I take care of myself. I want to be with Taylor, but he's right. I'm running on empty after the sleepless night followed by the long, difficult day. "Okay."

"That was easier than I expected it to be."

"I'm an agreeable kind of girl."

His snort of laughter makes me smile. "Sure you are."

After he gets into the driver's seat, I reach for his hand. "Thank you for coming with me on this dreadful mission. It's above and beyond the call of duty for a widower."

"Nothing you need is above my call of duty, love, even a trip to a funeral home. I'm not sure that Taylor would've had it in her to fight for what she and Will wanted the way you did."

"I felt bad about that. The woman just lost her son."

"Her son's wishes must be respected. You made sure they were."

"What an awful situation."

"It sure is."

On the way home, I get a text from my widow friend Joy. *Dear God, Iris, I just heard from Christy about Taylor's husband. I'm heartbroken for her. What can I do?*

Joy joined the group about six months before Taylor's last meeting.

I call her. "Hey, hon. There's not much we can do but be there for her. The wake is Sunday, and the funeral is Monday."

"I'll be there for both and take her some food in a week or two when the influx dies down."

"She'll appreciate that."

"Good Lord, Iris. How can this happen to someone twice?"

"It's impossible to believe."

"And with the baby due any time, too."

"I know."

"So I'm not sure if you've looked at your phone in the last hour or so, but Lexi sent a photo of her and Tom. They got engaged today."

"Oh, wow. That's fantastic news." I hold the phone aside to tell Gage, who smiles widely. "I'll text her when I get home."

"I got the feeling she doesn't know about Taylor."

"I haven't had the chance to call her, and I doubt Christy or any of the others will say anything about it to her today. Tomorrow will be soon enough."

"Yeah, for sure. What a day of soaring highs and crushing lows."

"For real."

"How are you doing? I'm sure you've been by her side since you got the news."

"Gage and I were with her at the hospital last night and today at her house. She's in shock of course and having a few issues with the pregnancy that might require an early delivery."

"When it rains... I'll be praying for her and her sweet kids."

"Thanks, Joy. I'll send more info after I get the chance to talk to Lexi tomorrow."

"Let me know if there's anything at all I can do for Taylor or for you. Anything, Iris."

"Thanks, love. I'll let Taylor know you're praying for her and the kids."

"Yes, please do, and make sure you take care of you while you're taking care of everyone else."

"I will. I promise."

"Are we still meeting this week?"

"I think we probably should. This news is shaking the foundation under all of us. We need to keep each other close."

"Couldn't agree more. I'll be there."

"Love you."

"Love you, too. Tell Gage I love him, too."

"I will."

I sigh as I end the call.

"Great news about Lexi and Tom," Gage says.

"Yes, for sure. I wish I didn't have to tell her about Taylor when she's so happy."

"She'd want to know."

"Yeah, she would."

Gage gives my hand a squeeze. "I heard what Mama Joy said about taking care of you while you're taking care of everyone else. I'm going to make sure you do that."

"Thank you for being my biggest supporter. All I can think

about is how I would feel if this happened to me." I glance his way. "You'd better never do this to me, you hear?"

"I hear, and I'm not going anywhere."

I want to make him swear to it, but that wouldn't be fair. We both know all too well that there're no guarantees in this thing we call life.

Nine

Angela

After it starts to rain at the park, Brad invites us to their house for homemade pizza. Since Jack perks up considerably at the word *pizza*, I accept the invitation even though I feel sort of guilty for enjoying my time with Brad and his kids so much when I'm supposed to be mourning my late husband.

Watching Jack play catch with Brad left me deep in my feels and stirred an aching grief for my son, who loved playing with his dad so, so much. It didn't matter what they were doing, Jack was enthralled by everything Spencer said and did. My little boy is hungry for the male attention he used to get every day from Spence. Brad gave him what he needed while I kept an eye on all the other kids, and afterward, Jack seems more animated than I've seen him in months.

I also feel guilty for thinking Brad is handsome and kind and, well, sexy. I love watching him care for his kids and respect the enormous amount of patience it takes to guide little ones who lack the ability to understand what's happened to their missing parent. The questions are relentless.

"Why did Mommy have to leave?"

"Will Daddy be there when we get home?"

"Can I call Mommy?"

"Do you think Daddy misses me?"

Just when we think they've asked us every knife-sharp question they have, there'll be another one to shred us.

We've fallen into the habit of texting the questions to each other, to the only person we both know who's going through the same exact thing.

I catch him watching me when he thinks I'm otherwise occupied, and each time that happens, a bolt of heat travels through me, landing in a flush on my face that I'm sure he must notice.

Do I care if he notices? Not the way I should. This entire situation has left me fresh out of fucks for things that would've been unthinkable before my husband died suddenly, leaving me with two grief-stricken little kids and a baby who'll never know his father. The only fucks I have left are for getting myself and my kids through each day and then getting up and doing it again the next day. Anything other than that barely registers with me.

However, Brad Albright is registering with me, and to be honest, that feels better than anything has since disaster struck.

He's tall, blond and muscular. The hint of blond stubble on his face and jaw is sexier than hell, and so's the way his faded jeans cling to his ass.

I'm going straight to hell for noticing another man so soon after I lost the husband I loved for more than ten years. Eighteen months later, I feel like I'm starting to come out of the state of deep numbness I've been in since that awful day at Camp David when Spencer wouldn't wake up.

Part of me wonders if my infatuation is the direct result of that disaster. Sometimes I feel like Brad and I are the only two adult survivors of an apocalypse, left with five kids to guide through the unthinkable on our own. We're both blessed with tremendous family support and friends who've shown up consistently since our losses, but at the end of the day, we're alone with our kids in homes we used to share with our spouses.

The loneliness of those long nights must be experienced to be understood.

Brad gets it like no one else, and I find myself turning to him more and more often when things go sideways—which they do far too often for my liking. Such as the day last week when Jack somehow managed to clog the second-floor toilet, and water was spilling onto the floor at an alarming rate.

I called Brad. He told me to shut off the water to the toilet, which hadn't occurred to me in my panic. Then, while his kids were at school and daycare, he came over to unclog the toilet for me.

Way above and beyond the call of new friendship, but he shows up for me, and I do for him, too. When Daphne spiked a high fever a couple of weeks ago, he brought Drake to my house while he took her to urgent care.

At some point over the last year, we've become each other's go-to person.

I sit at the island in his kitchen, holding Josh, while Brad supervises the four kids placing pepperoni on their pizza. Then he goes to the fridge and returns with a container of pineapple that he hands to Jack.

Jack smiles as he takes it from him. "You remembered."

"I did."

The look that passes between the two of them goes straight to my heart.

"What do you say, Jack?"

"Thank you, Mr. Albright."

"You should call me Brad. The mister thing is too formal for close friends like us."

"My mom says we have to be respectful to our elders."

"That's very true, unless your elder gives you permission to call him by his first name."

Jack shoots a wistful look my way. "Is it okay, Mom?"

"Since Brad suggested it, I think it's fine."

Brad extends a hand that Jack takes and gives a shake. "Looks like we have a deal, my friend."

I'm going to cry, and I can't do that in front of the kids. I get up and take Josh into the living room to cuddle with him.

Brad comes after me a few minutes later. "Pizzas are in the oven, and the kids are coloring at the table." He sits next to me on the sofa and puts his feet up on the coffee table. Photos of his late wife are all over the house, but the one from their wedding on the side table gets me every time. They were such a gorgeous couple.

"Thank you for getting the pineapple. That was very nice of you."

"I remembered he likes that combo."

"Not sure where he first had that, but he loves it."

"Are you okay?"

"Yeah, you know... Just seeing him smile... Thank you so much for today. It meant so much to him to play catch with you and to have the pineapple. Not to mention calling you by your first name."

"I should've asked you first."

"No, not at all. It was perfect just like that."

He runs a hand through his hair, leaving it disheveled as he releases a sigh. "Today started out rough and turned into a good day."

I want to reach over and straighten his hair, but I don't dare touch him. God knows what that'll lead to with five little kids underfoot. None of us is ready for anything more than what this is right now.

Friendship. Comfort. Understanding.

With a side of attraction tossed in for good measure.

I'm going straight to hell.

Lexi

TODAY HAS BEEN RIGHT out of a dream. Tom planned every minute, right down to a candlelight dinner at the restaurant where we reconnected after not seeing each other since high school. That was the night he casually offered me a way out of my parents' basement, where I'd been living since my husband, Jim, and I moved in with them after he was diagnosed with ALS.

More than a year after Jim's death, I was stuck in the place where my worst nightmare unfolded because I was saddled with crippling debt from his illness. Now, I'm in love with Tom, and my dear friend Joy found a way out of the debt through a program for people like me, and suddenly, life is sweet again—and getting sweeter all the time.

I had no idea Tom was planning to propose today. I thought it was just another autumn Saturday spent doing something outdoors. Every weekend is another adventure. We've hit a number of fall festivals, done some long hikes and taken a pumpkin-carving class at a local garden shop. So when he suggested Skyline Drive today, I didn't think anything of it beyond a fun day in a beautiful place.

As we ride home from the restaurant, I can't stop staring at my ring, which reflects each streetlight we pass. I told my Widows, because of course I did, but I still need to tell my parents, who'll be absolutely thrilled for both of us. He needs to tell his sisters. We'll do that tomorrow in person rather than with a call or text.

The news will keep.

After Jim's horrific illness and premature death, I honestly never expected to feel this kind of joy again. I thought that was over for me, and in a way, I was fine with it because my relationship with Jim was extraordinary in every way. I had my great love, and I was grateful for every minute I spent with him, even the difficult time at the end.

But then came Tom to show me that I still have a great big, beautiful life left to live and that joy and love are still possible.

He reaches over to put his hand on top of mine, his thumb caressing the stunning diamond ring he gave me earlier. "How're you feeling, hon?"

"Thrilled, excited, stunned, happy."

"All good things, right?"

"The best things. Thank you for the most amazing day."

"I was so nervous this morning. I'm surprised you didn't notice."

"Why were you nervous? You knew I'd say yes."

"I was worried about doing it at Skyline Drive. I debated that endlessly, but my gut kept pushing me in that direction. I wanted Jim there with us. I thought that was important."

"It was perfect, and the fact that you thought of him makes you perfect for me."

"He'll always be part of us. I promise."

"My widow friends talk about meeting guys who are threatened by the fact that they still love their late husbands. They can't handle sharing someone, even with a dead man. It means a lot to me that you're comfortable with keeping my love for Jim part of our relationship."

"Of course it is. He's part of you, and I love all of you."

"How lucky am I?"

"How lucky are *we*?"

"Very. I never take it for granted."

"I don't either."

Ever since his cardiac episode, he's stuck closely to a low-cholesterol diet and faithfully attended cardiac rehab until he graduated. Now he goes to the gym at least four times a week to continue the exercises he did in rehab. He's lost about fifteen pounds and is leaner, trimmer, more muscular as a result of the changes he's made.

I thought he was sexy before, but now he's even more so, especially since his hard work to get fit makes it more likely he'll live for a good long time. That's critical to my well-being, too. I simply can't exist in constant mortal fear of suddenly losing him, which is what I did for a time after his heart attack.

I went back to the therapist I saw after Jim died and worked through my anxiety about Tom's health, which was made worse by the fact that his father and his siblings died of heart attacks in their forties. Despite my experience with medical disasters, I'm determined to stay optimistic and not focus on the doom and gloom of it all. That's just no way to live.

Tom is doing everything he can to stay healthy, and that's what matters. If he were to die suddenly, it wouldn't be because he didn't take the risks seriously. The therapist has helped me to remember that we're all living with an expiration date, and we can't live in fear of something that may not happen for decades.

At home, he drives his truck into the garage, next to my car. I still can't believe this is where I live, that I get to be with him every day and sleep with him every night. Months ago, we moved my stuff from my former room over the garage into the main bedroom that I now share with him.

I walk into the kitchen to find a dozen red roses, congratulations balloons and champagne chilling in a bucket on the counter. Spinning around, I find him smiling as he comes in behind me. "How did you pull this off?"

"With a little help from Cora," he says, referring to his sister. "It's a good thing you said yes, or this would've been embarrassing."

I laugh at the grimace he makes as he says that. "So she knew about your plans for today?"

"She helped me choose the ring. I didn't feel qualified to do that on my own."

"She did great, and so did you." I loop my arms around his neck. "I love the ring, and all of this. Thank you for everything you did to make this a day I'll never forget."

"I'll never forget it either. It's not every day a guy gets engaged for the first time, to his high school dream girl, no less."

"Life is so weird."

"And wonderful."

I rest my head against his chest, feeling the strong beat of his heart against my ear. "That, too. Especially lately."

"Let's go finish this day in style, my love."

"What do you have in mind?"

"You'll see."

He takes me by the hand to lead me into our bedroom, which is awash in candlelight, with rose petals on the bed.

"You did not have your sister sprinkle rose petals on our bed!"

"I only asked her to light the candles when we were leaving the restaurant. The rose petals were all her."

"It's beautiful."

"So are you." He draws me into his arms and kisses me lightly at first and then more intently as the usual desire flares between us. His hands move over my back with increasing urgency as he removes my top and then pulls at the button to my jeans while I work on his shirt.

"No matter how many times we do this, no matter how many days we spend together, I can never, ever get enough of you, sweet Lexi." He drops his head to my shoulder. "Sometimes I still can't believe I get to love you for the rest of my life."

"Believe it. I'm here, and I'm not going anywhere as long as you love me."

"That's going to be a very long time." He eases me onto the bed and comes down on top of me.

The fragrant scent of roses and the candlelight combine to create a romantic setting as we make love for the first time as an engaged couple. Tom is always a tender, sweet, generous lover, but it's somehow so much *more* tonight after the commitment we made to each other today.

Everywhere he touches me lights up with sensation that travels through me like an electrical current. He takes me right to the edge of release before backing off and doing it again, until I'm pleading with him to move things along.

He chuckles as he pushes into me, going slowly for maximum effect. "So impatient."

"I've been very patient. Now let's go."

He gives me exactly what I asked for—and then some. Two orgasms in ten minutes, and he's not done yet.

I used to think I'd never do this again, but it took the right man at the right time, when I was ready to love again.

"Tom."

"What, honey?"

"I just want to…"

He raises himself up on his muscular arms. "What do you need?"

"I want to say thank you for everything. Not just today, but all of it."

"Oh God, Lex. I should be thanking you. I thought my life was great until I ran into you that night and found out I was barely existing when there was so much more." His lips find mine in a hungry, desperate kiss that has us clinging to each other as we move together toward another release for me that will include him this time.

Afterward, we stay wrapped up in each other for a long time, pulsing with aftershocks and drunk with contentment.

"I love you so much," he whispers. "More than I ever thought I could love anyone."

"I love you just as much. I can't wait to be your wife."

"Let's do it sooner rather than later."

"It's your first time. Don't you want a big wedding?"

"God no. I just need you and our closest people. Would that be okay with you?"

"Absolutely. I've done the big white wedding. I'd do it again if it was what you wanted."

"Nah, no need. Let's keep it simple—and soon."

"I can't wait to tell my parents. They'll be thrilled."

"They were very excited when I spoke to them last week."

"Thank you for doing that. I'm sure it meant a lot to them."

"Your mom cried. She's so happy for you—and for me, too. But mostly for you."

"I'm happy for *them*. It's a relief for them to see me coming out of the dark cloud of grief and finding my way forward again."

"You did that all on your own before we ever reconnected. If you hadn't, you wouldn't have been ready for me and this."

"It's nice to be with someone who tries to understand widowhood. I appreciate that you get it."

"I can't possibly know what you've been through, but I can see how hard you've worked to make a new life for yourself. I'm proud of you, and Jim would be, too."

"Means a lot to me that you think so."

"I know so. You've earned the right to your happily ever after, Lex. Now let's make sure you get it, shall we?"

I hug him tighter. "I've already got it. Anything else is just frosting on the cake."

Ten

Iris

Gage shakes me awake. "Wake up, Sleeping Beauty. We're home."

I fell asleep on the way home from checking on Taylor and the kids one more time after the funeral home. Thank goodness Gage still has his wits about him, because mine are gone.

"Wow, I was out cold."

"You fell asleep midsentence."

"What was I saying?"

"Something about the next Wild Widows meeting."

"I'm losing it."

"You're on overload, babe. Time for a good night's sleep."

"You're right."

"I usually am."

"Jeez, I walked straight into that."

He laughs as he meets me in front of the car and puts an arm on my back to send me toward the kitchen door. We remove our coats in the mudroom and hang them next to the empty hooks where the kids' coats should be.

It's weird to come home to a house with no children in it.

"I hate when the kids aren't here," Gage says, echoing my thoughts, as he so often does.

As much as I loved Mike—and I loved him very much—my relationship with Gage is deeper, forged on loss and grief and the understanding that only a fellow traveler could possibly have.

"I do, too. Even though they'd be asleep, we'd still feel their presence."

"I'll pick them up in the morning and get them back where they belong."

I turn to him and put my hands on his chest. "Thank you for everything today—and last night. I appreciate you stepping up the way you did for my friend."

He kisses my nose. "Whatever you need. And whatever Taylor needs going forward. We'll make sure she gets all the support we can give her."

"Do you think..."

"What?"

"I hate to even say it."

His brows furrow. "What's on your mind, honey?"

"Should we postpone the wedding?"

We've been counting down to Thanksgiving weekend, when we're set to tie the knot that Saturday. Next week, friends and family are coming from all over to celebrate with us. I get a queasy feeling in my stomach when I think about wallowing in my second-chance happily ever after when Taylor has lost hers.

He looks slightly stricken by the idea. "Uh, well... I guess that would be up to you. If you don't feel like you could go through with it..."

I feel terrible for having to even suggest postponing when we've been so excited about it. The kids can't wait to marry their Daddy Gage. "Not because of you or us. You know that's not it. I just wonder if it'd feel appropriate so close to Taylor's loss."

He wraps his arms around me. "Sit with it for a couple of

days and see how it feels then. It's still fresh, and emotions are running high."

"That's true." I rest my head on his chest. "Thank you for always being the voice of reason."

"Your voice is pretty reasonable, too, but like we always say, no big decisions right after a big loss, even if it's someone else's big loss."

"Thank you for being you, for always knowing what we all need and trying to get it for us. We're so lucky to have you."

"I'm the lucky one. Let's get you to bed before you fall asleep standing up." He surprises me when he picks me up and carries me up the stairs.

I fan my face. "Sexy."

"Haha, you're too tired for sexy tonight."

"How do you know? I took a nice nap in the car. I have a second wind."

"Your tank is on empty, and we've got a long few days ahead of us. You need sleep more than you need me."

"For the record, I need nothing more than I need you, even when you're being mean to me."

I love to make him laugh. It happens a lot more than it did when I first knew him, when he was still coping with the brutal loss of his wife and twin daughters. Every laugh I draw from him still feels like a victory, even after all this time.

I snuggle up to him in bed as he holds me close. "Sometimes it's all too much."

"Only sometimes?"

"A lot of the time."

"Can I say something potentially controversial?" he asks.

"What's that?"

"We don't always have to be as heavily involved in the Wild Widows as we are now. No one would blame us if we took a step back to focus more on the future than on the past."

"I'm not sure I could step away from the group."

"I know you feel that way, but maybe you should give it

some thought. Yes, we're doing a lot of good for people who truly need us, but what's the toll on us to be constantly immersed in the grief of others when we've worked so hard to survive our own losses?"

Raising myself on one elbow, I study his handsome face. "Do *you* want to step away?"

"Not particularly, but maybe we should. Is it healthy for us to be the first call for people suffering a tragic loss? Is it in our best interest to constantly be on the front lines of fresh tragedy?"

"I can't imagine walking away from people who need us so badly."

"It doesn't always have to be us who does the rescuing. I just want you to keep that in mind."

"You raise good points, but it makes me feel good to help others. Whenever I think it's too much, I remember Wynter when we first met her and how far she's come from that terribly unhappy place. She's proof that we're making a real difference for people who desperately need it."

"There's no doubt at all about that, but have you noticed that on Instagram, I write more about parenting my new partner's kids these days than I do about losing mine?"

"I have noticed that, and I love your posts about being Daddy Gage."

"My point is that life—and grief—moves on. It evolves and changes, and we change right along with it. I'm more focused these days on what I've gained rather than what I've lost, even if I think of Nat and the girls every day and remember something fun or funny or sweet about each of them. But those memories are finite now. The ones I'm making with you and the kids... Those are infinite. At least I hope they are."

I return my head to his chest as I consider what he said and how right he is—as usual.

"What're you thinking?" he asks after a long silence.

"My work with widows is a big part of who I am in the 'after.' I'm not sure what my life would look like without it."

"I'm not saying you have to quit it entirely or that you should quit it at all. I just want you to be aware that I see the toll it takes on you sometimes. You internalize the pain of so many others, and you carry it with you. I worry that might not be healthy for you long term, but only you can know if that's the case."

"You've given me something to think about."

"I don't mean to add to the load you're already carrying for Taylor, and nothing about this has to be decided any time soon."

"I know, but you make good points, and you didn't even mention that our house is ground zero for the Wild Widows."

"That, too."

"They've become family."

"And they always will be, no matter what."

I'm so tired, I can barely keep my eyes open, but as I drop into exhausted sleep, I can't deny that Gage has raised a very valid concern.

Adrian

I WAKE up at three in the morning to an empty bed. After I use the bathroom, I go looking for Wynter, checking first in Willow's room, expecting to find her doing a middle-of-the-night feeding. But she's not there, so I go downstairs, following a light on in the kitchen.

Wynter is on her knees, scrubbing the inside of the refrigerator, which has been completely emptied of its contents.

"Sweetheart, what're you doing?"

"Cleaning this disgusting mess of a fridge. If the Board of Health inspected us, they'd shut us down. Those tacos you brought home a week ago are still in there. Gross. Why am I the only one who ever cleans out the fridge?"

"I'll tell Xavier he needs to do a better job of that from now on."

"I'm not joking! It's gross."

"Does it need to be addressed at three o'clock in the morning?"

"I was awake, so I figured, why not get it done?"

"Can I help?"

"No, you're the problem."

I'd laugh, but she's not in a joking mood. "I apologize for my habit of abandoning leftovers and promise to do better in the future."

She looks up at me, glaring. "Are you patronizing me?"

"Would I do that?"

I lower myself to the floor, so she doesn't have to look up at me.

"Yes, I believe you would."

"Let me help you finish this so you can come back to bed."

"I can't sleep, so there's no point to being in bed."

"There's other stuff that can be done there."

"I'm not in the mood for that."

"Since when? You're always in the mood for that."

"Right now, I'm not." She doubles down on the scrubbing. "We need to be better about cleaning this thing before one of us dies from food poisoning."

"It's not that bad."

She glares at me again, this time with tears in her eyes. "It is that bad!"

When I slide close enough to put my arm around her, she goes stiff.

"What's really going on here, love?"

"I told you. The fridge is gross. It needed to be cleaned. I can't imagine having your sister over and her looking for something in there."

"She wouldn't care."

"Yes, she would. She'd never eat here again."

"Wynter... Talk to me."

"Nothing to say."

"When do you have nothing to say?"

"Right now, I have nothing to say."

"Is it because of what happened to Taylor?"

"I hardly know her."

"You know her, and you knew Will, too. It's devastating. I keep thinking about their kids and the new baby, who'll have a parent missing his whole life, like Xavier and Willow."

"It's not fucking fair. She already lost one husband, and the kids have now lost *two* fathers."

"You're right. It's not fair."

All at once, she seems to lose the head of steam that was powering her through the fridge cleaning.

"Let me help you put this back together. It's clean enough to do surgery in there."

That gets a small snort of laughter from her.

I get up, help her up and work with her to return the shelves and drawers to their places and replace the items that're going back in. A huge pile of containers sits on the counter by the sink. "I'll deal with that in the morning."

"Yes, you will, because it's all your crap."

"I'll take care of it, and I'll try to do better in the future. Can we go back to bed now? Our kids will be up in about two and a half hours."

"I guess."

She lets me lead her up the stairs, where I tuck her in and then get in next to her, rolling onto my side to cuddle up to her.

"You want to talk about it?"

"Not really."

"It's upsetting when we hear of things happening to other people that force us to revisit our own traumas."

"I said I don't want to talk about it."

"I know. I'm just saying... it's normal to be upset."

"Thank you for letting me know that."

By now, I know that Wynter gets mean when she's scared or anxious. I try not to let it bother me because I understand why she gets that way. I don't mind her taking it out on me. That's what I'm here for.

We're quiet for a long time, so long that I wonder if she's fallen asleep.

"If you die on me, I'll never forgive you. I just want you to know that."

I bite my lip to keep from laughing because nothing about this is funny.

"Thank you for letting me know."

"I mean it."

"I know you do." I tug her in closer to me. "Come here."

"I'm here."

"Not close enough."

She sighs dramatically and curls her sexy self against me, provoking the usual immediate reaction. "Put that thing away."

I snort with laughter. "He can't help himself. If you're around, so is he."

"How will she do it?"

"What? Who?"

"Taylor. How will she rebuild her life a second time?"

"She'll find a way. She has to for the sake of her kids."

"I couldn't do it."

"Yes, you could."

"No, I really couldn't. Somehow, I managed to survive losing Jaden, but you... If it happened to you... I'd never get over that."

"You'd find a way for the kids."

"I'm not sure I would. It's not like I'm a helpless woman who can't function without a man. That's not what I'm saying. It's that I can't function without *you*."

"Aw, babe, that's very sweet of you to say."

"I'm not being sweet. I'm being serious. We've risen from absolute ashes to put together a life for ourselves that we both love. I'm just saying I can't see myself doing that again."

"Neither can I, so don't you go anywhere either."

"I'll try not to."

I run my hand over her back, hoping she'll relax and get some sleep before the kids are up to run us ragged for another day.

"Adrian?"

"Yeah, hon?"

"I want you to know... I really, really loved Jaden. I loved him so much."

"I know you did."

"But this... After what we went through to get here... I just don't know how I'd survive losing you. And honestly? It never occurred to me that it could even happen until I heard about Taylor's husband."

"We've all got an expiration date. Some just get more time than others. Gage always says life is a fatal illness."

"I don't like that saying."

"I don't either, but it's true. That's why we have to make the most of the time we do have. We never know when we'll run out."

"That's a fucked-up way to live."

"These things were decided way before we arrived on the planet. Unfortunately, we're stuck with the system we were born into."

"I want to know where I can file an appeal."

"I'll look into that for you."

Her hand moves from my chest, over my abdomen, to cup my still-throbbing erection.

"I thought you said you weren't in the mood."

"I wasn't until you reminded me that every minute counts."

"I'll have to do that more often."

Her low chuckle feels like a victory of sorts—and a relief.

Her dark moods, which aren't as frequent as they used to be, can last for days. They usually occur around Jaden's birthday or the anniversary of his death.

When she climbs on top of me, I wrap my arms around her, holding her tightly to my chest. "I'm right here, love, and I'm not going anywhere as long as I have you and our kids."

"Make love to me, Adrian."

"Nothing I'd rather do." I draw her tank top up and over her head and toss it aside, sliding my hands from her narrow hips, over her ribs, to cup her full breasts. As I run my thumbs over her nipples, I love the way she reacts, pressing her heat against my hard cock and generally driving me crazy as only she can do.

She's wildly sexy, responsive and up for anything in bed, which are just three of the many reasons I love her with my whole heart.

Before she can take over, I turn us so I'm on top and set out to kiss every bit of soft skin I can get to. I suck her nipples until they're standing straight up, and then I bury my face between them, breathing in the fragrant scent of the woman I love.

After I lost Sadie, I couldn't imagine having this kind of connection with another woman, but Wynter has shown me what's still possible, even after disaster. But she's right when she says losing what we have would be a whole other level because of what it took to get to a place where we were not only ready to love again, but open to taking all the risks that go along with it.

She's lying when she says it never occurred to her that she could lose me, too. Of course it did. You don't survive what we did without a healthy dose of reality showing up to remind you that nothing and no one is safe. Taylor's tragedy is the latest reminder of what can happen with no warning and no way to prepare yourself.

I remove the scrap of fabric she calls panties and make myself at home between her legs. It drives her wild when I do this, and I never get tired of the way she responds to me. She makes me feel ten feet tall when she claws my back, pulls my hair and begs me for more. She always wants more, and I'm happy to give it to her.

By the time I push into her, she's already come twice, and I'm on the edge. She's so tight and wet that I have to force myself to take it slow, so I won't hurt her. For all her bravado, she's fragile in ways that would surprise people who don't know her as well as I do, and the thought of hurting her is abhorrent to me.

"I want it fast and hard," she says, panting from the effort to take me inside her.

"You'll get everything you want when you're ready."

"I'm ready now."

"No, you're not."

My Wynter can start a fight over absolutely anything, even this. "Wouldn't I know better than you?"

"Not about this."

"Because you're such an expert."

"I'm an expert on you, and if I plow into you, it'll hurt, so shut up and let me do my thing."

"Fine."

"Fine."

"Wake me up when it gets good."

I give her a light smack on the ass, which causes her to clamp down on me, impinging my progress. "You're such a brat."

"You knew that before you went all in with me."

"I'm trying to go all in with you, but if you keep doing that clamping thing, we're never gonna get there."

She throws her arms out and spreads her legs. "Have it your way."

"I'm trying to, but as usual, you're being a pain."

She's having one orgasm after another as I press farther into her, until I'm fully seated and doing everything in my power not to lose it before I take her on the wild ride she requested. I hold perfectly still for at least two minutes while she squirms under me, trying to move things along.

There's nothing in this world quite like making love to my Wynter.

Her fingernails score my back and ass, and knowing there'll be marks afterward only turns me on more.

She groans. "Don't get any bigger."

"That's your fault, banshee girl."

"Sticks and stones..."

"Hold on tight. Here we go."

I love the way she wraps her arms and legs around me. I love the sounds she makes and the way she comes so hard, she makes me see stars while I try to hold out for as long as I can because it feels so fucking good.

She gasps with shock when I abruptly pull out and flip her over, giving it to her from behind. By now, I'm fairly certain she's no longer thinking about what happened to Taylor or her fears of losing me or anything other than the incredible pleasure that pounds through me and into her. I reach around to caress her clit, making her come one last time as I give it to her as hard as I dare before letting myself go with her.

"Mmmm," she says. "That's what I'm talking about."

Since I'm still buried deep inside her, I give a little push to ride the aftershocks that're almost as good as the main event.

I take a little bite of her shoulder. "I love you."

She shivers. "I love you, too."

"Everything's going to be all right. I promise."

"If you say so."

"I say so, and you have to believe me because I love you."

"Love you, too."

Eleven

Angela

Okay, so I'm not sure exactly how this happened, but all three of my kids are asleep on sofas at Brad's, and he and I are in the kitchen, still talking, at nine o'clock!

We. Never. Went. Home.

What. Is. Happening?

"I, uh, I should go."

"You don't have to. You guys are welcome to spend the night. We have a guest room for when Mary Alice's parents come to visit."

I can't spend the night here. That would be crazy! And inappropriate. And a million other things. But the thought of waking my sleeping kids, driving home and battling them into bed is so repulsive that I find myself considering Brad's kind offer. "Jack and Ella would be up all night if I woke them now."

"Mine would be, too. So you'll stay?"

"It's weird, right? For me to stay here?"

"How so? We're friends, your kids are asleep, and it'd be a nightmare to move them at this point. No big deal."

"Right. No big deal."

"I'll get some blankets for the kids and make sure the guest room is set for you and Josh."

"Thank you."

While he goes upstairs, I text my older sister, Tracy. *Hey— just FYI we're hanging at a friend's house tonight. Didn't want you to panic if you come by in the AM and we're not there.*

Thanks for letting me know. Which friend?

I think long and hard before I reply, knowing that whatever I tell her will lead to more questions. *A new one.*

I've said very little to anyone, even my sisters, about the friendship I've formed with Brad. Since Sam introduced us at one of the hearings in the criminal case, we've kept in close touch, but no one really knows that. I can't bear the possibility that they'd think it's too soon for me to have male friends. I know that's not reasonable, because they both want the best of everything for me, but for some reason, I haven't told them.

Am I allowed to ask questions?

Not now!

Fine. Tomorrow, then. There'll be questions.

Thanks for the warning, now go away.

Hey, Ang?

WHAT?

If you're happy, I'm happy. Have fun.

Just a friend. Relax.

Love you.

Love you, too, busybody.

My sisters are my best friends, and there's no way I would've gotten through suddenly losing Spencer without them and their families. But along with world-class support comes curiosity about what happens next for me and my kids. The last thing in the world I'm ready for is anything romantic.

I like being with Brad. He's easy to talk to, and he's going through the same thing I am. That's all this is.

I've wandered out to check on the kids when my phone

buzzes with another text that I assume is also from Tracy, who can be like a bloodhound when she catches a scent on the wind.

But it's not Tracy. It's Luke, the doctor/widowed father of four I met through the Wild Widows. *Hey, can you chat? Crazy day around here. Could use a good vent.*

I've texted with him a lot since we met, and he's asked me to get coffee, but that hasn't happened yet.

Can't tonight. Maybe tomorrow?

Sure, sounds good. Have a good night.

You, too.

I no sooner send that text than Brad comes downstairs with blankets that he puts over my sleeping kids and a rolled-up something he hands to me.

"Sweats and a T-shirt to sleep in. Thanks to Mary Alice's incredible efficiency, we also have spare toothbrushes."

"Five-star accommodations. Thank you."

"My pleasure. It's fun to have the company."

I follow him into the kitchen and place the clothes he loaned me on a chair.

"How about a glass of wine, since you don't have to drive?"

I haven't had a drink in ages, not since I was first pregnant with Josh. One glass of wine probably won't hurt anything. "What do you have?"

He goes to the cabinet over his refrigerator and takes a look. "My sisters were here recently, so I have Rosé and Chardonnay." He opens a cabinet over the stove. "And Pinot Noir."

"Rosé, please."

"Coming right up." As he gets out glasses and finds a corkscrew, I watch the way his soft gray T-shirt clings to his muscular torso. Why am I so interested in how his T-shirt fits him?

He spins around to ask me something and catches me looking.

A slow, lazy smile spreads across his handsome face. "Whatcha looking at?"

I'm mortified to have been caught gawking. "I, um, I was just spacing out."

He smiles as he pours the wine and brings it to the table. "This is nice."

"What is?"

"Your kids and my kids asleep, and you here to hang out with. This is often the toughest time of day for me, when everything is done and I'm reminded once again of how alone I am."

"I get that. It's the silence after everyone else is asleep."

"No one to binge-watch shows with or talk to or just... anything. It's such a weird void after being married for so many years."

We've talked before about how he was married to Mary Alice for seven years, while I was married to Spencer for almost ten.

"Not to mention together for years before we got married," I add.

"Same." He takes a sip of his wine and then meets my gaze across the table. "I'm trying to figure out who I am as a single guy again. It's the weirdest freaking thing to accept I'm not married anymore. I can date if I want to. Not that I want to. Not really."

"You'll be ready for that someday."

"What about you? Do you think about that?"

We haven't talked about this before. Most of our conversations have focused on helping our kids through the sudden, traumatic loss of a parent and getting through the days without the help of our partners. We talk about the anger, too. There's been a lot of that over the way they died, even if we don't blame them. Most of the time, anyway.

"I think about it, but with three little kids, including a seventeen-month-old, I'm not exactly prime dating material."

"Don't sell yourself short. You're a beautiful, fun, smart, caring woman. Anyone would be lucky to date you."

"Oh... well... thanks."

"I didn't mean to embarrass you."

"No, it's fine. I just haven't thought of myself in those terms in quite some time. I've been very, very married."

"Yeah, me, too. It's incredibly strange to not be anymore."

"Do you think about taking off your ring?"

"Every day. I debate it over and over again, wondering why I still have it on when she's been gone for a year and a half and what it'll mean to take it off."

I glance down at my stunning diamond solitaire and the matching band. "I love my rings so much. I hate the idea of not wearing them anymore."

"Could you wear them on the other hand?"

"I've thought of that. I might switch them over at some point."

"Feels fucking final to take the rings off, even to put them on the other hand, doesn't it?"

"It really does, not that it hasn't felt fucking final for a while now. Sometimes I still can't believe it happened."

He grimaces. "And we've got the fucking trial to look forward to."

They'd both been notified by the U.S. Attorney's Office that they could be called to testify.

"Fuck this shit."

He laughs. "Fuck it to hell and back."

We're finishing our wine when I hear Josh stirring in the other room. I rush out to get him before he wakes Jack and Ella and bring him back to the kitchen, where Brad has dimmed the lights for us.

Josh has been fed and changed, so he's just looking for some mommy snuggles that I happily give him.

"He's a sweet little guy."

"I'm so lucky to have gotten an easy baby after losing Spence. If he'd been Ella two-point-oh, I would've been losing it. She had colic and barely slept the first year."

"Yikes."

"It was rough, but I had help. Spence was great with her. He spent a lot of nights walking the floor with her so I could get some rest."

"Drake was like that, too. I worked nights, so it was tough on Mary Alice."

"What's the latest on going back to work?"

He's been on an extended leave of absence while he adjusted to single parenthood. "It's on for the first of the year, and they're moving me to days, so my schedule aligns with the kids', but that means a whole new group of coworkers and possibly a different station—and still some occasional night shifts that no one can avoid." He shrugs. "Not what I would've chosen, but none of this is my choice."

"Reminder that the GoFundMe my friends did for me after Spence died raised a ton of money, thanks to my sister and brother-in-law promoting it. I'm happy to share it with my fellow widow friends."

Mary Alice didn't have life insurance, and while there were fundraisers for him and his kids that have sustained him while he was out of work, they didn't raise a fraction of what mine brought in thanks to Sam and Nick's support of the fundraiser that Sam's partner, Freddie, started. Before his death, Spencer had lost his job and his life insurance along with it, so I would've been totally screwed without the fundraiser.

"You're going to need that money, Angela. Don't give it away."

"I'll need a fraction of what was raised, and if I could help to make your life easier and the lives of other young widows, why wouldn't I?"

"I wouldn't feel right taking money from a friend."

"These aren't ordinary times, Brad. You should think about how it could make life so much easier for you during this difficult transition. You could work part time instead of full time or change direction altogether. Whatever works for you and your family."

"It's kind of you to want to help me."

"I want to help everyone who needs it. Young widowhood is a tough journey, especially for families like ours that didn't have life insurance."

"Who worries about things like that in their twenties or early thirties?"

"I didn't. Spence had it through work until he lost his job, and it never occurred to us to get it for me."

"Same here—I have it through work, but we never got it for Mary Alice because she was a stay-at-home mom. Obviously, it never occurred to either of us that she could die young and leave me in a mess."

I reach over to put my hand on top of his. "Let me help you."

He stares at our joined hands for a long moment. "I'll think about it."

"It would make me happy to help you. This terrible tragedy has led to new friends, and we're going to survive this together."

Brad blinks back tears that seem to take him by surprise. "That makes it bearable... Knowing we're going to survive together."

"Of course we are. We're friends forever after this."

"Friends forever," he says gruffly.

Taylor

I'm in bed with my kids asleep on either side of me and the baby playing an aggressive game of soccer in my belly as I stare up at the ceiling. I need to pee, but I can't move without disturbing the kids. It took hours to get them to sleep after another devastating day. They have a million questions about what happened to their daddy, where he is now, what happens next, can he still see us, will he get to meet the baby before he's born.

Each one is like a knife to my broken heart.

I don't know what to tell them because none of it makes sense to me either.

The outpouring of love and support from everyone we know has been overwhelming. Food has come pouring in, along with flowers and offers of help with the kids and anything else we might need. As much as I appreciate everyone, it's bringing back memories of the early days after Greg died, a time I'd prefer to never revisit.

But here I am, wallowing in the horror of losing two husbands. How is this our fate?

What am I going to do with two devastated kids and a new baby to care for on my own? The path before me feels dark and hopeless, but in all the madness, the one spark of light has been hearing from Will's insurance company that they're working on paying out his life insurance expeditiously. That'll make a huge difference for me as I stare down life without him.

All I want is for Will to come breezing in, flashing that sexy, irresistible grin and telling me everything is going to be fine the way he always did when my anxiety got the better of me. But he's never coming back, and I'm not at all certain that every-thing will be all right. Not this time.

I long for him, for his touch, his kind heart and his immense love for me and the kids. He infused my life with hope, optimism and faith that my best days were still ahead of me rather than behind me, as I'd believed after Greg died.

Now what?

My bladder is about to burst when I finally inch my way down between the kids, trying to get out of bed without waking them or peeing my pants, either or both of which is possible. I'm almost out when Miles raises his head.

"What's wrong?"

"Nothing, honey," I say in a whisper, praying Eliza won't wake up, too. "I have to go to the bathroom. Go back to sleep."

"Are you coming right back?"

"I will. I promise."

He drops his head to the pillow and sighs. I imagine he's remembering—again—that Will died, and that's why he's sleeping in our bed.

My bed. It's my bed now.

I make it into the bathroom just in the nick of time, relieving my bladder as tears slide down my face in a steady stream that feels like it might never stop this time. My head feels too heavy to hold up, so I drop it into my hands and bite my lip to keep from wailing. I wish I could, but that would scare my traumatized children, and I'd never want to add to their grief by making them worry about me, too.

Since I've been here, done this before, I'm well aware that I have no choice but to survive the loss of Will. I have no choice but to rally for my soon-to-be three children and to continue to put one foot in front of the other the way I did after we lost Greg. But I really, really, really don't want to do any of it.

If it was just me, I'd crawl into bed, pull the covers over my head and stay there as long as I could, until the searing ache in my chest let up enough for me to breathe comfortably.

That's not going to happen.

What will happen is the sun rising in the morning, the kids waking and looking to me for guidance on how to get through this devastating loss. I'll be there for them every step of the way.

Because I have no choice in the matter.

Twelve

Hallie

I'm on the deck, stretched out on the sofa, staring up at the stars, contemplating life and loss and the vagaries of both, when my partner, Robin, comes out with bourbon for me and wine for her. That she understands I need the hard stuff tonight is one of many ways she's perfect for me. She lives with me when her kids are with their dad, and we look forward to the time alone together.

I take the glass from her and sit up a little to take a sip. "Thank you, hon." She's tall, blonde and so pretty she takes my breath away, especially when she smiles.

"How're you doing?"

I've been spiraling since Joy called with the news about Taylor's husband. I don't know her very well and met Will only once, but the news of his death—so close to their baby's arrival—has left me breathless. "I'm... you know... unsettled."

More unsettled than usual, I should say. Robin has stage-four breast cancer, which is currently stable, but the unknown has been hard to manage for me after losing my wife, Gwen, to suicide.

"Have you heard from Iris?"

"She texted to say that Taylor and the kids are doing as well as can be expected. I guess she and Gage were with Taylor last night and most of today."

"They're good souls, those two."

"They really are. Always there for all of us." I swish the bourbon around in the glass. "I can't stop thinking about Taylor and what she must be feeling. The few times I've met her, she seemed so happy and settled. She'd left widow life far behind, not that she didn't still grieve for the husband she lost to brain cancer, because she did for sure. But she didn't dwell in Widowville with the rest of us."

"Widowville," she says with a chuckle.

"It's a town populated by people who get what it's like to lose a spouse and, in our case, a young spouse who dies far too soon. Iris and Gage are the mayors of Widowville."

"I'm comforted to know they'll be there for you when you need them again."

I glance at her, surprised to hear her say that, because we try to never talk about where this situationship, as we refer to it, is heading. I like to think that it'll be years before I have to think about losing her, but we honestly have no idea how much time we'll have. And yes, I know how crazy I am to be involved with someone staring down a fatal illness, but the reward of spending this time with her has been worth the risks.

Or so I tell myself until something like Taylor's loss happens to remind me of what's ahead. I try my best not to think about losing Robin. I'm focused much more on enjoying every minute we have together.

"I'm sorry to be such a drag tonight."

"Please don't apologize. Of course this news upset you. It upset me, and I don't know them at all."

"I just keep thinking about how much her kids loved Will and how they have a new baby due soon. It just boggles my mind that this could've happened to them."

"I know. It's terrible."

"The good news, I guess, is that there're resources available to her that she didn't have the last time. Thanks to her and Iris and Christy, she'll have the Wild Widows to fall back on."

"You guys will get her through it."

"We'll do our best. Joy said this has her questioning everything."

"Is she still seeing that guy? What is his name?"

"Bernie. Yes, and as far as I know, it's been going well, but she said she's tempted to never leave the house again."

"Which she knows is no way to live."

"She said that, but the temptation is real."

"For you, too?"

I glance her way to find her watching me in that all-seeing way that's usually a source of comfort to me. Tonight, I fear she sees too much. "Nah."

"Liar," she says with a chuckle.

"I don't want to feel that way."

"But you can't help wanting to run and hide, especially in light of our situation."

"Something like that."

"It's okay, Hal. Don't feel like you have to dodge me on the hard stuff. I'm here for all of it."

I reach for her hand and am immediately comforted by her touch. "I can't bear to think of a time when you won't be here."

"Likewise. I mean, it's unlikely, but I could lose you before you lose me."

I make a face at her.

She laughs. "What? It's true. Look at what happened to Will. Leaving the house can be dangerous."

"Luckily, I don't work on scaffolding."

"We're all thankful for that."

I'm a well-documented Calamity Jane who'd have no business working anywhere that involves high places. "I keep thinking about what he thought of as he was falling, probably knowing he was going to die."

"I'm sure his every thought was for Taylor and the children."

"Definitely."

"Will you do something for me as you process this terrible tragedy?"

"Yes, of course. What do you want me to do?"

"Talk to me about it. Don't curl up in a ball and try to muscle through it. That doesn't work, and it's apt to make everything so much worse."

"I promise I'll talk to you about it, but I may not have much to say."

"That's fine, too, as long as you don't bury it and think it'll go away, because it won't. It'll just fester."

"I know," I say with a sigh. "Sadly, this is far too familiar to me. Thinking about what Taylor is going through brings it all back with Gwen. The initial shock, those first few days, the people, the food, the disbelief. I haven't taken a trip down that memory lane in a while."

"I'm sorry you're hurting all over again."

"I'll be okay. Don't worry about me."

"I can't help it. I love you, and I hate to see you suffering."

"Is it weird to be suffering over someone I hardly know?"

"You understand what she's going through, and that's why you're suffering. You know how hard she worked to get to where she was with Will, only to be put back to day one as a widow."

"That's it exactly. You're good at this."

"At what?" she asks with a laugh.

"Getting to the heart of the matter and making me feel better about being grief-stricken for the friend of a friend."

"She's a fellow traveler. That's who you're grief-stricken for."

"I hope she comes back to the group."

"She may decide that was too much a part of her first time around and want something different now."

"Maybe, but I still hope we can help her somehow."

"I admire how that's always your first thought: 'How can I help?'"

"Our whole group is like that. It's what we do."

"It's a beautiful thing, but at a time like this, you need to be keeping an eye on your own well-being while you reach out to others."

"I hear you, and I'll be okay. I promise. This was tough news today. I needed a minute to process it. I'm sorry it cut into our time together."

"You're not apologizing for being upset, remember?" She slides closer to me and puts her arms around me, bringing my head to rest against her. "One of the things I love best about you is how deeply you care about the people in your life. You cared so much for Gwen that you still mourn her all these years later. You care so much for your widows, even the ones you don't know well, that their hurts become yours."

"It sounds more like an illness than a positive quality."

"Hush," she says with a chuckle. "Your big heart is your best quality, and I hope you never change. But..."

"There's always a but."

"Not always, but there is this time. I want you to be careful with that big heart. You feel so much for Taylor, but you're not obligated to show up for her, even though I'm sure you will."

"How can I not?"

"You can. Of course you can, but don't take on her grief and make it your own. You're already dealing with enough of your own—and that includes the anticipatory grief that comes from knowing you're probably going to lose me sooner than we'd both like."

"Shut up with that. You're not going anywhere."

"Hallie."

"Robin." I raise my head off her shoulder and look her in the eyes. "Shut. Up."

"Fine, but I hope you heard the rest of what I said."

"I heard it, and I appreciate it. You're right, as usual. I want to bring in the cavalry to help Taylor, but that's not my job in this situation. I'll be there for her in any way that I can, but I won't lose my mind over it. I promise." I stroke the back of her hand, marveling as I do every day over the softest skin I've ever touched. "Thank you for caring."

"You're easy to care about, and I can't bear to see you suffer."

Her deep sigh says what I don't want to hear—that someday, I'll probably suffer deeply over her, but she's worth it. Every minute with her is a gift.

I give her hand a light tug. "Let's go to bed."

Joy

TODAY HAS BEEN A DAY—AND a half. I'm absolutely crushed for Taylor and her kids. And for poor Will, who was such a good guy. The way he stepped up for her and those babies endeared him to all of us who knew Taylor before she met him.

We're in bed watching a movie, but I lost the plot an hour ago and can't be bothered with catching up. The raw feeling I've carried around since Christy called with the news reminds me so much of the day I woke up to realize my husband, Craig, had died in his sleep.

That still ranks as the most shocking moment of my life. He'd been fine the night before when we had dinner with friends, went to bed, made love and fell asleep. Only one of us woke up the next morning. Two autopsies were "inconclusive," and his death was determined to be "natural causes." Whatever the hell that means.

I can very easily put myself in Taylor's position after the sudden loss of someone irreplaceable, and dwelling in that space for hours has made a wreck of me.

"That was awesome," Bernie says when the movie ends. "I loved it. What did you think?"

"It was good."

"You didn't hear a word of it, Joyful."

I love that he's given me a nickname that no one other than my grandmother has ever used for me. He's a gorgeous man with smooth light brown skin, warm brown eyes and a show-stopper of a smile. That smile was the first thing that attracted me to him, and it still gets to me every time he directs it my way.

"I'm sorry. I'm just distracted."

"Thinking about your friend?"

"Yeah, and her kids, and the rest of our widows, who'll take this harder than most of the people in Taylor's life, even the ones who barely know her. Many of them are courageously creating new lives for themselves and their children with new partners. This'll be a reminder that none of us is safe from disaster striking again."

"Does that include you?"

"What do you mean?"

"Are you courageously creating a new life for yourself with a new partner and fearing disaster striking again?"

Realizing what he's asking me, I give him the side-eye. We've been seeing each other for more than a year. He's the first guy I've slept with since Craig died. I'm enjoying him, but I'm not ready to put labels on it.

"That's a really long pause after a question."

"I was trying to think of the nicest way to say I'm not sure yet what I'm doing here, and I'm sorry if that's not what you want to hear."

He takes my hand and kisses the back of it. "It's okay. I'm not in any rush to call it something. I want you to know how much I enjoy being with you."

"Same."

"Okay, then. We'll continue doing what we're doing. But can I ask you for one thing?"

"Sure."

"Don't let this awful, terrible, tragic thing that's happened to your widow friend lead you to think it'd be easier to be alone than to take another chance with your heart."

I place my hand on his muscular chest. He works out every day and has the body to prove it. I've never been with a guy who has an actual six-pack, only his is more like a twelve-pack.

"It'd be a crying shame to mess up a great thing over something that happened to other people," he adds.

"I know."

"So let's not do that, okay?"

"I'll try very hard not to."

"I understand how something like this must bring it all back..."

"It does."

"Will you talk to me about it? I can't possibly know what you've been through or what news like this does to you unless you tell me. Will you do that?"

"I can try."

"Only if you want to. I'm here for you, Joy. Not just for the fun stuff, but for the hard stuff, too. We've been all about the fun, which has been great, but we've both been around long enough to know there's more to life than fun and games."

"Yes, there is, but the fun and games have been just what I needed, so thank you for that."

"Is that all we're going to be? Fun and games?"

"I... I'm still trying to figure out what I'm capable of in the 'after,' as we refer to this widow life. I don't know if I can go all in again, or if this is all I can do."

He moves closer to me and caresses my face. "I think you, beautiful Joy, are capable of a tremendous amount of love for the people in your life. I think they're incredibly lucky to be loved by you, that anyone would be. I would be."

Damn him and his sweetness, which has me blinking back tears.

"I don't want to push for more than you can handle. I know this much has been a big deal, but I'm falling hard for you. I thought you ought to know that."

I rest my forehead against his, ridiculously moved and terrified of the big feelings I've had for him for a while now. I was getting closer to doing something about those big feelings when I got the news about Will. Since then, I've been in a spiral that I can't seem to pull myself out of, no matter how hard I try.

"Talk to me, Joyful. Tell me what's going on."

"I've taken this news about my friend's husband hard. I wish I hadn't, because my rational brain says it's silly to let something like this resurrect all my old hurts. But the emotional part of me, the part of me that loved my Craig with all my heart and will never get over losing him so suddenly... That part of me is running the show tonight, as much as I wish it wasn't."

"That's totally understandable."

"I'm glad you think so, because it's pissing me off."

I feel the rumble of his low chuckle against my ear as he holds me close to him.

"Even a badass like you can have a setback every now and then."

"I don't like setbacks. They irritate me."

"Yes, I can see that, but the thing about setbacks is they're usually temporary. So it'd be foolish to make decisions about anything while you're dealing with one. Right?"

"Yeah, that's true."

"So let's table this conversation about what we're doing and where it's going until you feel up to it, okay?"

"That'd be good," I say on a sigh of relief. "Thank you for understanding."

"I can't possibly understand any of this, but I'm more than willing to follow your lead through it."

"That makes you a rare and special guy, Bernard."

He scowls. "Only my mother calls me that."

I laugh for the first time in hours as the tightness in my abdomen lets up somewhat, which is a relief. I carry my trauma in my belly for some strange reason, and when it aches like it has for hours today, it brings back memories of that horrible morning when I realized Craig was dead.

"Do you want me to go?" Bernie asks. "I promise I won't be hurt if you say yes—as long as I can come back another time."

"I don't want you to go."

"Oh, good, because that would've been a bummer."

I look up at him, smiling. "Thank you."

"For what?"

"You've handled today's emotional firestorm just right, and it's very much appreciated."

"Tell me what you need, and I'll do what I can to make sure you get it."

"A gal could fall in love with a guy who says things like that."

"The guy in question—if we're talking about you and me, that is—would be fine with that."

For the first time in hours, I relax and allow myself to wallow in the sweet comfort he offers so willingly. From the start, he's been amazing in all the ways that matter to a widow attempting to start over after a devastating loss.

He listens more than he talks. He tries to understand while acknowledging he never can. He's never once pushed me for more than I'm ready to give. And he makes me laugh—a lot. That last one has been a tremendous gift in addition to all the others.

"Bern..."

"Yeah?"

"Thank you for being patient with me."

"You need to stop thanking me for things I'm happy to do."

"Not everyone would be, you know?"

"You wouldn't be with someone who couldn't handle it. You'd have kicked me to the curb a long time ago if I were like that."

"You're right about that. I've kicked a few others to the curb over the years."

"Their loss, sweetheart."

Thirteen

Brielle

With my son, Charlie, asleep, I settle on the sofa with a glass of wine, my phone and the dating app I recently joined. I can't get over the flood of messages that've poured in since I posted my profile four days ago. Every message is full of bullshit, platitudes, nonsense. I can't imagine how I'll ever sift through the swamp full of crap to find someone I might want to get to know.

I text my widow friend Naomi, who helped me set up the profile after months of pleading with me to give it a whirl. *This app is ridiculous!*

She responds with laughing emojis. *You gotta kiss a lot of frogs before you find a prince.*

Ew. I'm not in the right frame of mind for this tonight.

I get that. I've been a mess all day, and I barely know her— or him.

I keep thinking about poor Lexi hearing this news, which she will eventually.

I know. Me, too. I'm glad she got to have today, though. No one deserves a happily ever after more than she does.

True.

Lexi took care of her husband, Jim, who had ALS, and was left with crushing medical debt that was finally alleviated thanks to our friend Joy, who found a grant program for family members burdened with medical debt. What a miracle that was for Lexi—and what a miracle Joy is for all of us.

Seeing Lexi happily in love and now engaged to Tom Terrific was just what the rest of us needed today while dealing with the awful news about Will.

Naomi calls me. "So there's not one dude who sparks the slightest interest?"

"There's so much crap, I don't even know what to look for. I'm not sure that this is the right thing for me."

"Brielle... You're a single mom who can't go out and meet new people the way most singles do. Without the apps, you're going to turn to moldy cheese while your son is growing up."

I nearly choke on the sip of wine I was taking. "Moldy cheese? Seriously?"

"I read that hymens can grow back if there's not enough traffic."

"That is not true! Shut up."

She cackles with laughter.

"You're ridiculous."

"Am I wrong? Are you or are you not collecting dust at home while life marches forward with terrifying speed?"

She's not wrong. Charlie will soon be *four*, which is impossible to believe, as is the fact that his dad, Mark, has been dead four years already, too, killed in a skiing accident while at his brother's bachelor party weekend. I was left to deliver and raise our son on my own, which has been my sole focus for all this time.

Lately, though, the loneliness has become harder to handle. I confided that to Naomi, thus the dating app.

"I'm collecting dust. You're right. I can't believe it's been four years already. How is that even possible?"

"I know. It's crazy. It'll be three years for David soon, which is so hard to believe. I didn't think I'd survive a day without him, let alone *years*." Her fiancé died of lymphoma, and because they never got the chance to be married, she jokingly refers to herself as a widow wannabe. Not that anyone would want to be, but we tell her she's as much a widow as the rest of us.

"You're doing great, Nai."

"Eh, I guess. In many ways, I'm still on the starting blocks in the aftermath."

"At least you're out there meeting people and having some fun."

"It's not as much fun as I make it out to be."

"Really?"

"Nah. It's the same bullshit you're seeing on the apps, only in person. In some ways, that makes it worse because they're lying right to your face, hoping to get laid."

She's slept with a couple of them, but still hasn't felt a connection with anyone, so she keeps looking and hoping.

"Was it like this when we were dating before?" I ask her.

"Not like this. It's gotten kinda feral out there. My single friends say the same thing. Guys aren't interested in relationships. They want one thing and one thing only—and will say and do whatever it takes to get it."

"That's profoundly depressing."

"Yep."

"So what's the point of even bothering if that's the playing field?"

"What else should we do? Curl up in a ball and give up?"

"That's actually sounding pretty good to me right about now."

"Today was a shit day. I'll give you that. But we can't give up."

"Why not?"

"Because! You're in your early thirties, Brielle. You've got decades left to live, and you can't exist solely for your child, who'll grow up and leave you eventually."

"My Charlie will never leave me."

"Whatever you say. Come on. Try, will ya?"

"If I must."

"You must. And remember, a lot of people have met their one through the apps. It just takes time and patience."

"I've got the time. It's the patience that's the problem."

"Nothing ventured, nothing gained."

"Are you reading self-help books again?"

Naomi laughs. "Always, but that's the truth, and you know it."

"All right already. I'll keep looking."

"There's got to be *one* diamond in the rough."

"I guess we'll see. Are we still meeting on Wednesday?"

"Iris said it's still on," Naomi says, "and she'd let us know if anything changes."

"I'm sure she's been with Taylor nonstop. I worry about the toll it takes on her."

"She's always there for everyone."

"That's what worries me. When does it become too much, you know?"

"I'm sure she'd say so if that happened."

"Would she, though?" I ask. "I think she'd soldier on, even if she was buckling under the weight of it."

"Maybe we should talk to her about that at some point."

"We may get the chance at Wednesday's meeting. I'm sure Taylor's loss will be first on the agenda."

"Definitely. Do you think she'll come back to the group?"

"I don't know her well enough to say what she might do. I hope she does if she thinks it would help."

"I do, too. Well, I'd better get to bed. Gotta work in the morning."

"Thanks for calling and for giving me a push."

"You got it. Text me any updates."

"Will do."

I'm so thankful for friends like Naomi who understand the struggle to move on and give me a push when I need it. Mark would be pissed with me for standing in place for so long after he died, even if I've had my hands full raising the son he never got to meet. My love was a get-things-done kind of guy, and sitting still was never his thing. I wonder sometimes if he'd already be remarried if I'd been the one who died.

He sure as hell wouldn't be sitting here years later, alone and lonely, trying to take the first step toward a new life.

Or maybe he would. Who knows? Grief makes a mockery of even the most confident people. Mark loved me passionately, so maybe my death would've wrecked him the same way his did me. He was so larger than life that after all this time, I still can't believe he actually died. If you'd asked me before the skiing accident that took him from us if he would die young, I would've laughed. I would've said, "No chance. He's invincible."

Of course, no one is invincible, and we learned that the hard way. His poor brother... Mark died at his brother's bachelor party, and though he and his fiancée were eventually married in a smaller, scaled-back wedding, the marriage didn't last. It was doomed from the start by grief and guilt. I'm still in touch with my ex-sister-in-law, who's suffered almost as much as I did over losing the man she loved to the same tragedy that took my husband.

Eh, enough of this morbid shit. Time to get serious about finding my chapter two. With that in mind, I get back on my phone to read the flood of messages I've received, hoping to find that diamond Naomi promised me.

Kinsley

I'VE DEBATED THIS ENDLESSLY, to the point of madness, really. Lately, all I've thought about is reaching out to Luke, one of the newer members of the Wild Widows. He lost his wife and the mother of his four children to colon cancer.

My husband, Rory, died of pancreatic cancer, so I have an idea of what Luke endured. I want to tell him I get it, that I understand some of what he went through and offer any help I can.

Today of all days, with the news from Taylor heavy on my heart, I should be worried about my own little family and not thinking about Luke and his kids. But the desire to reach out gets stronger by the day and hasn't been dampened in the least by today's tragic news.

One thing is keeping me from going for it.

Well, two things.

The first is that he has *four* children. The oldest is eight, and the youngest is three and a half. Christian, my eldest child, is eight, and my Maisy is six. That's a lot of little kids underfoot.

Second thing... is the spark of instant attraction I felt when I first met him at Iris's house the summer before last. That hasn't happened since Rory died. I haven't had so much as an ember of interest in any other man, so to have a full-blown spark is unsettling, to say the least.

Luke is gorgeous, with light brown hair that always looks like he's been running his fingers through it, golden-brown eyes and a smile that belongs in toothpaste commercials. Not to mention the rippling muscles that were visible through the button-down shirt he wore to Iris's gathering. When Lexi's boyfriend, Tom, fainted at Iris's house that night, Luke jumped into action to help Tom.

While everyone was naturally focused on Tom—who was thankfully okay—I watched Luke and was impressed by his quiet competence and obvious skill as a doctor.

He's been to a few meetings since then, but I've thought about him every day since the first time I met him, wondering how he's holding it together with four young kids and a busy job that must keep him away from home for long hours. I want to know about his wife, Isabella—he called her Bella—and what she was like. He said she was diagnosed when expecting their youngest child, Phoebe, and postponed treatment to safely deliver her daughter. She died when Phoebe was eighteen months old.

I found him on Instagram and devoured his posts about losing his love and raising their children alone, and after reading his heartfelt posts, I was more than halfway in love with him, which is another reason I haven't reached out.

I feel like a weirdo stalker with a high school crush on the big man on campus.

Ridiculous.

And getting worse by the day.

Fuck it. I pick up my phone, find the contact info Iris sent to all of us after we first met him and start writing.

Hi, Luke, it's Kinsley Davis from the Wild Widows. I've wanted to reach out to say hello as a fellow cancer widow. You've heard a lot of our stories, so as a refresher... My husband, Rory, had pancreatic cancer for all of forty-two days, and was thirty-eight when he died. Our kids, Christian and Maisy, are eight and six now, and are doing better after a rough few years. Anyway, I just wanted to say hi and...

And what, Kinsley? What else do you want to say? Perhaps you should mention you think he's hot and you haven't thought that about anyone since Rory died. Or maybe that might be too much to mention in the first text...

I laugh at my own stupidity and stare at my phone screen for several minutes before I finish that sentence.

...you have friends who understand what you're going through. Hope to see you at a meeting soon. Best, Kinsley

Before I can talk myself out of it, I send the text and then take a big sip from my wineglass. This feels way too much like high school redux, not that texting was as much of a thing then —thank God. It was bad enough without cell phones and social media. I can't imagine the drama that must go on these days.

I nearly jump out of my skin when I see reply bubbles pop up on my screen. Oh my God, he's writing back!

I'm practically hyperventilating by the time his response comes through.

Hey, Kinsley, thank you so much for reaching out. I so appreciate all the support I've received from the Wild Widows.

It occurs to me then that some of the other single women from the group, who are also my closest friends in the "after," might've gotten to him before me. That thought is as deflating as a pin stuck in a balloon. They saw what I saw, and naturally, they'd be interested. Who wouldn't be?

PC is the worst of the worst, and I'm so sorry you and your family lost Rory to it. I'm glad to hear your kids are doing better a few years out. Mine are a day-to-day situation. Some days are better than others. My older two have suffered tremendous grief since Bella died, while the younger two barely remember her. I'm not sure which is more heartbreaking, to be honest.

We're getting through it, thanks to tons of support from family and friends, as well as an amazing nanny who makes it possible for me to work without worrying about what's going on at home. That said, I'm always worried about what's going on at home and hoping I'm doing the right things by my kids. I'm sure you can relate.

Anyway, I've gone on long enough here. I really appreciate the friendship and support from you guys. It's made a big difference to know I'm not alone. I really want to get to the meetings more often and I hope to see you Wednesday. Fingers crossed for no work or life disasters!

I read and reread his messages until I feel like I could recite them from memory. He hopes to see me on Wednesday. Or does he hope to see all of us? It occurs to me that he's met so many of us, he probably has no idea which one of us is Kinsley.

That makes me laugh at my own stupidity. He has no idea who I am, and I've thought of him every single day since I met him more than a year ago. Being a widow has made me weird in more ways than I can count on one hand. Acting like a foolish teenager in the throes of a crush is just the latest entry on that long list.

"Time to call it a night, Kinsley." Did I mention I also talk to myself all the time? Yeah, weirder and weirder by the day. That's me.

I go around to check that the doors are locked, which I did earlier, but you can never be too cautious when you're home alone with two kids. Upstairs, I look in on my sleeping angels. They've saved me in every way a person can be saved, giving me a reason to go on when I wanted to die, too.

After I get in bed, I read through the text exchange with Luke again, wondering if he's waiting for me to reply to his last message.

Shit, is he watching the screen for bubbles like I was before? Or did he send that message and promptly forget all about me?

"Oh my God, Kinsley, I hate your guts right now. You're such a simpering fool."

That may be true, but if only I could forget the impact of meeting him for the first time and realizing I felt *something* for a man for the first time since I lost my husband. It was so overwhelming that I didn't even tell my widow friends about it, mostly out of fear that the single ones felt the same way I did.

After all, he spent most of that first gathering talking to Angela, the other new member who joined us that night. Maybe they've been seeing each other ever since and I'm a total idiot for thinking someone hasn't snapped him up. Who wouldn't want a sexy young doctor with a broken heart and four precious babies who need a new mommy to love them? He might very well be the most eligible bachelor in Northern Virginia.

Disgusted with myself and everyone else, too, I put my phone on the charger without replying to him and shut off the light. The morning will be here long before I'm ready to face another day of more of the same.

Fourteen

Christy

I'm in bed before Trey, who's basically living with us. My children love him as much as I do and are enjoying having a father figure again, even if they'll never stop missing their dad or reliving the day we lost him. That memory lives rent-free in all our minds as much as we'd like to forget the horror of him dropping dead right in front of us.

Will's death has brought those memories to the surface as I try to put myself in Taylor's place, wondering how in the hell she'll see her kids through yet another tremendous loss. It's simply unimaginable, and all day, I've been forced to wonder whether I'm doing the right thing for my kids by letting them fall in love with Trey. What if we lose him, too? How would we ever survive such a thing after what we've already been through?

I'm in an anxiety-fueled spin. I know it, but I can't seem to make it stop.

I've been so, so happy since I decided to go all in with Trey. The kids have been, too. He's gone above and beyond to connect with them without trying to force them to accept him. The four of us are slowly becoming a family, which has brought joy back into our home. Not that we need a man to make us whole. We don't. If it was just the three of us forever, we would've been fine, and we'd have found plenty of joy on our own.

Trey brings new energy, new interests, new everything.

I love him madly, deeply, desperately, all of which makes me vulnerable in a way I never would've chosen to be again. But when love is standing right in front of you, daring you to take the risk, what else can you do but live and love and hope for the best?

He comes out of the bathroom, fresh from the shower, whistling a jaunty tune as he strolls bare-ass naked into the bedroom that's become ours over the last few months. We even went to the store to pick out new bedding and towels that are "ours" to replace the ones that were just mine. Like everything we do, Trey made that fun by joking about the various patterns and which ones were chick-only and which ones were for chicks with dudes.

The lease on his townhouse expires at the end of next month, but he's mostly moved out already. Trey lives with us now. He's part of our family. He's helping to raise my children. He drives them to practices and picks them up at friends' homes after sleepovers. He knows all their friends' names and has inside jokes with most of them. Even homework has become more bearable because he's willing to help wherever he's needed. Thankfully, he gets algebra and geometry, which is such a blessing because I'd be in big trouble with that on my own.

As he gets into bed and comes to my side to snuggle up to me, I wish he wasn't here—and that's a first. I'm well aware of why I'm feeling this way tonight, but that doesn't make it any easier to cope with.

Trey, being Trey, picks right up on my unusual lack of enthusiasm for bedtime. "Want to talk about it?"

"No."

"Can I do anything for you?"

"No."

"Do you want me to sleep somewhere else tonight?"

I glance at him, trying to determine if he's pissed, but the only thing I see is the usual loving support I always get from him. "No."

"Any time you need some space from me and/or us, all you have to do is say so. I understand there're parts of you I don't have access to, and that's okay. But I'm right here if I can help."

My chin wobbles and my eyes fill as he says the perfect thing, as usual. "Thank you."

He takes my hand and laces his fingers through mine.

I can't stop thinking of Taylor's face, flat with shock and disbelief, reminiscent of how I felt the day we lost Wes. When tragedy comes with no warning, it seems to take longer to accept. For weeks after Wes died, I didn't believe he was really gone. I didn't have months or years of terminal illness to prepare me for his eventual death.

That morning, I'd had sex with my perfectly healthy, almost-forty-year-old husband, who later went to do some work in the yard and came in gasping for air before dropping dead in the mudroom. My scream brought the kids running toward us. I've regretted that scream every hour since then. If only I'd held it together, I might've spared them from witnessing their father's death. But I had literal seconds to process that he was dying right in front of me.

It's been a long time since I dwelled on the events of that day. They tend to live in a back corner of my mind that I keep sealed off so I wouldn't be regularly retraumatized as I worked so hard to rebuild our lives without Wes. We've done a good job of that, in my humble opinion, but Taylor's tragedy has reopened the old wounds, as much as I wish that wasn't the case.

I have a whole new life, one that I love as much as I loved the old one. I love Trey the same way I loved Wes, with my whole heart and soul, and my kids do, too. Life is good for all of us, the way I once wondered if it ever would be again. We did it. We survived something that could've destroyed us all, and we did it with courage, perseverance and determination to rediscover joy and optimism. We did it with the help of so many people who made sure we were ready when Trey came along.

And now... My sweet, sweet friend Taylor is back to day one a second time, and the very thought of it is almost more than I can bear to imagine. She's been one of my closest people since we were introduced in the aftermath of our initial losses by a mutual friend who thought we might benefit from having someone to talk to who understood.

Oh, how we benefited. Taylor and I hit it off from the first time we met for coffee and quickly became everyday best friends. I was one of her attendants when she married Will, whom I also adored. My heart is shattered for both of them and their kids.

But especially for Taylor. The thought of her having to rise up from the ashes—a second time—and guide herself and her children through another tragic loss is just so abhorrent to me that I feel like it's happening to me, as crazy as that sounds. That's how deeply I feel for her.

A sob erupts from my chest.

Trey wraps his arms around me and holds me as I dissolve into grief and heartbreak.

It's so fucking unfair.

I wish I could run away and hide from this situation, but I'd never leave my dear friend at such a time. I'll stay and support her every step of the way, but my heart is broken once again, and it won't be put back together overnight.

Iris

I HAVE to tell Lexi about Taylor's loss before our usual weekly meeting tonight, but she's been so deliriously happy since she and Tom got engaged last weekend that it's making me sick to think about making that call.

"You have to tell her," Gage says over morning coffee after he took the kids to school.

"I know, and I'm not sure why I'm being such a wimp about it. She barely knows Taylor."

"But the news will upset her anyway, and that's why you're putting it off." He leans in, his expression as serious as it ever is. "Can you see the toll this takes on you, love? This is what I'm talking about. You feel a responsibility to tell Lexi news that'll be devastating to her, which means first, you have to be devastated on her behalf."

He's the wisest person any of us knows, and he sees me in a way that Mike never did, as much as I hate to compare them. Gage has the "benefit" of having lived through one of the worst tragedies I've ever heard of, which has given him hard-won insight and understanding of the human condition that Mike never had.

Mike was devoted to his family and to flying. That was it. After he died, I found out he was also devoted to Eleanor, the mother of his other child, Carter, both of whom I've since met and formed a bond with. But Mike wasn't emotionally intelligent the way Gage is.

"I see it, and I feel it, but I need to be there for them. In so many ways, my work with widows has given my life purpose that it never had before I lost Mike. Yes, being a mother is my primary purpose and the one that brings me untold amounts of joy every day. But my widows... They give me something I never had before, a feeling that I was born to do this work, even if that sounds nuts. I mean, who's born to be a widow, you know?"

"I do, and I get what you're saying. I feel that sense of purpose, too."

"It's different for you because you also had a very successful career. I've done some cool things professionally, but I never had a runaway success until I helped found the Wild Widows. We've done so much good through that group and gained so many friends who are like family. It's begun to feel like a true calling to me, and the idea of walking away from it because it's hard sometimes doesn't seem right."

I glance at him, feeling shy as I ponder whether to share the other thing that's been on my mind lately.

"What?" he asks, brow raised in inquiry.

"I've actually been thinking lately... just here and there..."

"About?"

"Your book... I was thinking maybe I could participate in some way. Not that you need me to make it great, but our story is pretty cool."

"You'd want to do that?"

"I think maybe I would."

"I'd love to work on the book together. I've been kind of all over the place with it. Maybe if we did it together, you could keep me focused."

I get up to refill our mugs. "I don't want you to feel like you have to take me on if you don't want to." When I return to the table, I find myself on his lap with his arms wrapped around me.

"As you know, I *love* taking you on." He punctuates that sentences with a kiss to my neck that sends a shiver through me and makes me giggle.

"Be serious."

"I'm deadly serious about you."

"Don't say 'deadly.' It's bad juju when we've had more than enough of that."

"Yes, dear. And yes, I want to write a book with you. Let's do that. We've got one hell of a story to share between the two of us."

"So much for backing away from the widow scene."

"I heard what you said about it being a calling, and I'd never want to get in the way of that. My concern will always be that you're taking care of you—and letting me take care of you—while you're taking care of everyone else."

"Thank you for caring so much about me, and for seeing me the way you do. That's an incredible gift to me in this new life of ours."

He nuzzles my neck and holds me tight. "I hate that four people had to die for us to have this, but I love every fucking thing about this new life of ours."

"I do, too, and I feel the same push-pull of grief and joy that you do every single day."

"I honestly don't think I could've moved on with someone who wasn't also a widow."

"That was the first thing that attracted you? My widowness?"

"Haha, as you know, the first thing that attracted me was your naked ass in my bed."

I absolutely love when he brings up that night, which we still "argue" was an accident on my part, a case of mixing up the rooms in a weekend rental. I'm such a liar. It was totally on purpose, which he also knows. But I'll never cop to that. "So that was the first time you were attracted?"

"Not even kinda, but that was the first time I couldn't stop myself from acting on it."

"And look at us now."

"Look at us now."

"What're we going to do about the wedding?" I ask. "If we decide to postpone, we need to do it sooner rather than later, so we can tell people who are traveling."

"I don't think we should postpone."

"But—"

He plants a soft, sweet kiss on my lips. "Hear me out on this. After we attend Will's funeral and do everything we can to help Taylor and the kids through these first days, it might be good for everyone to have a reason to celebrate."

"I'm not sure I can do that to Taylor."

"What would she want you to do?"

I drop my head to his shoulder. "She'd want me to have the wedding, even if she's not up for attending."

"Then that's what we ought to do. It might be just what the rest of our widows need to restore their faith in optimism."

"You're right, as usual. I just don't want to appear selfish in the midst of Taylor's unimaginable loss."

"Iris, my love... That's the last thing anyone who truly knows you would ever think you are."

"That's nice of you to say."

"It's the God's honest truth. You're the least selfish person any of us has ever met."

"You know I'm a sure thing, right? I'm going to marry you, so you don't need to fill my head with sweet nothings."

"I'll always fill your head with sweet everythings."

"I'm so glad I ended up naked in your bed by mistake."

His snort of laughter makes me laugh, too. "Mistake, my ass."

"There's nothing about your ass that's a mistake. It's a work of art."

"If you say so."

"I say so, and as the wife, I'm always right."

"Is that a fact? Maybe I should reconsider this wedding."

"Don't you dare."

"Wouldn't think of it, love. I can't wait to be married to you."

"I can't wait either," I say with a giddy little laugh that I instantly regret when I think of what Taylor must be feeling this morning.

"Don't do that, Iris."

"Don't do what?"

"Feel guilty for being happy. Taylor wouldn't want that either."

"Quit knowing me so well. It's maddening."

That earns me another big laugh, every one of them a victory when I think about the somber man who joined our group after the most tragic of losses.

"What do you say to marrying me on Thanksgiving weekend?"

I smile as I kiss him. "I say, I do."

Taylor

After another fitful night, the morning arrives with the surreal reality that Will is dead.

Will is dead.

I glance at the wedding photo he kept on his bedside table, the two of us, smiling, each holding one of the kids in our arms. A brand-new family and a happily ever after that didn't last anywhere near as long as it should have.

I stare at his handsome face. That face... My God, he had me at hello with that face, perfect cheekbones, lips to die for and shockingly blue eyes that never looked at me with anything other than pure affection and love.

I let my mind wander to that first day he came to look at my roof. He'd been referred by a friend who'd filled him in on my widow status, which was actually a relief because he never asked to speak to my husband, like so many others did when they came to do work on the house while Greg was sick and after he died.

From the minute he arrived, he was nothing but helpful, sweet and genuine. I was immediately impressed—and a bit dazzled, if I'm being honest. It'd been four long, lonely years since Greg died when Will strolled into my home and seemingly never left. In all that time, I'd never had a single encounter with a man who made me think, hey, I'd like to get to know this one.

Until him.

It was immediate chemistry as we talked about the roof and other repairs I needed to have done to the house, things that'd been ignored as I dealt with more pressing issues, such as two young, grieving children. Not to mention my own despair over losing my first love far too soon, and after so much suffering.

The suffering undid me. I'll never forget the helplessness of realizing there was nothing I could do to ease Greg's pain or his despair over knowing his precious babies would grow up without him.

That suffering is why I stepped away from the Wild Widows after Will and I were married. I couldn't bear to dwell in that space any longer than I already had. I give Iris and Christy and the others so much credit for sticking with it, even after they've moved on to happy chapter twos. I couldn't do it anymore.

And now here I am, right back in the place I started seven long years ago when Greg died, leaving me with two young kids to raise on my own. This time, I'll have *three* kids to care for as a single mom.

I'm exhausted and hasn't even been a full week since disaster struck once again.

I long for Will. He'd put his strong arms around me and tell me everything would be okay, that he'd make sure of it. Without him here to tell me that—and then make it so—it's hard to believe that anything will ever be okay again.

Miles stirs next to me. As his eyes open to a new day, I can see the exact second when he remembers what's happened. Within seconds, his eyes are full of tears that spill down his cheeks. I reach for him, and he burrows into my embrace, his little body racked with sobs that break my heart all over again.

How in the world do I encourage him and Eliza to have faith in the future when life has already been so incredibly cruel to them? How do I find that faith myself?

Oh, Will... We loved you so much. You were everything we wanted and needed, and you showed up right when we were ready for you. I've always believed Greg sent you to us. I hope the two of you have found each other in heaven and that you'll keep an eye on things for us.

The baby chooses that moment to give a swift kick that makes Miles giggle. "That's so weird," he whispers since Eliza is still asleep.

"How do you think I feel?"

"It's like having an alien inside you."

"You were in there once upon a time. Were you an alien, too?"

"No," he says, laughing. "I was just a boy."

"He's going to need you to show him the ropes."

"I'll be the best big brother. I promise."

"I know you will."

"Mommy?"

"What, honey?"

"I feel bad for laughing when Daddy is gone forever."

"Oh, baby, he wouldn't want you to feel bad about anything. He loved you so, so much. He'd want you to laugh and play and do all the things that bring you joy."

"I'm so sad."

"I know. I am, too. But we're going to be okay. I promise." I have no idea if that's true, but I know it's what he needs to hear. I suppose it's probably true, since we've survived it once before, even though that seemed impossible at the time. Somehow, we did it then, and we'll do it again. What choice do we have?

The day has just begun, and I'm exhausted by the challenges that lie ahead. First and foremost, we have to get through the wake and funeral, which I'm dreading. People will say the dumbest things.

At least you're young and you can fall in love again.
At least he didn't suffer.
He's in a better place.

Whatever. And fuck off. Can I say that out loud? Last time, I held my tongue when people said things like, *At least the children are too young to remember him*, as if that was some sort of blessing. This time, I might not be so polite. I might actually tell them to fuck off with platitudes that do more damage than they can ever imagine, having never been through what we have.

The thought of making a scene has me smiling. After what Will learned from me and my friends about the pitfalls of widowhood, he'd approve of a full-blown scene at his wake or funeral. I have no doubt about that.

Roni

ON WEDNESDAY MORNING, Derek and I ride to the White House together after getting the kids settled with the at-home daycare provider who watches them while we're at work. My entire being has been upset since we heard the news about Will's death. I feel like I'm standing on the side of a glacier without the right equipment to keep me from sliding into the dark ravine, or something equally dramatic.

Everything feels uncertain all of a sudden, when last week, I was confidently charging forward in my new life with Derek, his daughter, Maeve, and my son, Dylan.

Today, I'm a wreck again, back in the headspace of early grief when everything was raw, scary and devastating. I hate it here. I hate how the sick feeling that lasted for months, starting the minute Sam Holland told me my husband had been killed, is back with a vengeance, even though I barely know Taylor and Will.

I know what she's been through, and I'm trying to understand what it would be like to go through it a second time.

Derek is tapping along to the music as he drives. It's hard to believe something that's become part of my everyday routine—the ride to work and his drumming to the beat, along with all the other things he brings to my new life—could be snatched away from me as suddenly as Patrick was.

"Derek."

"What's up, hon?"

"Can you pull over for a second?"

He glances at me and then ducks into a spot that has a no-parking sign over it.

I open the door, lean out and throw up.

"Gross," a guy walking by says.

"Roni, oh my God, are you all right?"

I'm dry heaving through sobs that make me feel ridiculous as well as grief-stricken for people I hardly know.

Derek puts a hand on my back. "What can I do, sweetheart?"

I shake my head. There's nothing he or anyone can do to rid me of the trauma that resides within me, resurfacing at times like this to remind me that the horror of Patrick's murder is hard-wired into my soul and always will be. Derek tossed and turned all night, too, no doubt triggered by memories of Victoria's murder and the grim days that followed.

"What do you say we take a day off?"

"Too much to do." We both have a full day of meetings that would have to be rescheduled.

"It'll keep until tomorrow, and we have people who can cover for us. Let's take today and just be."

"Okay."

While Derek calls us out of work, I try to pull myself together, using a tissue to wipe my mouth, followed by a sip of cold water from the cup I bring to work every day. Lilia calls that cup my assistant because it's always with me. I hate to feel like I'm letting her down, the best boss I've ever had and now my close friend, too. Not to mention Sam, who gave me the ultimate dream job as communications director to the first lady. Hopefully, they'll understand, as it's my first unscheduled day off since I started the job.

As Derek drives us home, I rest my head against the seat and focus on breathing. One breath at a time. That's how I got through Patrick's sudden death, and it's how I've gotten through everything since then. One breath at a time. I remember that first day, wondering how I'd survive it and how I focused on taking the next breath and then the one after that.

At home, Derek pulls off his tie the second we walk in the door and tosses it onto the kitchen table. His suit coat is slung over a chair as he takes my work bag, grabs the lunch I made for myself to put in the fridge and then puts the bag by the door for tomorrow when we'll try again to go to work. Hopefully, it'll go better then.

Taking me by the hand, Derek leads me straight upstairs, where he helps me change into my favorite at-home attire— track pants and one of Patrick's long-sleeved T-shirts. While I go into the bathroom to brush my teeth and rinse the foul taste out of my mouth, he goes into the closet to finish removing his work clothes and emerges in basketball shorts and a T-shirt from a 5K he did last year.

Derek sits next to me on the bed. "What can I do?"

"This is what I needed. Thank you for making it happen."

He puts his arm around me, and I drop my head to his shoulder.

"I'm always thankful for you, but never more so than when widow shit arises."

"I get it."

"I know you do—and I'm sorry that you do." We stay like that for a long while, absorbing the comfort we can get only from each other. "I thought this kind of setback was a thing of the past."

"PTSD doesn't work like that. It says when and what and how."

"So I'm discovering. I'm not a fan."

He grunts out a laugh. "Nor am I."

"Will it always be this way? Ten years from now, will I hear about something happening to someone else, someone I don't even know all that well, and it'll cause a spiral for me?"

"I hate to tell you that it's apt to be a thing for the rest of your life."

"Great."

"You know what the good news is?"

"There's good news?"

"Always. It's that you loved Patrick so deeply and so truly that you'll suffer over losing him for the rest of your life. So many people never get to experience a love like that."

I raise my head so I can see the face that's become the center of my life in the after. "Or a love like this one."

"We're truly blessed to have found it twice."

"The most blessed people have the most to lose."

"That's also true. Life is just a series of risks that hopefully add up to something beautiful."

"I can't take it sometimes. I really can't."

"And that's totally fine. When you feel like that, take the time you need to feel stronger again. This widow thing isn't just the first few months after a loss. It's a life sentence, and there'll be days when it's too hard to carry and other days when it barely shows up."

"I'd like a schedule so I can better prepare for the days when it rears its ugly head."

"Wouldn't that be nice? But think of it this way... If you had a schedule, dreading the upcoming bad days would take the joy out of the happy days."

"You've gotten good at this."

He laughs. "Gee, thanks. Just what I always wanted—to be a successful widower."

"You're a good man first and foremost."

"I'm a better man now than I was when I was married to

Vic. I have a lot of guilt about that, as you know. But all we can do is all we can do, you know? When we know better, we do better."

"Hell of a way to know better."

"Yeah, I'd take a hard pass on the murder shit if I had the choice."

"Right there with you."

He gives me a tight squeeze. "I'll always be right here with you—and Dylan and Maeve and maybe another one someday. And whenever the PTSD shows up, we'll get through it together."

"There's tremendous comfort in that."

"For me, too."

I reach out to put my hand on his face and bring him in for a kiss. "I love you."

"Love you, too. So, so much, and I hate to see you suffering."

"This too shall pass."

"Yes, it will, and in the meantime, we have an entire kid-free day to do whatever we want. What shall we do?"

"I can't think of a single thing. You?"

His hand moves in slow circles over my back. "I've got a few ideas."

"Is it the same idea you have most nights at bedtime and during weekend naptime?"

"Very similar in many ways, the only difference being that naked time can last all day."

I laugh and lean into him. "Sounds good to me."

Sixteen

Iris

Taylor has turned over the planning for the funeral to Will's family because she said it matters more to his religious parents than it does to her. She's staying focused on her kids and preparing for the birth of her new baby. Thankfully, the swelling in her ankles has subsided, and she's feeling better than she was.

Today, I had no choice but to call Lexi and fill her in on what's been going on while she was celebrating her engagement.

"Oh my God," she says. "I feel like such a jerk."

"What? No! We're thrilled for you and Tom. Please don't feel bad. You had no way to know about Will, and none of us wanted to steal your hard-won joy. Trust me, your good news has been a light at an otherwise dark time."

"I hesitate to ask how Taylor and the kids are doing…"

"It's been rough, but they're soldiering through."

"And her baby is due so soon, too."

"It's all so fucking tragic."

"I'm so, so sad for her and the kids and everyone who loved Will."

"I am, too."

A somber group gathers in my living room on Wednesday night.

There's none of the usual friendly bickering and laughter that have become such a big part of our weekly get-togethers.

"How's everyone doing?" I ask when we're seated in a circle, each of us with a plate of appetizers that Joy and Christy brought.

There's much exchanging of glances before Lexi says, "I'm so sorry to all of you who know Taylor and Will better than I do."

Christy dabs at her eyes with a tissue. "It's been hard."

"Very, very hard," Joy adds.

"I hardly know them," Roni says, "and I've had the worst few days in a long time—and I feel guilty for even saying that because it's certainly not about me."

"It's about all of us," Gage says. "Taylor's loss is a stark reminder that we're never completely out of the woods in this thing called life."

He does such a great job of summing up what we're all feeling.

"I'm so fucking angry at the universe," Wynter says. "How dare she have to do this twice?"

"That's a very good question, Wynter," Brielle says, "and one that's been on my mind—and I'm sure all of yours—since I first heard what happened. It's grossly unfair."

"How's she doing, Iris?" Naomi asks.

"It's a minute-by-minute thing. She's hoping to get through the wake and funeral before the birth."

"It's all too much," Joy says tearfully. "Just too damned much."

"Do you think she'll come back to our group?" Adrian asks.

I've been wondering that myself. "I don't know. She certainly knows we're here if she feels it'll help at some point."

"It's sobering to hear of it happening to someone a second time," Angela says.

"I agree," Luke says.

As two of our newer members, this is the last thing either of them needed to hear. Hell, it's the last thing any of us needed to hear. We were glad he was able to come tonight, as he's rarely able to make our weekly meetings.

"Here's the thing, guys," Gage says. "As we always say, ain't none of us getting out of here alive. Some will get more time than others, which is a simple fact of life."

"When I first started coming to the meetings and buying what you people were selling," Wynter says haltingly, "I had this notion that I'd eventually get over Jaden's death and move on with my life with someone else or by myself. Either way, I'd leave the past where it belonged. It's been hard to realize it doesn't work like that."

"I've had those same thoughts this week," Roni says. "Derek and I have talked a lot about PTSD and how, no matter how much hard work we've done to cope and move on, it still shows up out of nowhere to remind us that we're never again going to be who we were before disaster struck."

"I hate that," Hallie says. "I hate it for all of us—and I especially hate it for Taylor."

"She wanted me to thank you all for the outpouring of support, the food and all the other things you guys have done. She said no one shows up for a widow like other widows."

"We wish it could be more," Christy said.

"She'll need help long term," I remind her. "There'll be lots of opportunities to show up for her and her family. And I want to say one more thing with my whole chest this time... Those of you who don't know Taylor and Will—and meeting them here a time or two doesn't count as knowing them well—are under no obligation to attend the services."

"Iris is right," Gage says, adding, "and I'm not just saying that because I'm sleeping with her."

That makes everyone laugh, which was no doubt his goal, and serves to break some of the unusually gloomy tension hanging over us.

"Please, guys," Iris adds, "take care of your own mental health and don't worry about Taylor. She'll be very well supported by an army of friends and family."

"Thanks for saying that, Iris," Lexi says. "I was thinking I should go, but I wasn't sure."

"Don't go. Be there for her for what's ahead. That'll matter most."

"Let's talk about some good news, shall we?" Gage says. "Starting with a huge congratulations to Lexi and Tom Terrific on their engagement. We couldn't be happier for you guys."

The others clap and cheer for Lexi, who takes it all in with a big smile, even if her eyes are sadder than they've been in a while. The news about Taylor's loss is still new and raw for her, while the rest of us have had a few more days to wrap our heads around it.

"Thanks, guys," Lexi says. "I can't say enough about how much all of you contributed to me being ready for this next step. Or at least I thought I was ready until Iris called earlier."

"You're ready, Lex," Joy says emphatically. "You've done the work and taken the time to heal. This is your moment with Tom, and you deserve every happiness. Please don't let anything stand in the way of that."

"I'll try not to, but it's hard to be elated when someone else is hurting."

"Someone else is always hurting, which is why we have to take the joyful moments where we can find them," Gage says.

"True, thanks for the reminder."

"Any time you need it, pal."

"When's the wedding?" Kinsley asks.

"We're hoping to do it next summer. Something fun and chill at home. He doesn't care about having a big wedding, and I've been there, done that, so we're keeping it simple."

"We can't wait to celebrate you guys," Roni says. "We're so proud of you, Lex."

"Aw, thanks."

"How's the new job?" Derek asks.

Lexi recently took a job as the volunteer coordinator for the Northern Virginia Chapter of the ALS Association. We've worried about how she'd cope with being surrounded by the illness that took her husband, Jim.

"So far, so good. I really like the people I work with, and I've met several of the local families who are relying on us for help. It's nice to feel like I'm making a difference at work, which is a huge improvement over the data-entry gig."

"Anything would be an improvement over that job," Naomi says.

"Who else has good news?" I ask.

"I, um, I swiped right," Brielle says, her face flushing with a rosy glow. "For the first time."

The news sets off a round of applause that mortifies Brielle.

"Oh stop. It's no big deal."

"It's a huge deal," Naomi says, "and we're proud of you."

"Don't get too excited. It's nothing much so far. Just a few messages exchanged. I'm not as good at this as you are, Nai. Thanks for the encouragement. It's really helped."

"Please... It's not like I'm an expert or something."

"You'll keep us posted, right?" Joy asks Brielle.

"If there's anything to tell, you'll be the first to know."

"Excellent," Joy says, smiling. "And you'll never meet him or anyone without someone knowing who you're meeting and where, correct?"

"Yes, Mama Joy, I'll be careful. Promise."

"I have some good news," Hallie says. "Robin had a scan this week, and her cancer is stable. That's four months in a row."

"Wonderful news," Roni says. "We're happy for both of you."

"Don't you guys ever get sick of this shit?" Wynter asks in an angry burst of words that takes us all by surprise.

"What shit in particular?" I ask her.

"The widow shit. The constant cheering of tiny steps forward. The ridiculous optimism in a world where someone can lose *two* husbands tragically. The platitudes, the this-too-shall-pass nonsense, when we all know it'll never pass. It'll always be there. It's starting to feel like total bullshit to me."

Her outburst is met with stunned silence.

I have no idea what to say to that.

"Allow me," Gage says to the rest of us. Then he looks right at Wynter. "It's all bullshit. Every single bit of it is bullshit. The tragedy of it all, the shit people who don't know better say, thinking they're helping. The sayings, the platitudes, the cheering of small successes. Every bit of it is total bullshit."

He's making me nervous. "Gage..."

"But here's the rub." He never blinks as he gives Wynter his full attention. "What's the alternative? Sitting alone in a dark room for the rest of our lives, rolled up in a ball, stuck in the place we were when it first happened? I don't know about you, but I never again want to be in that place and hope to God that none of us are ever there again. I *ache* for Taylor, Will and their children. But the ache isn't stopping me from loving Iris and our kids or being excited about our wedding and all the good things to come. What the fuck choice do we have, Wynter?"

By the time he's done, I'm wiping away tears, and so are most of the others, including Wynter.

"So very well said, as always, Gage," Derek says as he takes a subtle swipe at his face.

Adrian slips an arm around Wynter.

"I never wanted any of this," she whispers on a sob.

I glance at Angela and Luke, who are looking at the floor.

"None of us want this, sweetheart," Gage replies. "But it's the hand we were dealt, and if I do say so myself, I think we're doing one hell of a job playing that hand. We've got two couples from this group making new lives for themselves and their children. We've got Lexi engaged to Tom Terrific. Christy and Trey are creating a new family. Joy's got her Dr. Bernie, and Hallie has her Robin. Naomi is dating, and Brielle swiped right. Kinsley talks more about possibly taking the plunge into dating than she used to. Angela and Luke came back for more of us after having had the time to think about whether or not they wanted what we're offering."

"I'm sorry," Wynter says to Angela and Luke. "I shouldn't have spouted off."

"Why not?" Angela says. "Everything you said is true. Some days I feel like I'm wading through hip-deep bullshit. I feel that way every day, if I'm being honest."

"Same," Luke says. "I appreciate your honesty, Wynter. I'm just over two years out, but I'm still so pissed off that this happened to my family—and to Bella, who so didn't deserve to suffer the way she did. Despite being surrounded by incredible love and support from everyone in our lives, every minute is a struggle, and it's exhausting."

A lot of us are nodding in agreement.

"That said," Luke adds, "I was looking forward to tonight, to being with people who get it, which makes a difference. This group makes a difference, and I, for one, am thankful for the outlet."

"Same," Angela said. "I wish I'd joined sooner."

"You came when you were ready," I tell her with a smile. "Well... How about some dessert?"

Everyone stands and stretches, except for Wynter and Adrian, who stay where they are, heads bent together in silent communication.

I follow the others into the kitchen and go directly to Gage, who sees me coming and wraps me into a hug. "That was intense."

"Yeah, but I think it was healthy to talk about the rage a bit. We don't do that very often."

"I worry about a setback for her. She's been doing so great…"

"I know."

"You were magnificent."

"Aw, thanks. I was flying by the seat of my pants."

"Your pants do good work."

He laughs, and we're soon surrounded by others needing hugs and reassurance and all the things we're here to give.

"Look at you, swiping right," I say to Brielle.

"Don't be too excited. It's a total shit show."

I watch as Kinsley's gaze seeks out and lands on Luke, who's talking to Roni and Derek. Interesting…

She looks back at me in time to realize I saw who she was looking at. "Don't make a thing of it."

"Is it a thing?"

"I don't know what it is. I find myself thinking about him and his kids a lot."

"Nothing wrong with that."

"I know."

"Go talk to him. You're among friends."

"I don't want to be a weirdo."

"Oh please, you're the furthest thing from that, and PS, we're all a little weird in Widowville." I give her a nudge. "Go. What've you got to lose?"

"Is that a multiple-choice question?"

"Haha. He's looking over here."

"No, he isn't."

"Is, too."

She ventures a glance, and when their gazes connect, something electric passes between them.

"Oh my," I say. She seems frozen in place. "He's coming over here. I'm out."

"No, Iris… Don't go."

"I'm already gone."

Seventeen

Kinsley

Damn her! I thought she was my friend! I have about two seconds to prepare myself for his arrival. He is carrying a small plate with several of Naomi's chocolate chip cookies and offers me one.

I take it. "Thanks."

"They're crazy good."

"Naomi makes them. We can't get enough."

"I can see why." He looks toward the living room, where Wynter and Adrian are still seated and talking quietly. "Will she be okay?"

"I think so. She was like that all the time when we first knew her. She's climbed mountains since then, and we're so proud of her—and Adrian."

"They seem like a great couple."

"They are."

He shifts his gaze back to me, and I feel as if I've looked directly at the sun. What the hell is that about?

"I appreciated your text the other night. You couldn't have

known, but it arrived at a moment when I really needed it. So thanks for that."

"Oh, um, sure. I'd been thinking of you and had been meaning to reach out. Cancer is a heck of a thing to have in common with someone." *Stop talking, Kinsley.*

"Yeah, for sure. Would you want to get a coffee or lunch sometime?"

"I'd love that. Any time."

He smiles, and I'm done. *Finished.* "I'll text you."

"Okay." How will I live until I get that text, and when did I transport back to middle school, anyway?

"Let me ask you something..."

"Sure."

"Has hearing about what happened to Taylor's husband have you all..." He waves his hand as if searching for the right word.

"Fucked up?"

He laughs. "Yeah. That."

"Big-time. It's been rough for all of us."

"So it's not just me feeling grief-stricken for someone I don't even know?"

"Not at all. After what we've been through, you can't help but put yourself in her place and then run from that thought as fast as you have it."

"There you go, making me feel better again."

"Oh, well..." I can't remember the last time I blushed. That's Brielle's thing, not mine, but damn if my face doesn't feel hot.

Roni and Derek come to say good night, forcing me to focus on something other than Luke, which is a relief. He's overwhelming in the best possible way.

"I'll walk out with you guys," he says. "I might make it home for bedtime. Thank you, Iris and Gage, for hosting. Appreciate all the support from this group."

After he says goodbye to the others, he comes back to me. "Talk soon?"

"Sounds good."

I watch him walk away, noting the way his faded jeans fit just right.

Iris reappears next to me. "So…"

"We're having coffee. Soon."

She lets out an excited squeal that has everyone else looking at us. "Nothing to see here, folks. Just Luke asking Kinsley out for coffee."

"Iris!"

"Sorry, did I say that out loud? I didn't mean to."

"Yes, you did."

She laughs, and I can't help but join her because her laughter is so infectious.

"Is Iris minding other people's business again?" Gage asks as he puts an arm around her.

"You need to do something about her."

"I've tried. She's incorrigible."

"I'm sorry, Kins," Iris says. "I couldn't help myself. We're in bad need of good news around here."

"It's just coffee."

"Okay."

"Iris!"

"What? I said okay."

I shake my head with amusement and go to get the plate I brought with the brownies that are all gone. Good thing I held some back for the kids, who are at home with my mom.

I say my good nights, dodging questions and comments about Luke, and head out to my car, wondering how long I'll have to wait to hear from him.

Angela

I drive home toward the District, thinking about Wynter's outburst and how on the mark she was with what she said. I haven't been part of the group for long, but I already know her message is not the one they promote. The Wild Widows are all about moving forward with optimism and courage and hope.

On most days, I agree with Wynter. It's all bullshit. The stuff about optimism and hope gets old when you're taking care of three young kids without the person who was supposed to be your partner in all things. Hope is the last thing on my mind when I have a hungry baby, a crying toddler and a little boy suffering from tremendous grief that seems to be getting worse with time, not better.

I'm so worked up that I decide to call Brad, because he'll understand exactly how I feel.

"Hey," he says, "how was the meeting?"

"It was good, but tougher tonight because we were talking about Taylor and Will. People who knew them well are really upset, and people who hardly knew them are traumatized from hearing about it."

"I get that. I didn't know them, but it's all I've thought about since you told me. I read some of the news coverage of the accident, and that didn't help."

"Why'd you do that?"

"Professional curiosity, I guess."

"That was dumb."

He chuckles. "I realized that pretty quickly."

"One of the younger members went off on how something like this brings home the fact that the whole hope-and-optimism message is total bullshit."

"Yikes, how'd that go over?"

"There's this one guy, Gage, who's a bit older than the rest of us. He lost his wife and twin daughters to a drunk driver."

Brad's wince is audible.

"He agrees it's all bullshit, but then he said something to the effect of, What choice do we have but to at least try to make something of the life we have left? He said it much more eloquently than I did, but that was the gist."

"He's the one who writes the Instagram posts, right?"

"Yes."

"I read all his posts one night recently. If he says we have to make something of the life we have left, I'm down with it. The guy gets it like no one else I've encountered since this happened."

"He's great, but they all are. I still say you should come to a meeting. Tonight was an exception, but I usually leave feeling uplifted and energized to face the days ahead. That doesn't last for long, but I'll take the temporary high where I can get it."

"I've been thinking about checking it out."

"Can't hurt to come once and see what you think. Next week?"

"I'll see how I'm feeling."

"Sounds good. I won't pressure you."

"It's okay if you do. I like being pressured by you."

I can't contain the nervous laughter. "Whatever that means."

"I enjoy your company, Angela, and not just because you get what I'm going through in a way that no one else in the world can."

"Oh, well... I enjoy yours, too, and not just because of how we met."

"Would you consider..."

"What?" I ask, feeling as breathless as I sound.

"It's probably too soon."

"For what, Brad?"

"To ask you out on a real date. No kids, just us."

"Um..."

"It's too soon. I know it is, but you've been the brightest light to me in this hellish situation, and all I seem to want lately is more time with you." After a long pause, he adds, "And I've said too much and made it weird."

I laugh because how could I not? He's too funny. "You've been a bright light to me, too, and I find myself wondering all the time what you'd think of whatever is happening at the moment."

"So it's not just me?"

"Definitely not."

"Well, that's a relief." Another long pause follows. "But it's still too soon, right?"

"My Wild Widows have taught me that there's no such thing as too soon or not enough or too much or whatever the rest of the world dictates widowhood should look like. Our journey is ours and ours alone, and we're not bound by rules set for us by people who'll never know what we've been through—and are lucky not to know."

"I wish I was taking notes right now. That was very well said."

"I can't take credit for Wild Widows material. It's validating—and freeing—to hear them say there're no rules, no expectations, no need to meet anyone else's requirements."

"I like the way they operate."

"I do, too. It's why I keep going back. I need to hear that I'm allowed to do this my way, not the way someone else thinks I should do it."

"My wife's sister is judgy about everything. She actually said to me, 'If you start dating, don't tell me. I can't bear to picture you with anyone other than Mary Alice.' Like, gee, thanks for the support. That was the last thing I needed to hear from her."

"That's her own grief talking. She's so lost in it that she can't see the forest for the trees. I have to think if she was thinking clearly, she'd never say such a thing to you."

"I'd like to think so, but who knows? Maybe that's what she really thinks, that I should be alone for the rest of my life in some sort of tribute to Mary Alice."

"If she cares about you, she'd never think that."

"Anyway, enough about her. Are you going to answer my

question or leave me hanging like an eighth-grade boy who asked the prettiest girl in school to the dance and didn't get an answer?"

"Did that happen to you?"

"More deflection, Angela."

Speaking of middle school, my nervous giggle is right out of seventh grade, except that nothing this exciting ever happened to me then. "I'd love to go out with you sans kids for once."

"Phew. That was a long wait from question to answer."

"It was kind of a big question."

"True, but let's not make it into the big deal that everyone else will. Let's just go out and have some fun. Can you think of any two people who deserve that more than we do?"

I pull into the driveway at home, cut the engine and turn off the lights. "I can't."

"Do you have someone who can watch your kids who won't need to know every detail of where you're going and with whom?"

"I can tell my sister Tracy that I'm meeting friends. She'll be glad I'm getting out. She and Sam worry about me too much."

"They love you. That's why they worry."

"I know, but it can be too much at times. They want me to say I'm okay, that everything is all right, that things are getting back to 'normal.' Whatever that is now. What I've learned from Iris and Gage and the other widows is that I'll never again be who I was before I lost Spencer, and I'm still figuring out what my new normal looks like."

"Again, I feel like I should be taking notes because I've been trying to explain that to some of the people in my life. They're hovering on the periphery waiting for it to be safe to reengage with me. They're waiting for the old me, the guy I used to be, and they haven't figured out yet that he died along with Mary Alice."

"Yes, he did, and now New Brad is figuring out the rest of his life."

"He's trying, anyway. What should we do on our big night out?"

"Let's not put pressure on it by calling it big."

"Right," he says with a chuckle. "What should we do?"

"I'd be up for a dinner where I don't have to cut anyone's food or wipe faces."

"That'd be nice, right?"

"Uh-huh."

"You said you love Mexican, right?"

"I did."

"There's a place we used to go… before everything happened. The food is really good, and it's quiet, off the beaten path. We could check that out."

"Will you be triggered by memories if we go somewhere you've been with her?"

"I don't think so. I've been to some of our places and done okay. But thank you for thinking of that."

"It's the little things that make for a successful outing for a widow."

"Life is like a minefield for us."

"Yeah, seriously. Hopefully, the mines won't always be active."

"That'd be nice."

"So I'm home, and I need to let my sister go home. Can I call you back in a bit?"

"I'm here all night."

I laugh at a line we've said to each other frequently. Without a partner to rely on, we can't go anywhere once the kids are in bed.

"Okay, talk soon."

"I can't wait."

My heart is in my throat as I end the call and get out of the car. So, that happened. He asked me out, and I said yes. In truth, we've been heading toward this for months. Not that I actively thought of him as a potential romantic partner. I've been too busy surviving every crazy day with two traumatized kids and an infant. Who has the time to think about romance?

But one phone call at a time, one playdate with the kids at a time, a thousand texts later, a friendship has blossomed into the possibility of something... more.

Am I ready for something more? Probably not, but when will I ever be ready for such a thing? Until Spencer died so tragically, it'd never occurred to me that I might one day have to date again. That I'd have to start over with a new partner—or not. If I were to stay permanently single, I feel like that would be fine, too. It's not like I need a man to make me complete. I've never been that girl. I needed *Spencer*, not just any man.

But as I find myself on the precipice of whatever this might be with Brad, I've begun to wonder if maybe I've become that girl who can't be without a man—not that I'd ever judge such a girl. I never would, but I didn't think that label applied to me. Maybe it does now.

And so what if it does?

I like Brad. I like talking to someone who freaking *gets it* in this strange aftermath of disaster. We both had our lives upended by the same criminal enterprise.

Are we building something real for ourselves, or is it a house of cards built on shared catastrophe? And how would I even know the difference at this point?

Eighteen

Angela

I walk into the house through the back door to the kitchen and hear Josh crying, so I drop my bag on the table and go to relieve Tracy.

"There's your mommy, buddy," Tracy says when she sees me.

Josh immediately calms when he sees me coming. He's the sweetest, easiest baby, and I'm so thankful for his presence to give us all something new and exciting to focus on, and I'll always be thankful to Josh for that and so many other things.

"How were they?" I ask Tracy when Josh is happily snuggled into my arms on his way back to sleep.

"A few tears at bedtime, but otherwise, they were great. We played Chutes and Ladders and two games of Candy Land. Ella won the second one, to Jack's great dismay."

I laugh as I picture my competitive son being outraged to be bested by his baby sister. "I hope he wasn't mean to her."

"Nah, he was a gracious loser."

"He was? Really?"

"Well, not really, but aunties don't tell tales."

"Ah, I see how it is. Thank you so much for always being willing to help me out."

"I love every minute with them. How was the meeting?"

"It was a tough one this week because one of their widow friends lost her second husband. She was one of the cofounders of the group after she lost the first one."

"Jeez."

"Did you see the thing on the news about the construction worker who fell from the scaffolding?"

Tracy nods. "I did. They said he had two kids and a baby on the way."

"Sounds familiar, right?"

"All too. Did they say how the wife is doing? Which sounds like a stupid question the minute I ask it."

"As you would imagine. Such a tough thing, and the news has hit some of the widows in the group like a fist to the gut."

"Understandable. Is it having that effect on you?"

"No more than anything else. I think I might still be numb in some ways. I don't react to things the way I used to. Who knows if I ever will again?"

"You will. Eventually."

"Something happened recently that made me good and mad."

"What's that?"

"Jack told me how Spencer said he'd want us to be happy if anything ever happened to him."

Tracy gasps. "When did he say that?"

"Summer before last, when they went fishing. I'm so freaking outraged that he'd put something like that on Jack. Imagine how worried he must've been about his daddy after Spence said that."

"Yeah, that's a lot for a little kid to process. Did he seem upset when he told you about it?"

"Not at all. He was sort of matter of fact about it, as if he'd had a lot of time to process it and it wasn't a big deal anymore. At least I hope that's the case. I guess we'll see."

"I'm sorry Jack had to hear that, but it's further proof of how sick Spencer must've been. He never would've said that under normal circumstances."

"No, he wouldn't have." I pause before I decide to tell her about Brad. "In other news, something interesting happened tonight."

"Do tell."

"My widow friend Brad asked me out."

Tracy's eyes go wide with glee. "Please tell me you said yes."

"I did."

She lets out a whoop that scares Josh.

"Sorry, buddy," Tracy says with a laugh as I resituate the baby. "Your mommy told me the best news."

"Please don't tell anyone, even Mike. I don't want it to become headline news for everyone in my life."

"I won't tell anyone. I promise. But I'll tell you how happy I am for you and how proud I am of how you've managed the unimaginable for yourself and your kids."

"That's nice of you to say. Most days, it feels like a sausage factory from the inside. No one should ever see what goes on here."

"Your kids are clean, well-fed and well-loved. You're slaying single motherhood."

"Only because of the fundraiser that solved my most pressing problem. Brad is struggling financially and won't let me give him some of the money."

"Find a way to do it without him knowing where it came from."

"He'd know it was me."

"Lie and deny."

I laugh at the way she says that, without an ounce of irony. "That ought to be on a bumper sticker."

"If it gets the job done."

"I'll think about how I might pull that off."

"And you need to think about what you're going to wear on your date."

"I'll just wear jeans or something. I'm not getting all dressed up."

"Put a little effort in."

"He sees me all the time in mom mode. He knows what to expect."

"Which is all the more reason to wow him a bit."

"I'm not sure if I want to wow him." Suddenly, my eyes are full of tears that I quickly brush away. "I don't want you to think…"

"What, honey?"

"That I've forgotten Spence or moved on from him or what happened, because I haven't. Not at all."

"I'd never think that, and neither would anyone who knows you."

"I worry about what his family would think if they heard I went on a date."

"How would they hear that?"

I shrug. "People know who we are because of Sam. What if someone sees us and posts it or something?"

"That's a long shot."

"But it could happen."

"Yes, it could, but most likely it won't, and you shouldn't worry about it because you wouldn't be doing anything wrong having dinner with a friend."

"You know how people spin stuff like that."

"Ang, honey, as long as you know you're not doing anything wrong, which you're not, then you shouldn't worry what anyone else thinks. No one else has walked in your shoes or his. If they criticize you, then they can fuck off. And you should feel free to tell them your older sister said it was okay to say that."

She always makes me laugh. "Got it, thank you."

"You'd better ask me to babysit that night."

"Who else would I ask?"

"Mom, Celia, Sam…"

"I'd always ask you first."

"And I'll always say yes."

Thank God for sisters and friends who get it and sweet babies who give me a reason to keep going. Despite the heaviness of the meeting tonight, I feel more optimistic than I have since that horrible morning at Camp David when life as I knew it ended forever, and a whole new, unwanted and unexpected life began.

Kinsley

I'M ALMOST home when Luke calls me. I'm so flustered to see his name pop up on my dashboard screen that I nearly press the cancel button instead of taking the call.

"Hi there," I say, thinking I sound calm and cool when I'm a rattled mess because my crush called me. *You're an idiot, Kinsley.*

"Hey," he says, "are you home yet?"

"Not quite."

"Where's home?"

"Lorton. What about you?"

"A few blocks from Iris and Gage. My Beckham is in the same grade as their Tyler."

"Ah, I see. How are you feeling after the meeting?"

"A little shaken, to be honest. It's hard to hear about one of the original Wild Widows losing her second husband so tragically. Especially when they're about to have a baby."

"A few of our members have had babies after their husbands died. Brielle had her Charlie, and Angela had her Joshua. Roni had Dylan after her Patrick died. She didn't even know she was pregnant when he was killed."

"It's all so sad."

"It is, but they're doing well, thriving as much as they can in the after."

"I heard the second year is harder, and I'm finding that to be true. People have moved on from our tremendous loss, not that I expected them to stay close or anything."

"People who don't know better think everything gets better after you survive the first year. Some of my widow friends found it was years two, three and four that were the real bitch, and I thought year two was harder than year one in many ways."

"Ugh, so it can still get worse before it gets better?"

"From what you've shared, it seems like you and your kids are doing as well as can be expected. Or is that what you want us to think?"

"No, we are. There're still some tough days, though. My older two remember Bella and miss her desperately, while the younger two are aware someone is missing, but they're fuzzy on the details. That makes me so sad for them. Thank God for videos and letters and all the things Bella did before she died so she'd be present for them throughout their lives. She even wrote letters to them for their graduations and wedding days, the birth of their first child. She made it so she'll be present for all the big moments."

"My Rory did, too. I have them in a fireproof safe."

"I need to get one of those. They're in a metal file cabinet now."

"That's not good enough."

"I'm realizing that. I'll get a fireproof safe tomorrow. Thanks for the tip."

"You could also have them scanned so you have them saved digitally, too."

"I don't want anyone else to see them. It's like they're private between the kids and their mother. Does that make sense?"

"It does. I get that. I've never looked at the ones Rory left for the same reason."

"I never thought this would be my life, protecting the last letters my wife wrote to my kids. Fucking cancer."

"Couldn't agree more. I hate cancer more than just about anything. It's taken so much from so many."

"If there's an upside, at least they had the chance to write the letters and make the videos, and we had time to prepare ourselves for them to leave us."

"I had forty-two days, which is still surreal. From jaundiced on day one to dead in forty-two days."

"That's unbelievable."

"It really was. He was in perfect health until that summer when he started having trouble eating and was losing weight for no apparent reason."

"With hindsight, those are signs of pancreatic cancer coming on."

"We chalked it up to getting older and naturally things would start to change. We didn't think anything of it until the jaundice appeared."

"And by then, it's usually too late to do much of anything."

"That was the case for us. They said he wasn't eligible for surgery because it had already spread to his liver."

"It must've been so shocking."

"I think I was in shock for a full year. I have gaps in my memories from that first year."

"It's all a blur for me, too. You're in survival mode at first, and the days run together."

"They do."

"How old were your kids when Rory died?"

"Four and two."

"So they don't remember him?"

"Christian has some distinct memories, but not a lot of them. Maisy doesn't remember him at all. I'm not sure which is worse, honestly—the one who has some memories he's trying desperately to hold on to or the one who has no memories of someone who should be there."

"They're both the worst. It's so unfair. My heart breaks for my kids every day. I see the older ones glomming on to their friends' mothers, and it just makes me so sad. Bella was such an amazing mom. She should be here with them."

"I feel the same way, but such is the hand we were dealt."

"It's a shitty hand."

"In many ways, yes, but in other ways, it's brought some incredible new people into my life who've become so important to me. My widows are some of the best friends I've ever had."

"I can tell there're a lot of tight bonds in that group."

"I'm not sure I would've survived without them. I give Iris and Christy and Gage so much credit for holding us all together, when no one would blame any of them for moving on from the group at this point."

"Iris described it to me as somewhat of a calling for her."

"Yes, for sure. She and Gage are our Yodas."

"I felt sad for Wynter tonight. She seemed so upset."

"She's had such a tough time of it. She was so young when she lost her Jaden. I don't even think she was twenty, and they'd been together for years."

"That's rough."

"I wish you could've known her back in the beginning. Despite her outburst tonight, you wouldn't believe the progress she's made."

"She and Adrian seem like a great couple."

"They are, but as in all things in widow life, none of it came easy for either of them."

"I'm sure it didn't. Are you home yet?"

"About ten minutes ago."

"Who's with your kids?"

"My mom."

"Does she live close?"

"Right around the corner. Not sure what I'd do without her and my dad. They're always willing to help out."

"I've got my parents and Bella's nearby, too. They're a godsend."

"It's nice to have people in our daily lives who love the kids like I do."

"For sure. That makes such a big difference. So do you work in addition to managing two kids on your own?"

"Part time from home for a nonprofit, doing social media and online marketing. I work while the kids are in school, which is perfect for us. I was one of the lucky ones—Rory had great life insurance through his work, so I wasn't left in desperate straits like some of my widow friends were."

"That's such a blessing. Bella had life insurance, too. We have a friend who's a financial adviser, and he told us to get it the minute we were expecting our first child. He made the argument that even if Bella was going to be a stay-at-home mom, if anything ever happened to her, I'd need help that wouldn't come cheap. I can't tell you how thankful I am for that advice every day."

"I'll bet. People don't think about stuff like that when they're young, with their whole lives ahead of them—or so they think."

"No, they don't."

"Why would they, really?"

"Yeah, true. Well, this conversation has taken a morbid turn," he says with a laugh.

"I've learned from my Wild Widows that it's healthy to talk about it. Keeping it bottled up inside won't get you anywhere but pissed off and hopeless."

"I can already see the benefit of airing it out."

"It helps to be around people who understand the struggle and don't say stupid things like, 'He or she is in a better place.'"

"Oh my God, I might punch the next person who says that to me."

"Don't do that."

"I won't, but I want to."

"Right there with you. That and 'It's God's will' are two of my least-favorite platitudes. How could God have wanted this for us?"

"Exactly. It's infuriating to hear that crap from people who'll never know what we've been through."

"Joy's had people say, 'At least you and Craig didn't have kids,' as if that somehow makes it all better that she lost her young, healthy husband to natural causes."

"That makes me see red for her."

"She tells them that doesn't help, and they should think before they say something stupid to a widow."

"She comes right out and says that?"

"Yep. After years of biting her tongue, she doesn't anymore."

"Good for her."

"I agree. Why should she have to listen to that shit?"

"No one should." After a pause, he says, "So, um, do you want to grab lunch one day this week?"

He's asking me out, and I'm dead, done. Good thing I'm seated, or there might've been swooning.

"Kinsley? Are you still there?"

Say words, you fool. "Sorry, yes, I'd love to have lunch with you."

"Great. I need to look at my schedule for the week, and then I'll text you to set up a time and place. Does that work?"

"Perfect. I'll look forward to it."

"Same. I'm really glad you reached out."

"I'm glad, too. Talk to you soon."

"Yes, you will."

I left Iris's feeling sad and unsettled after talking about Taylor's loss, but I'm absolutely giddy as I get out of the car to go inside.

"There you are," Mom says. "I heard the garage a while ago, but I was watching the end of my show."

"I was on the phone."

"I figured it was something like that."

"I was on the phone with a boy who asked me out."

My mom's eyes go wide as her face lights up with the biggest smile I've seen from her in a long time. "I'm going to need details about this boy."

"Well, he's actually a man—a doctor, in fact—and the single dad to four kids eight and under after losing his wife to colon cancer two years ago."

"Oh my. That's a lot."

"Sure is."

"What's his name?"

"Luke."

"What kind of doctor is he?"

"An internist."

"Very interesting. Four kids, though. That's a lot."

I dodge that comment because I'm having lunch with him, not offering to raise his motherless children. "Speaking of kids, how were mine?"

"Delightful as always, even if Miss Maisy avoided bedtime for as long as she could."

"That's getting worse all the time. The child can function on very little sleep, which isn't ideal for her mother, who needs a good eight hours."

"You've been like that since you were a baby. You were my best sleeper."

"I love sleep. It's my favorite thing."

"Remember when you were a teen and I used to wake you up at one o'clock on the days you could sleep in and you were always groggy, even at that hour?"

"Ah, the good old days of sleeping the day away. That's ancient history now."

"I'd better get home before Dad comes looking for me."

"How's he feeling?" He's had a terrible cold for more than a week.

"Much better. Not as congested as he was yesterday. He's eager to get back to being with the kids."

"They've missed him at school pickup."

"He misses it, too. He'll be back soon."

I hug her at the door. "Thank you so much for everything. All the time. Every day. I couldn't do this without you guys."

"We love every minute with you and the kids."

"Just so you know how thankful I am. Not everyone has the kind of support I have, and I never take it for granted. The way you guys uprooted your lives and moved here to help me…"

"Of course we did, sweetheart. It was the best thing we ever did."

"Thank you."

She hugs me one more time. "Love you. Love your kids. Loved your Rory. And I love that you have a date with Luke."

"Don't tell anyone, okay? I don't want everyone asking me about it."

"I won't say a word. I promise." With a side-eyed glance, she adds, "As long as you tell me everything."

"Haha, good night, Mother."

"Good night, daughter."

After she drives off, I lock up, shut off the lights and go upstairs to check on my sleeping babies.

I love to run my fingers through their soft hair while they sleep and to kiss their sweet faces. They're always on the move when they're awake, so snuggling with Mommy isn't high on their to-do list.

"Love you to the moon," I whisper to each of them as I adjust the blankets and leave them to have sweet dreams.

Their bedrooms have a bathroom in the middle that they share, and I think it's adorable that they want the doors open between their rooms during the night. That won't last forever, but for now, they take comfort in the nearness of their best friend. I'm aware that best friendship probably won't last through the teenage years, but I think they'll always be close due to the early trauma that most siblings luckily never have to experience.

Even though they were very young when Rory fell ill and died, they recall that time and often ask questions about what happened and why, as if trying to keep the memories present as the years have passed since tragedy struck.

As I get into bed fifteen minutes later, I glance at his side of the bed as I've done every night since he left, looking for Rory's smiling face as he waited for me to join him. I was always the last one to bed because I was making lunches or folding clothes or doing something to make all our lives easier the next day. He was a wonderful, hands-on father, but he wasn't great with the details of the kids' daily lives.

That was fine. He worked hard to provide for us, and I handled most of the "home" stuff while working part time. Before he got sick, he used to joke about how screwed he'd be if I ever died, so he said, "Please don't do that to me." And I'd say, "I won't if you won't." We'd seal the deal with a kiss any time the subject came up.

He said that often enough that I wonder if he suspected that one of us might die young or if he had a premonition about his own health. His illness and death transpired so quickly that I never thought to ask him about that. We were so overwhelmed by the speed of his decline that we had little capacity for anything else during those surreal forty-two days.

However, he told me every day about how much he loved me and the kids and how sorry he was to be leaving me alone to raise them. His heart was broken over leaving us. I had no doubt about that.

I'm surprised to discover tears on my face as I emerge from those painful memories. For a while after he first died, I thought I'd never stop crying, but it's been a while since I shed tears over losing Rory. I feel guilty about that realization, but I refuse to feel guilty about getting on with my life the way he would've wanted me to.

And I refuse to feel guilty for being excited about my plans with Luke.

For the first time in what feels like forever, my last thoughts before I fall asleep aren't about Rory. No, I fall asleep with a smile on my face, thinking about Luke and how excited I am to see him again.

Nineteen

Taylor

I haven't been this exhausted since Greg was in hospice, but I can't sleep no matter how hard I try to clear my mind and focus on keeping myself healthy for my children, especially the one who isn't here yet and is still relying on me for everything. The baby moves restlessly at night, as if he's aware that his life has been altered irrevocably before he's even born.

Every time I close my eyes, I see Will falling off that scaffolding, and I try to imagine what he must've thought in the seconds before he landed. I know for sure that my face, the kids' faces, the baby and our life together were foremost in his mind, as we always were. As much as I ache for myself and my kids, I'm heartbroken for Will and the baby he wanted so badly and for the special relationship they'll never get to have now.

We'll do our best to bring Will to life for the baby, but it won't be the same as experiencing him as a living, breathing, loving father.

I feel so cheated by his death on behalf of myself and all three of our children, and I'm honestly not sure if I can go on without him by my side. Having that thought makes me sound like a feeble, helpless woman who can't survive on her own. That's not me at all. I've already done this once before, and not only did I survive, but I thrived as a single mother for years before I met Will and took another chance on love.

It's not that I *can't* do it. It's that I don't *want* to do it on my own again.

Single parents are often lauded as heroes, and yes, that title is well deserved, but most of us would rather have a partner to help us raise our kids than be held up as heroes. I don't want to be a hero. I want to be a wife and a mother and part of a family that includes Will.

How can he be gone forever? It makes no sense to me.

After having now been through both, I've decided the sudden tragedy is far worse than the long illness. At least Greg got the chance to record videos and write letters to the kids to keep him present for them going forward. He had the opportunity to say goodbye to me and the kids, to say all the things we needed to hear to live without him for the rest of our lives. Will had no such opportunity before he was ripped from our lives forever.

We had time to prepare for Greg's death, even if I wouldn't wish his suffering on anyone. We knew for months that he was dying and planned accordingly to make sure everything was in order for the aftermath.

After we were married, Will and I updated our estate documents to make each other the beneficiary should the worst happen to either of us, but that process in no way prepared me for the reality of his premature death.

I turn on my side, seeking relief from the baby's nightly soccer match, and come face-to-face with the framed photo of our wedding on my bedside table, illuminated by the nightlight I leave on in case the kids need me now that they've returned to their own beds for the first time since Will died.

God, he was so handsome and fun and funny and sexy and all the things. After having zero interest in men or dating for the years following Greg's death, I was a goner for him from the first minute we met. Our wedding day was one of the happiest occasions of my life—and my kids' lives. From the minute I introduced them to him, several months after we met, they, too, were in love with him.

When he proposed to me, he also proposed to them, with gifts for each of them and a special, heartfelt promise to always be there for them and to be the best possible stepdad he could be.

We all said yes with no hesitation whatsoever.

My friends and family were thrilled for us, and I embarked on my chapter two with great excitement and anticipation for the future, largely leaving my widow life, which included active participation in the Wild Widows and other groups, in the past, where I thought it belonged.

How naïve I was.

Since sleep isn't happening, I decide to get up and take care of some things that are weighing on me and probably keeping me from getting the rest I need so badly. One of those things is the dreaded task of writing my husband's obituary. His family offered to take care of it for me, but I said I wanted to do it with their input. His mom sent their notes yesterday, and with the services looming this weekend, I need to get it published so people will know when and where.

I take my water bottle and reading glasses with me to the office downstairs, where Will used to do invoicing and paperwork for his business. I haven't yet figured out what will become of the business, but there'll be time to worry about that later. Bryan, Will's foreman, told me to reach out when I'm ready to talk about next steps. That's on my to-do list, but not in the top ten until after the services are completed. I trust Bryan and the others to keep things running until I have time to catch my breath.

Everything in this room reminds me of my Will. From the faint scent of his cologne to the photos of me and the kids on the desk to the sports memorabilia he collected with such relish. I realize that any time I want to feel close to him, I need only come in here and sit at the desk where he held court, as I liked to say.

With the computer powered up, I open the email from Will's mother, which includes details from his life that save me the time of confirming the years he graduated from high school and college and started his business. I use the same file his mother sent me and start writing.

William Ellington Lonergan Jr., 38, of Falls Church, died on Friday, November 12, in an accident at work. He was the proud owner of WE Lonergan Construction for the last fifteen years.

He's survived by his wife, Taylor Cummings-Lonergan, and their children, Eliza Cummings and Miles Cummings, as well as a much-loved and highly anticipated unborn son expected next month. Will was an incredible husband, father, son, brother, uncle, friend and employer, who was loved by everyone who knew him.

He came into the lives of Taylor and her children several years after her first husband and the children's father, Greg Cummings, died of brain cancer. Will took on the role of husband and stepfather as if he'd been born to it, while always being incredibly respectful of Greg's memory. We loved him deeply.

In addition to his wife and children, Will is also survived by his loving parents and grandparents, two sisters, a brother, four nieces and two nephews.

I insert the family rundown my mother-in-law sent with the correct spellings of names, which saves me from double-checking all that.

Will was a faithful, lifelong fan of all the Washington-area sports teams as well as his beloved Virginia Tech Hokies.

I include his school information as well as the wake and funeral details.

When I'm finished, I send it to his mother for her approval, asking her to send it back to me when she's happy with it.

It's not that I don't trust her, because I do. I have no reason not to, but I've learned that grief makes people do things they wouldn't ordinarily, such as possibly rewrite the obituary their daughter-in-law drafted for their son.

To avoid that, I make it clear in my message that I want to be the one to submit it to the funeral home, along with the photo I've chosen to accompany it.

With that dreaded task completed to the best of my ability, I leave the office and go into the kitchen, where I spend the early morning hours cleaning up after the wild influx of friends and family and food over the last few days.

My sisters have been tidying every day, so the kitchen doesn't really need cleaning, but it brings me comfort to do a "normal" task at a time when nothing else feels normal. What even is that anymore? And why do I have to keep redefining it for myself and my kids while others have the same husbands and fathers for fifty or sixty years?

I'll probably spend the rest of my life alone, because who'd want a twice-widowed woman as a partner? Wouldn't they be worried the whole time about a black cloud hovering over their own head?

Now that's a morbid thought. But seriously, who'd want to be with me after the last two men I loved ended up dead long before their time?

I start to laugh, and the sound is maniacal as it echoes off the walls of the kitchen Will and I designed together before his workers gutted and fully renovated it to our exacting specs.

Before long, laughter turns to sobs, and I lean over the countertop we chose, remembering the day we spent "deep in the bowels" of the stone emporium, as he'd so eloquently put it.

Our relationship wasn't perfect. We often disagreed about little things, such as whether the bed needed to be made the minute we got up (me: yes, him: no) or how to load the dishwasher or why every sock he owned was always inside out. But the rest of it... That was as close to perfect as any two people could get while still being flawed human beings.

I'll miss him forever.

Iris

"Will's obituary is online," I say to Gage when he comes downstairs, fresh from the shower on Friday morning.

He leans in for a good-morning kiss, and I breathe in the unique scent of body wash, shaving cream and cologne that comes with him.

"I sent you a link."

"Thanks."

"Taylor did a nice job with it."

"I can't imagine her having to do that twice in one lifetime. Once was more than enough for me."

"Me, too."

"Have you heard from her today?"

"Just a quick text to let me know she's still alive and breathing, which is what I most wanted to know."

"I wish there was something more we could do for her and the kids."

"As we both know, the most important thing we can do is continue to show up long after the hoopla has died down."

"Yes, and we will. I talked to Mimi today," he says of his former mother-in-law, who, along with her husband, Stan, is still close to Gage and now to me and my kids, too. "They're excited to get here next Tuesday and for Thanksgiving and the wedding."

"I can't wait to see them."

He puts his arms around me. "I know you're exhausted in every possible way, so let me know what I can do to help. You don't have to power through what's supposed to be a happy time for all of us."

"Thank you for saying that, because I'm all over the place right now, emotionally and physically drained and not sure how I'm going to pull off the next week of houseguests and holidays and a wedding on top of it."

In one of the strangest developments since becoming widowed, I'm close to Eleanor, the woman my late husband, Mike, had another son named Carter with. Mike's deception cut me—and Eleanor, who had no idea we existed—deeply, but the kids and I have come to love Eleanor and Carter, and they've become part of our lives and family. Life is so weird—and beautiful—sometimes.

They're flying in for the festivities, and Eleanor had wanted to get a hotel because she thought I had enough going on. However, I insisted they stay with us so the kids could have more time together.

"Ask for help, Iris. Ask the Wild Widows to pitch in. They'd do anything for you, and you know it."

"They have their own families and holidays to tend to. I wouldn't feel right asking them for help at such a busy time for everyone. I'm still not even sure we're doing the right thing, having a wedding the same week Taylor buries her second husband."

"The wedding was planned months before Will died. Taylor knows that, and she loves you, Iris. She wouldn't want anything to stand in the way of your happiness."

"No, she wouldn't, and I know that for certain, but I'm struggling with the timing of it all just the same."

"I understand, love. And I'm sorry you're struggling."

"I'll be okay. It's just a lot all at once."

"Yes, it is, and we'll get through it together. I'm right here and will do anything I can to make this time easier for you."

"And you wonder why I love you so much."

"I don't wonder."

I laugh—hard—which makes me feel better right away.

He's magic that way, in how he can always find a way to lift me up when I need it.

"Will you do me a favor?" he asks.

"Anything for you."

"Will you try to enjoy this time? I know your heart is heavy on Taylor's behalf, and mine is, too, but you and I deserve this, Iris. After what we've been through and all we've tried to do for others in the same boat... We deserve to celebrate our love and to move into this new life together with joy and true happiness. I don't want anything to take away from that for you."

"And I don't want anything—especially me—to take that away for you. No one in this world deserves happily ever after more than you do."

"More than *we* do."

"Right. We all deserve this, and it's going to be an amazing week of friends, family, holidays and celebration."

"I don't want you to fake it until you make it. If your heart is aching, I want you to talk to me. Do you promise?"

"Yes, I promise. I don't have to fake being happy with you, Gage. You know that. And the kids are out of their minds with excitement. I'm going to stay focused on you and them and enjoy the moment. I'll be okay."

"I love you, and I can't wait to marry you and our kids."

"I can't wait either."

Twenty

Gage

This morning's conversation with Iris stays with me as I spend the day in my office, working on the book, which I'm calling *Surviving the Unsurvivable: Moving on from Great Loss to Find New Joy*. I'm about three-quarters of the way through the writing of the first draft, and it's still kind of all over the place. I'd hoped to finish it by the end of the year, but I'm not optimistic about meeting that goal. Now that Iris has expressed interest in participating, I'm looking forward to seeing what she wants to add to the story, even if that will make for a more complicated writing process. As with all things with her, I'm sure it'll be fun to collaborate.

I'm used to putting my innermost thoughts about loss and widowhood out into the world through my daily Instagram posts, but the book goes even deeper into the subjects of loss, grief, moving on and rebuilding a shattered life than the posts have.

Writing the book has reopened some old wounds and forced me to dwell in the place of early grief once again so that I might fully capture the experience I somehow managed to survive.

The writing hasn't been productive today as I wrestle with Iris's obvious stress as we prepare for a week we've looked forward to for a year. Before we can celebrate our happily ever after, we have to attend the wake and funeral for Will and immerse ourselves in Taylor's new tragedy.

It's all too much sometimes, and to see Iris buckling under the strain is worrisome, mostly because she's the one who usually carries the rest of us through the tough times. The more I think about it, the more I'm sure that our closest friends would want me to tell them that Iris needs their help and support this week as we count down to the wedding.

As I compose a text to the Wild Widows outside of our usual group chat, I hope I'm doing the right thing by calling in the troops.

Friends, as you know, our wedding is next weekend, and we couldn't be more excited to celebrate with all of you. However, before then, we have to see Taylor through the services for Will, and there's a holiday looming, with houseguests incoming as well. I'm starting to see signs of Iris buckling under the weight of it all, and I'm asking for some help. I don't even know what she/we need, but I figured you guys might have some ideas of how we can all help her through these next ten days. She would have my head for sending this message, so be careful to reply only to this thread that doesn't include her. I'm going to quit while I'm ahead here and thank you all in advance for any ideas you might have. Much love.

Roni replies first. *I know I speak for all of us when I say there is literally nothing we wouldn't do for you and Iris. My first thought is to have Friendsgiving at Wednesday's meeting, and we'll provide the food. Then you guys can pick at leftovers the next day and take it easy. What does everyone think?*

A flood of responses arrives in support of Roni's brilliant

idea. Within fifteen minutes, everyone has stepped up to take food assignments, including pies.

You guys humble me with your kindness.

And you have no idea what a pleasure it is for us to do something for the two of you who do so much for all of us, Joy says. *I'm so, so thankful you reached out, and now we also get to have Friendsgiving with all of you before we spend the next day with our own families.*

Christy chimes in next. *What Joy said. I'm so glad you asked us to help our precious Iris. While she stands by Taylor's side this week, we'll stand by hers.*

Not to play the realist, Derek says, *but how do we keep her from preparing Thanksgiving dinner?*

Always the buzzkiller, Roni says with teasing emojis for her fiancé.

Someone has to be the voice of reason in this group, Derek says.

Lots of laughter emojis follow their exchange.

I'll talk to my MIL, Mimi, and FIL, Stan, and plot a scheme whereby the three of us take over Thanksgiving dinner.

Good idea, Gage, Naomi says. *She'll buy that—and appreciate it.*

You guys are the best. Thank you for this. Iris will kill me for involving you, but whatever it takes to get her to the big day without an overload of stress.

I'll be dropping off two of my famous breakfast casseroles for your guests, Joy adds. *We got you, boo.*

Love you all so much.

I text Mimi to bring her and Stan in on the plan for Thanksgiving dinner.

I love that—and I'm sorry I didn't think to volunteer to take it on. I'd never want to step on Iris's toes, especially as a guest in her home.

Iris loves you to pieces, so you could never step on her toes, I reply. It's been one of the great joys of my widow life to see my new partner become so close to my late wife's parents—and for them to have all but adopted Iris's kids as their grandchildren. *I think it'll be great to celebrate Friendsgiving with you guys and the Wild Widows on Wednesday and then have a chill day for all of us on Thursday before the wedding festivities begin. No shopping, no cooking, no cleanup.*

How do we pull that off without appearing to prepare?

We could tell her we ordered dinner and it's all being delivered Thursday morning?

Yes! Perfect. Tell her Stan and I took care of everything. I love this! She'll be delighted when her friends come rolling in, bringing dinner.

And she'll have my head for organizing this, but I'll take my chances.

She'll know you did it out of love and concern for her. We can't stop thinking about her friend's tragic loss and how hard that must be for all of you.

It's been a tough one for sure. Wake is Sunday and funeral is Monday.

My thoughts and prayers are with you, Iris and everyone who loved Will. We'll be thinking of you. And we can't wait to hug you all.

Same. Thank you for all the love and support. Means the world to us.

We are so, so thrilled for you, Iris and the kids. Love you all to the moon.

I've written an entire chapter about Mimi and Stan and how the loss of their only child and their twin granddaughters could've been the end of them. Instead, they stepped up for me and have supported every move I've made in the aftermath of tragedy, which has been an incredible blessing to me as I rebuilt my life. I've heard from widows whose in-laws fought them every step of the way in dealing with their late spouse's estate and belongings. They've fought over money and decisions to sell the home where their late child lived. They've ended up in court, fending off grandparents who think they should have a say in how their late child's children are raised. And so on...

Mimi and Stan have been two of the best friends I've ever had and are as much my parents as my own parents are. Our shared grief for Natasha, Ivy and Hazel brought us closer together rather than driving us apart, and I'll always be thankful for their presence in my life.

I reach for the framed photo of my girls that I keep on my desk, so I'll see their sweet faces every day. I use my sleeve to wipe off the dust that's just another indicator of the relentless march of time. My daughters would be teenagers now, probably giving us the business and making us long for the day they'd leave for college as Nat and I pulled together to survive the chaos. Soon, we'd be teaching them to drive, and they'd be fighting over the car we'd make them share. They'd be thinking about college and what they wanted to do with their lives.

Instead, they're frozen forever at eight years old, when they were perfect and funny and insightful and delightful and all the things you could ever want from daughters.

And Nat, my beautiful, amazing, complicated Nat... How I loved her and the life we'd built for ourselves with our girls. I miss her every day, even as I count down to my wedding with Iris. That's the push-pull of grief. It's always there, even during joyful times in the after.

I kiss all three of their beautiful faces through the glass on the frame and return it to its place of honor on my desk. When I took that photo years ago on a family trip to San Francisco, I never could've imagined that someday, it would be all I had left of them. Along with the memories I'll carry with me forever, the photographs are priceless.

With a deep sigh, I soldier on with my work for the day, acknowledging the weight of grief is heavier than it's been in a while as I stare down the wake and funeral for a man I barely knew. I'll support his wife and children in any way I can for the long haul because that's what we do, but nothing about this

widow life is ever as simple as the things we took for granted in
the old one.

Adrian

WYNTER HAS BEEN quiet since our meeting with the Wild
Widows on Wednesday night. She goes through the motions of
taking care of our kids, but with none of her usual enthusiasm
for everything the two of them do.

I'm worried about how shut down she's been for days now,
and I have no idea how to reach her when she's like this.

I've been useless at work, so I ask my boss, who also
happens to be my brother-in-law, Mick, if I can leave early on
Friday afternoon.

"Everything okay with you? You've been quiet this week."

"It's been a rough time in the widow world. The friend of a
friend, one of the original founders of the Wild Widows, lost
her second husband in an accident last week."

"Oh God, so the first one died, too?"

"Yeah, years ago from brain cancer."

"Jeez. That's awful."

"They have a baby due any minute, and two kids from her
first marriage who've now lost their second father before they're
ten. Wynter is taking it hard. I think it was a huge blow to her to
realize it can happen again, even if she knew that intellectually."

"Hearing about that would be a kick in the teeth to anyone
with empathy for others, let alone what you guys have been
through."

I rub the back of my neck where the stress of this week has
landed in tight knots. "It's not about us, but it's hard not to
internalize the misfortunes of others at a time like this."

"I totally get that. Go on and be with your family. Take
Monday off, too. It'll be a slow week with the holiday coming."

"Thank you for everything always. You're the best."

"You're my top performer. I gotta keep you happy."

"I find that so hard to believe."

"It's true. I'm not shitting you."

"Well, that's good. I'm glad to be good for something around here."

"The customers love you. I get nothing but praise about you from them, and they leave glowing reviews online, too."

"That's nice to hear."

"I've told you that. Go on and get out of here. Take a break. I'll see you Tuesday. And give Wynter our love."

"I will. Thanks again."

"Sure."

I drive home, thinking about Wynter and wondering what I'll find at home. One day this week, she tore apart Xavier's room and cleaned every square inch of it before putting everything back in new places, which meant I couldn't find anything. When I asked her to show me where things were kept now, she said I needed to figure it out.

While I get that she's going through something, I sure as hell didn't appreciate that response. I've kept my distance from her ever since, which feels necessary but painful at the same time. Wynter and I are about closeness, not distance.

I've barely even gotten to hold Willow this week because Wynter has been holing up with her in the nursery with the door closed. I can take a hint even if I don't like the message she's sending.

I'm sort of dreading this weekend. All week, I've hoped she might work through the rage she's feeling over Taylor's loss so we can get back to normal. But that hasn't happened, and I'm running out of ways to manage it. I may take Xavier to my sister's house if things are still tense at home.

Although, the last thing I need is Nia asking me a million questions about what's going on between me and Wynter, especially when I have no answers. I mean, I know what caused it, but I'm not sure how to fix a PTSD-fueled grief reaction that can happen to any of us at any time after what we've endured in the past.

I was a disaster for most of the time Wynter was pregnant with Willow, fearing I could lose her the way I lost Sadie after she gave birth to Xavier. For all that time, Wynter stood by me, trying to calm my fears with her gentle reassurances that everything was going to be fine with her and the baby, that she felt it in her soul that Jaden was watching over them and protecting them.

Wynter was good to me when she had her own fears about childbirth and motherhood to contend with. She never once made me feel like I was one more thing she had to manage during that time. I want to be there for her the way she was for me, but she's pushing me away when all I want is to bring her closer to me.

I could demand that she talk to me... Right. I laugh at that thought. No one successfully "demands" that Wynter do anything she doesn't want to do. That won't work. Maybe I could plead with her to let me in so I can help. I could try that... I don't know. This feeling of walking on eggshells is uncomfortable and frightening.

After the awful ordeal of losing Sadie and then her mother a few months later, I've been feeling settled in my new life with Wynter and our children. If she's changed her mind about me —and Xavier—I'm not sure what I'll do. She and Willow have become part of me. I need them both. I need our little family to succeed, but I can't make that happen on my own.

My stress level is through the roof when I arrive at home, three hours earlier than usual. The kids should be napping, so I walk quietly through the house, looking for Wynter. I find her upstairs in our bedroom, putting piles of folded clothes on the bed.

"Hey," I whisper, fearing that I'll scare her with my early arrival.

She spins around, seeming shocked to see me.

"I got out of work early."

Usually, that would make her smile. She'd come to me and wrap her sexy self around me, thrilled to have a little time to ourselves while the babies are sleeping. But today she goes back to what she was doing, as if I'm not there.

"Wynter."

"What?"

"What're you doing?"

"Getting some stuff together."

"For what?"

"I was thinking I might take Willow to see my mom for a couple of days."

Her mother recently got married and is at her new husband's condo in West Palm Beach for a few weeks.

"What about Xavier?" *And me*, I want to add. *What about me?*

"I figured you wouldn't want me to take him."

I step closer to her, noting the odd way she's holding herself, as if her entire body is riddled with tension. I'm afraid she might break if I touch her. "Maybe we could go with you."

"Can we afford that?" We try to live on the money I make and not touch the life insurance money she received from Jaden and his parents.

"Can we afford not to?"

Her expressive face projects multiple thoughts in the span of seconds. "What does that mean?"

"I'm scared of the distance you've put between us this week."

Tears immediately flood her eyes, making me feel guilty for addressing the elephant in the room.

I take the final step toward her, close enough now to put a hand on her shoulder. "I don't want distance between us. I want you to run to me when you're hurting, not push me away."

"It makes no sense," she says gruffly.

I'm relieved that she's not pushing me away. "What doesn't, sweetheart?"

"I barely know them," she says softly, "and I feel like it happened to me."

"You certainly understand what she's going through."

"But I don't. It's happening to her for the *second time*, Adrian. How does anyone survive that?"

"The same way she survived it the first time, one minute at a time."

She shakes her head. "I couldn't do it again. I simply could not."

"Yes, you could. You'd have to for our kids."

"No."

"Yes, Wynter, you would. You'd never leave them to fend for themselves in this world."

Still shaking her head, she dissolves into sobs as I begin to understand why she's pushed me away the last few days. If she makes me hate her, she won't have to fear losing me. The thing is, though, I could never hate her.

I gather her in close to me. "I'm not going anywhere."

"Will didn't think he was either."

"That was a random, freak accident. The odds of that happening to us or any of our widow friends are probably as astronomical as getting struck by lightning. It's not going to happen."

"Please don't pretend that we aren't as vulnerable to more loss simply because it's happened before."

"We can't live in fear of it, though, or we'll ruin the time we have left worrying about something that's probably not going to happen."

"'Probably not' isn't good enough for me."

"It's all we have. That's the best I can do in the way of assurances."

"We should be there for Taylor."

"No, we shouldn't. Like you said, we barely know them,

and like Iris said, we're not under any obligation. Hopefully, she'll rejoin the group and become another close friend, but for now... We're not going to that funeral."

Her muscles go rigid again. My love doesn't like being told what to do. "What if I want to go?"

"It's not in your best interest, and your absence wouldn't hurt her in any way."

She sighs and sags into my embrace. "I hate when you're right."

That makes me laugh. "Mick gave me Monday off. What do you say we go visit Grandma and Grandpa for the weekend?"

"You really want to go?"

"I want to be wherever you are, and I think getting out of here for a few days would be good for both of us."

"Yes, it would. Let's do it. We'll use Jaden's money. He'd approve."

I hug her tightly. "I love you more than anything, and I can't bear to see you suffering."

"I'm sorry I was mean to you."

"You were hurting. I knew it."

"But I was still mean, and you don't deserve that."

"Good thing I love you so much that I forgive you the minute it happens."

"Please don't ever leave me. I really wouldn't survive it."

"I'm not going anywhere except to Florida with you and our babies."

Twenty-One

Taylor

On Saturday afternoon, I arrange some time alone with the kids in Eliza's room. We have a houseful of family and friends, so I shut the door, hoping we won't be disturbed.

My poor babies are looking at me with dread that I quickly put to rest so they won't think something else has happened. I sit on the floor, my back to Eliza's bed, and they sit on either side of me.

"I want to talk to you about Daddy's wake and funeral."

"What's a wake?" Miles asks, his little brows knitted adorably.

"It's when everyone comes to tell us they're sorry that Daddy died and that they love us. And then the next day, we have the church service, where they'll pray for him and us."

They're quiet as they process the information.

"I wanted to ask if you'd like to go or stay home. And before you answer, I want you to know that either answer is the right one. If you don't feel comfortable going, you don't have to."

"What if we want to go?" Eliza asks.

I tuck a strand of her soft hair behind her ear. "Then you're more than welcome to. Before you decide, I want to tell you more about the wake. At the front of the room, there'll be a wooden box that's called a casket. Daddy's body is inside that box. Sometimes, they open the casket so people can say a final goodbye to the person. Other times, they keep it closed. I've asked for it to be closed, because I want to protect his privacy. So if you come to the wake, you wouldn't have to see his body or anything like that."

"Even if we wanted to?" Miles asks.

"I don't think that's a good idea, buddy. It's much better for you to remember him the way he was when he was alive and here with us, than to have the other picture in your mind."

"Would you let us see him if we asked to?" Eliza says.

I think about that for a moment. "I'd probably say no, because I understand better than you do that sometimes, when you see something upsetting, it overtakes all the good memories. Does that make sense?"

They nod as they think about what I said.

"It's better for you not to see him. I need you to trust me on that."

"Okay," Eliza says. "Will it be hard for you to go to the wake and funeral?"

"Oh yes, honey. It's a very hard thing because everyone will be so nice and so kind, and all I'll want is to be home with you guys and Daddy, not at the funeral home or the church."

"We should be there with you." Eliza glances at her brother, who nods in agreement. "You shouldn't do that alone."

"I won't be alone, honey. Gram and Pop will be there, and so will Auntie Laura, Auntie Amanda, Auntie Kate and Auntie Iris, as well as Grandma and Grandpa Lonergan and Daddy's brothers and sisters. And I'll have lots of friends there."

"I want to go," Miles says. "I want to be with you. The three of us are a team, and a team does things together."

"Even the sad things," Eliza adds.

"You guys…" I gather them in close to me. "You make me so proud every day, but especially this week. I'm so, so sorry this has happened to you again. No one should ever have to lose two daddies."

"We were lucky to have them," Eliza says.

I blink back the tears that've been threatening since I walked into the room. "That's a nice way to look at it."

"Some kids have no daddies," Miles says. "We got to have two."

"That's true."

We sit together for a long time, drawing comfort from each other the way we have in the years since we lost Greg. "When the baby comes, we'll add him to our team and make sure he knows how very much his daddy loved him."

"Daddy was so excited," Eliza says. "He was silly excited."

Smiling, I say, "Yes, he was."

"We'll take good care of our brother," Miles says. "Always."

"Love you guys the mostest."

"That's not a word," Eliza says with third-grade disdain.

"It's a word if I say it is," I reply in a teasing tone. "I'm the mom."

"Mommy," Eliza says tentatively, "when will we go back to school?"

They've stayed home this week. "Maybe after the Thanksgiving break, if you feel ready?"

She nods. "I miss my friends."

"I'm sure they miss you, too."

"What do we wear to the wake and funeral?" she asks.

"Let's go see what our options are and figure that out, and, guys… If you change your mind about going, it's totally fine. Daddy doesn't expect you to put yourself through this if you don't feel up to it—and I don't either."

"We won't change our minds," Eliza says as Miles nods in agreement.

I've never been prouder of them.

. . .

Derek

ON SUNDAY, Roni is quiet and introspective from the minute we get up, through our morning coffee ritual and breakfast with Maeve and Dylan.

Maeve tries to get Roni to sing one of her silly songs for her, and Roni tries, but her song doesn't have the usual joyful frivolity.

Later, when Dylan is napping and Maeve is having quiet time in her room with her stuffed animals and books, I go looking for Roni and find her in the laundry room, folding the mountain of clothes two young kids produce.

"Hey."

"Hey."

"What's up?"

"Just folding. You?"

"Are you okay?"

"Yes, why?"

"You haven't been your usual happy self this weekend."

"I know. I'm sorry. I'm just..."

"Processing it. I know. Me, too."

"I want to go to the wake and funeral."

"Roni... You've met them twice."

"I know, but I want to go for Iris."

Leaning against the dryer, I cross my arms and sigh. "I get that, but you don't have to put yourself through it, even for her. She'll have Gage, Christy and Joy with her. She'll be okay."

"Other than you, she's my very best friend in the after, and Taylor is one of *her* best friends. I need to be there for her."

"Okay, then we'll go."

"You don't have to."

I really don't want to, but... "Do you honestly think I'd let you do that alone?"

"I won't be alone. I'll be with the others."

"And with me."

She gives me the exacting look that women have been giving men for all of time.

I give her the mulish look that lets her know I'm not backing down.

"Fine."

"Fine."

"What's the plan for the kids?"

She reaches for her phone. "I'll ask my mom to come over."

"Mine would do it, too, if yours can't."

"Okay. Are you mad at me?"

"What? No, I'm not mad at you. How can I be when I love you for your big heart, which is aching for Iris today?"

"I'm aching for all of them. Iris, Christy and Joy, who got to watch Taylor fall in love with Will and move into a new happily ever after, only to have it snatched away so suddenly. I'm aching for Taylor's kids and their unborn baby. It's all so sad."

"It really is, and I've felt that this week, too."

"I know. You've been tossing and turning every night."

"Brings it all back. Even when you don't know the people well, you certainly understand the experience."

"That's it, exactly."

Her phone lights up with a text. "My parents are happy to hang out with the kids for a few hours this afternoon."

"Did you tell them where we're going?"

"Nah. We'll tell them after, so they don't try to talk me out of it."

"Which tells me you know this isn't the best idea you've ever had."

"Haha, yes, I know. But I'm still going."

I reach for her, and she comes to me, relaxing into my embrace. "I love you for caring so much about your friend that you're willing to put your own well-being on the line to be there for her."

"I'll be okay."

"I'll make sure of it."

We plan to meet the others outside the funeral home in Falls Church before the wake so we can go in together.

I get a text from Iris as I'm getting dressed. *I feel like Roni is coming to support me, but she really doesn't have to do that.*

Try talking her out of it.

Sigh.

See you soon.

Love you guys.

Love you, too.

I've been blessed with tremendous friends in my life, but my Wild Widows are a cut above the rest, and while the last thing in the world I want to do on a Sunday afternoon is attend a wake for a man I barely knew, I understand why Roni needs to be there for Iris. Despite my reluctance, I want to be there for her, too, the way she's always there for us any time we need her.

I decide against wearing a tie, and as I put on a suit jacket, my gaze wanders to the photo of Victoria that sits on my dresser. Though I notice that photo every day, I rarely look closely at it the way I did when she first died, and I was desperate for answers as to why she betrayed me. I found out later that she didn't, that her loyalty to me led to her murder.

It's been almost three years since that grim day when I came home from a weekend at Camp David with then-President Nelson to find her dead on the floor of our kitchen and our daughter missing for a time. The days that followed were the darkest of my life, an experience so dire I'd rather be dead than ever go through it again.

I simply can't fathom what Taylor must be feeling, how surreal it has to be to have lost her second husband, too.

Will seemed like a great guy, the sort who's friends with everyone. He had an easy smile and a quick wit, and I enjoyed the brief time I spent with him at Iris's house. The most recent was last summer when they came to swim in the pool on a hot

August Sunday. I remember how great Will was with Taylor's kids, giving them his full attention even when surrounded by other people. I recall her son, Miles, with his arms around Will's neck as Will towed him around the pool, making boat noises that delighted the young boy.

It's so fucking heartbreaking.

"Keep an eye on us today, will you?" I ask Vic. "It'll be a tough one."

I head downstairs, where Roni is getting the kids settled with her parents. Maeve loves them as much as she loves mine, and they've treated her like a granddaughter since they first met her.

Taylor's tragedy is a reminder of how lucky and blessed we are to have this second chance at happiness.

"You kids have a nice time," Roni's mom says as we leave.

Roni and I share a grimace on the way out the door. Nothing about this outing will be "fun," except the kid-free time with her, but even that's tinged today by the dreadful occasion.

The ride to Falls Church is quiet, but we hold hands the whole way, drawing strength from each other the way we have from the start. She's given me a whole new lease on life that I didn't realize I needed until she came along. At first, I thought she was stalking me, which put me on high alert due to the bizarre series of events that resulted in my wife's murder. Later, she confessed that I reminded her of her late husband, Patrick, from behind, which had her following me, looking for something that was lost forever.

Then she appeared at the White House as the first lady's communications director, and I found out we had widowhood in common when she attended a Wild Widows meeting. I'd been a member of the group for a while by then. After that, it seemed like fate wanted us together, even if it was far too soon for her. We were close friends for a long time, including through the birth of her and Patrick's son, Dylan, before our relationship became romantic.

"Thank you for this," she says after a long silence.

"No problem."

"Sure it isn't," she says with a laugh.

"I owe Iris, Christy and Taylor so much for starting the group that saved me in many ways. There's no way I would've been ready for you and this if it hadn't been for them. Taylor was long gone by the time I joined, but I'm still thankful to her for what she helped to start and for what a big difference it's made for me."

"All that said, you're really doing this for me."

"Ninety-five percent is for you, two percent is for Iris and Christy, and three percent is for Taylor."

"Leave it to you to make a math problem out of it."

The droll comment is much more in keeping with her usual chipper personality, which is a relief. "I've been taking the fun out of things for nearly forty years now."

"Speaking of your four-oh, we need to have a party."

"We absolutely do not."

"Do."

"Don't."

"We'll see."

"I don't like surprises."

"Whatever."

"Roni, I mean it."

"I heard you."

The difference between Vic and Roni is that Vic would've heard what I said and acted accordingly. Roni heard what I said, but I can't be sure of what she'll do. I try to never compare them because I love them both, but life with Roni is full of surprises that I don't really mind, despite what I said about a possible party.

If I've learned anything from my own loss and those of my friends, it's that life is to be celebrated, even milestones we'd much rather ignore than celebrate. Vic and many of our widow friends' spouses and partners never made it to forty. I see it as the gift it is, even if I'd rather not make a big fuss of it.

Luckily, I won't be alone. Several of my closest friends are right there with me, hitting the big four-oh over the next year or two.

Not to mention the wake we're about to attend for a thirty-eight-year-old who would've loved to be forty someday.

I have no complaints.

Twenty-Two

Roni

Though I was adamant about coming to the wake, as we wait in the enormous line outside the funeral home, I'm less confident about it with every passing minute. It's an unusually warm, sunny November day, and the gorgeous weather is making a mockery of this solemn occasion.

When Iris sees us coming, she gives me a "what the hell are you doing here?" look and a smile as she hugs me. "You didn't have to."

"Yes, I did."

Christy's Trey and Joy's Bernie insisted on attending with them, which makes my heart happy for my friends.

This the first time we've met Bernie, so Iris suggests we grab dinner together after the wake so we can get to know him. That gives us something to look forward to as we make our way inside to sign the guest book and take a copy of the prayer card that bears Will's handsome, smiling face.

My chest aches as we round the corner and see Taylor and the children standing in the receiving line with Will's family next to his closed casket.

That's a relief.

I'll bet they made the decision to keep it closed out of concern for the kids, who might be more traumatized by seeing him than not.

Taylor looks beautiful in a black dress, with her hair falling in long curls around her pretty face, which is red and swollen from crying. She clutches a tissue in her left hand as she greets each person who's come to offer their condolences.

Miles, wearing a gray suit, and Eliza, in a navy dress, stand by their mother's side, also shaking hands with everyone who comes through. Their poise and strength are astonishing.

"The kids, though," Derek whispers to me.

"God yes. I was just thinking the same thing."

When we reach the front of the line, we stop as a group to say a prayer at the casket and to view the many floral arrangements and photos of Will and his loved ones.

This is absolutely brutal.

Christy goes first, introducing Trey to Taylor, who hasn't met him yet, and the kids.

"Thank you so much for being here," Taylor says. "It means the world to us."

Joy and Bernie are next, followed by Iris and Gage.

Iris reintroduces us to Taylor, which I appreciate.

"It's so good of you to come," Taylor says when I hug her.

"We've been thinking of you all nonstop since we heard. We're here for you."

"That means a lot. I'll probably need my Wild Widows again, not that I thought I'd ever say that."

"What you all started has been a sanctuary for so many of us. We will be again for you when you're ready."

"Thank you." She hugs Derek. "Thank you both for coming. Will and I enjoyed the time we spent together at Iris's."

"We did, too," Derek says.

We move on to shake hands with the kids, who are so polite and composed, they take my breath away.

Then we meet Will's heartbroken parents, siblings and their partners, expressing our condolences to each of them.

What a fucking tragedy.

I'm thankful that the others head straight for the exit after we're through the receiving line. I take deep breaths of cool, fresh air once we're outside, relieved to have shown up, expressed our condolences and gotten the heck out of there.

"I don't know about anyone else," Joy says, "but I need a big, fat drink, and I need it immediately."

"Right there with you," Gage says.

Iris

I'M SO TOUCHED that Roni and Derek came to support those of us who were close to Taylor and Will. We end up at a pub that Bernie suggests that has great food and the big drinks we all need so badly.

Bernie knows the owner and tells him our group needs VIP treatment after attending the wake of someone who died far too young.

They have the promised drinks in front of us in no time at all.

I raise mine in a toast. "To Taylor, Will, Eliza, Miles, the baby and everyone who loves them."

The others touch their glasses to mine.

"To life, love and friendship," Joy says.

We're happy to drink to that, too.

"What a nightmare." Christy dabs at raw eyes with yet another tissue. "A fucking nightmare."

We murmur our agreement.

"It's really messed me up," Christy says. "I keep waiting for Trey to tell me he didn't sign on for this level of emotional despair."

Trey puts his arm around her. "I'm here for all of it."

She rests her head on his shoulder. "Feels wrong to make it about me."

"Adrian said Wynter is feeling the same way, but she seems better since they got out of town for a few days."

"It's about all of us who understand better than anyone else ever could," Gage says.

"Except we can't quite understand having to do it a second time," Derek reminds him. "And thank the good Lord for that."

"You're an inspiring group," Bernie says. "I've heard so much about you that I feel like I already know you all."

"This is a small fraction of the whole," I tell him.

"I'm sorry there's such a demand for what you offer and for the losses that brought you all together."

I glance at Joy. "Someone has prepared you well for your first meeting with her widows."

She's been determined to keep their relationship casual until she was ready for more, which is why we haven't met him yet.

"That's all him," Joy says, smiling. "He came preprogrammed."

"Even better," Gage says. "What teams do you follow?"

While the guys debate the Commanders' chances this season, Joy says, "I can't stop thinking about Eliza and Miles in that receiving line. Those poor, sweet babies."

"I know," Christy says. "Such courage."

"Taylor told me she explained what a wake is and gave them the choice of whether they wanted to come," I tell them.

"God bless them," Joy says. "I'm not sure if I could've done that at their age."

"No kidding," Christy says. "I could barely handle it at my age."

"It was good of you and Derek to come," Joy says to Roni. "It meant a lot to Taylor."

"And to me," I add, knowing they did it for me.

"I've rarely felt sadder for anyone than I do for them," Roni says. "It's really hit me hard, which makes me feel guilty to even say."

"We've been where she is and can't imagine being there a second time, which makes it about all of us."

Roni shudders. "That. Exactly that."

"I'm glad to hear Wynter is rebounding," Joy says. "I've been worried about her."

"I know," I say with a sigh. "I hate to see her so undone. She's come so far from where she was when we first knew her."

"She'll be okay," Joy says. "She needs a minute to process it all. She'll bounce back."

"I hope so." Wynter is one of my proudest accomplishments with the Wild Widows, and I'm deeply invested in her successful chapter two with Adrian.

"It's a very strange thing," Christy says, "for someone else's tragedy to become so personal to the rest of us. I've been a disaster all week. Poor Trey is going to run for his life."

Trey leans back toward her. "No, he isn't."

Christy smiles at him, but her eyes are so sad.

I hand her a tissue across the table, hating to see her so undone, too. "Can I ask you guys something?"

"Of course," Joy says.

I glance at Gage, who's engaged with Derek, Bernie and Trey. They've moved on to the Capitals hockey team. "Are we being selfish having the wedding next weekend?"

"What?" Roni says, her face flat with shock. "No. No way."

"It feels... weird to be marching forward with my happily ever after when my close friend's life has been shattered."

"She wouldn't want you to cancel, Iris," Christy says. "She'd hate to be the cause of that."

"It wouldn't be her fault. It's just the circumstances and the timing... I don't know what to do."

Joy reaches across the table for my hand. "I'm fairly certain I speak for all of us when I say *no one on the planet* deserves their happily ever after more than you and Gage do. I can't wait to dance at your wedding next weekend and to celebrate two people who deserve every good thing life has to offer. Please don't cancel or postpone. We all need this celebration right now more than ever."

"Mama Joy is right as always," Roni says. "Your happy day is just what we need."

"What do I say to Taylor?"

"I'll talk to her," Christy says. "I'll tell her you'd love to have her there if she's comfortable but totally understand if it's too soon for her to attend."

"Will you let me know if you pick up on a vibe that she thinks I shouldn't do it?"

"There'll be no vibe, Iris. She loves you. She's happy for you, Gage and the kids. She'd never want you to postpose the wedding because of her."

"We'll be there for Taylor forever," Joy says. "She'll be begging us to leave her alone. In the meantime, the rest of us have to stay the course and live our lives. It's all we can do."

Even though I still don't know if going ahead with the wedding is the right thing to do, I've heard what my closest advisers had to say and will go ahead as planned.

After a fun but subdued dinner with our friends, we part with hugs in the parking lot and orders to Roni and Derek not to worry about coming to the funeral. They have more than stepped up for us by attending the wake.

"We'll be thinking of you all," Roni says when she hugs me. "Call me after?"

"I will. I promise."

"Love you."

"Love you, too. I'll never forget what you did today, and I know Taylor won't either."

"Nowhere else I wanted to be."

We tell Joy and Christy we'll see them in the morning and head home.

"What did the girls have to say about the wedding?" Gage asks when we're on the road.

"I wondered if you heard that."

"I was trying not to eavesdrop, but my curiosity was piqued."

"They said to go ahead, that it's what Taylor would want and that we shouldn't feel anything but joyful about it."

"I like that advice. Do you?"

"I'm coming around to it."

When we get home and send my mom home with hugs and thanks for watching the kids, Gage takes me by the hand and leads me to the sofa.

"What's up?" I ask him when he's got me seated on his lap.

"I want to say one thing about the wedding before we decide for sure to go ahead with it."

"What's that?"

"I want our wedding to be one of the best days of our lives. I want it to be a day in which we celebrate surviving something that should've broken us but didn't. I want to celebrate with the people we've helped to move forward and the ones who've made it possible for us to do that. More than anything, I want you, the center of our universe, to have a wonderful, carefree, beautiful day. If you can't do that so close to Taylor's loss, then we'll postpone until you can, and I'd be totally fine with that."

This man… This beautiful, wonderful, thoughtful man… "I love you so much. More than you'll ever know."

"I love you just as much, and I want your happiness—and the kids' happiness—more than I want my own. Sleep on it tonight. See how you feel after the funeral, and we'll meet right back here tomorrow night to make a final decision, okay?"

"Sounds like a plan. Thank you for understanding that I'm conflicted. It means so much to me."

"I love how much you care about everyone in your life. I can't just love that when it's convenient for me."

"The kids would be so disappointed if we postponed, so

that's weighing heavily on me, too. They're already sad about Eliza and Miles losing their new daddy."

"Of course they are, but they know better than most kids that death is part of life."

"Yes, they do."

"Now let's get some sleep. Tomorrow will be a rough one."

As we head upstairs to check on the kids and go to bed, my heart is heavy for my dear friend and her sweet kids as they prepare to say a final farewell to their beloved Will.

Twenty-Three

Christy

I'm awake before dawn and on my second cup of coffee when Trey joins me in the kitchen.

"I woke up alone, and that never happens."

My endless need for sleep is a source of constant amusement to him. I'm usually asleep before him and still asleep long after he gets up. Now that my kids can get themselves moving on school mornings, I get even more rest than I used to when they relied on me to get them up.

"First time for everything."

He takes my hand and brings it to his lips. "What can I do?"

"Nothing specific, but thanks for asking."

"What time do we have to leave for the funeral?"

I look over at him. "You don't have to go to that. You have work."

"I took the day off. I couldn't let you go through it alone."

His kindness brings tears to eyes that're raw from days of them. "This is above and beyond."

"Nah, it's the bare minimum. I can do much better with the above-and-beyond category."

Even when I'm filled with despair, he makes me smile. "Thank you for everything this week. I've seen you stepping up even more than usual for us, and it's very much appreciated."

"I wish there was more I could do."

"You've done everything I needed—and then some."

"So what time are we leaving?"

"A little before nine? The service is at ten."

"I'll be ready."

"Thank you for coming."

"No problem."

"That's hardly true."

"Even though I hate what we have to do and why, I love that I get to spend a random Monday with you. That doesn't happen very often."

"No, it doesn't."

"Lean on me today, babe. I've got you."

I nod because a huge lump has formed in my throat, and that's the best I can do.

We meet up with Iris, Gage and Joy outside the church and go in together to find the church packed with mourners.

"Bernie wanted to come but couldn't move his appointments around in time. He sends his best to everyone."

"I like him," Iris says. "He's the real deal."

"Yes, he is," Joy says on a sigh as we settle in one of the wooden pews.

"Why do you not sound happy about that?" I ask her.

"I am happy, but you know... It's always tinged with other shit now."

"You said 'shit' in church," Iris says with a scandalized whisper that nearly sets us off. At any other time, there would've been laughter.

"What're we doing here?" Joy asks. "What *in the heck* are we doing here?"

"Is this seat taken?"

We gasp when we look up to see Aurora, who was a regular

member of the group before she stopped coming to meetings. As always, every one of her blonde hairs is perfectly styled, and her makeup is artfully applied. But there's a sadness about her that I can certainly understand.

"Oh my goodness, it's so good to see you!" I hug her and introduce her to Trey as one of the Wild Widows. Her husband was arrested, charged with rape and convicted at trial. When she asked to join our group, we agreed she was as much a "widow" as the rest of us since her life was changed irrevocably by her husband's crime. We've worried about her since she checked out of our group around the time of his trial.

"We've missed you," Iris says.

"I've missed you, too." After she hugs Gage and Joy, she takes a seat next to me. "I'm so, so sorry for Taylor. It's such a tragedy."

"It sure is."

"Is she... How's she doing?"

"As you might expect. Shocked but functioning somehow for her kids."

"And a new one coming soon... It's so sad."

We lean on each other, heads on shoulders, hands clasped until the service begins with a soaring hymn sung by the church's choir. The casket is rolled down the center aisle by the pallbearers, followed by Taylor, holding hands with her children.

It's unbearable.

The Catholic mass is familiar to me from a childhood of Sundays spent going through the motions of stand, sit, kneel.

Will's sister, Catherine, makes her way to the altar to read the twenty-third Psalm.

The Lord is my shepherd; I shall not want.

He maketh me to lie down in green pastures: he leadeth me beside the still waters.

He restoreth my soul: he leadeth me in the paths of right-eousness for his name's sake.

Yea, though I walk through the valley of the shadow of death, I will fear no evil: for thou art with me; thy rod and thy staff they comfort me.

Thou preparest a table before me in the presence of mine enemies: thou anointest my head with oil; my cup runneth over.

Surely goodness and mercy shall follow me all the days of my life: and I will dwell in the house of the Lord for ever.

Memories of those words from Wes's funeral come rushing back to me in a tsunami of emotions that take me right back to that dreadful day when I was the widow following the casket with two young kids clinging to my hands.

It's all too much.

And then Taylor stands and heads to the altar to eulogize her husband.

My breath is caught in my throat as I try to brace myself for what she has to say.

"On behalf of myself and our children, Eliza and Miles, as well as Will's family, I want to thank you all for being here today. Will would be so honored that you're here and by the outpouring of love and support you've provided over this last surreal week."

I wonder how she can do it.

I wanted to eulogize Wes when he died, but I couldn't. So I wrote something that his brother read for me.

"I want to especially thank my parents and sisters, my amazing neighbor Kate and my widow friends, especially Iris and Gage, who've been by my side from the first minute I got the call that Will was in an accident at work all the way through to today. Nothing like having widow friends, including Christy and Joy, on call who know what to say and do when you're widowed a second time. I never thought my life would unfold this way, but who could ever plan for such a thing? I want you to know that in the deep fog of grief, there's also tremendous gratitude for the joy Will brought to our lives.

"My sweet, wonderful, precious Will..." Her voice breaks

before she recovers and presses on. "I'll miss watching *Love Island* with you and hearing your predictions, which were usually spot-on. I'll miss your unwavering love of all tacos, no matter what was in them. I'll miss your chronically inside-out socks and our arguments over whether silverware should be sorted going into the dishwasher or coming out. For the record, the answer is coming out, and you were wrong the whole time, my love."

The congregation laughs at that.

"I'll miss seeing you with our kids and how you all loved each other with your whole hearts. Watching you become a dad, one careful moment at a time, never stepping on the toes of the man who gave them life as you helped to mold them into people we could be proud of, was one of the most wonderful things I've ever experienced. Eliza and Miles want you to know how much they love you and miss you. They want you to know they'll never forget you.

"I'll miss the way you loved me with everything you had and then some. You took on a widow and her heartbroken children and somehow made us whole again while making that look easy when it wasn't. And more than almost anything, I'll miss getting to see you with our son, who'll never get to meet his wonderful daddy." She takes a moment to recover her composure. "We'll do everything we can to keep you alive for him, so he'll know how lucky he was to have you as his father.

"Before this awful thing happened, I already knew that life wasn't fair. Now I know it can be downright cruel. Despite that reality, my children and I will carry on. We'll endeavor to make Will proud of us as we surround his son with all our love and continue to survive and thrive as we have for seven long years since we lost Greg.

"Will was the brightest light in our world. We'll miss him always and love him forever. Rest in peace, my love."

We're wrecked by Taylor's heartfelt words, delivered with

such courage and fortitude. Tissues are passed between the five of us as we mop up a flood of tears.

When the service concludes, we're invited to lunch at a nearby restaurant.

"Can you join us for lunch, Aurora?" Iris asks.

"I wish I could, but I've got to get back to work." She hugs us all. "It was so, so good to see you guys."

"We'd love to have you back in the group," Iris says.

"I might get there one of these days. I appreciate you keeping me in the group text. It's nice to hear what everyone is up to. Congratulations on your engagement, you two. When's the big day?"

"This weekend," Iris says with a grimace. "Timing is everything."

"I hope you have the wonderful celebration you both deserve."

"Thank you."

"I'll be in touch. Please give Taylor all my love."

"We will," Joy says. "It'll mean a lot to her that you came."

She blows us a kiss as she heads for her car.

"Well," Iris says, "that was a lovely surprise."

I wave to her as she drives off. "It's nice to see her looking well."

"I hope she comes back," Joy says. "She looks great as always, but her eyes are sad."

Nodding, I say, "I saw that, too. I'd love to have her back with us."

Gage offers to drive to the restaurant, where parking is at a premium, and we pile into his SUV.

Not a single word is spoken on the short ride as we reflect on the service and all the emotions it aroused.

Other than Trey, we've all been where Taylor was just now, with all eyes on her as she led their family and friends through a ritual as old as time.

Again.

A subdued group gathers at the restaurant for the buffet lunch.

We pick at our food, none of us really interested, but trying to be polite.

Taylor comes around to each table with Eliza and Miles to hug us all, to thank us for coming and for the support over the last week.

"Iris, could I have a minute?" she asks.

"Absolutely." Iris gets up to talk to Taylor while Eliza and Miles return to their grandparents.

Iris

TAYLOR LEADS me to an outdoor patio off the main room where the guests are gathered. It's another warmer-than-average sunny November day, which feels almost unkind in light of the occasion.

"Your eulogy was magnificent. Will would've been so proud."

"Thank you. I wasn't sure until the last minute if I would do it myself. My sister was on standby, just in case."

"It was beautiful."

"I still can't believe I had to write another eulogy for a husband," she says with a grim chuckle.

"It's surreal."

"It really is."

"Did you see that Aurora was there?"

"No! Really? How is she?"

"She seems good. She wanted us to give you all her love."

"It was so nice of her to come. So listen, I want to talk about your wedding."

"Oh, Tay... Not today. It's fine."

"No time like the present," she says with a crooked grin, "and I can't help but assume you're struggling with the timing and whether to go ahead, and I just want to say *please, please* go forward with great joy and excitement and all the things you and Gage so richly deserve."

I give her a side-eyed look. "Have one of our mutual friends been telling tales out of school?"

"No one has said a word to me, but I know you and how I'd feel if I were you in this situation. I'm not sure yet if I'll be there, but please don't change your plans because of what's happened. *Please.*"

I hug her tightly. "Thank you for saying that. I have been struggling with it."

"I had no doubt. We need some joy around here, and who better to provide it than you two?"

"Thank you for taking the time today, of all days, to think of me."

"Iris... You really have no idea what you mean to all of us, do you?"

"Oh, well..."

"Our Wild Widows have been amazing. I've heard from so many of them, people I barely know who've vowed to be by my side every step of the way. They need your celebration of joy, especially now."

"That you're thinking of others at such a time..."

"It's a tough thing for widows to learn it can happen again. I can only imagine how rough it's been for them."

"Bless you for caring, and our group is waiting to welcome you back with open arms as soon as you feel up to it."

"We'll see how it goes but thank you for saying that. I wouldn't blame them for shunning me after I went skipping off into my chapter two without so much as a single glance back."

"Oh please. You're as welcome with us as you always were."

"I really hope to be there to celebrate you and Gage on Saturday."

"Only if you feel up to it. Don't feel obligated."

"I don't. I've been very much looking forward to it."

She hugs me again, and we hold on tightly to each other for a long time, the way we have for years now.

"Thank you for being there for me, for coming to the hospital, for handling the funeral home... All of it. You're one of the best friends I've ever had."

"Likewise, my love."

"Hardly, but if you say so..."

"I say so."

She hooks her arm through mine as we go back inside to rejoin the others. "Iris and Gage will be getting married as scheduled on Saturday with my full blessing and all my love."

"Thank you, Taylor," Gage says softly. "That means everything to us."

Twenty-Four

Wynter

The time away is just what I needed. My mom and Lou are thrilled to have us visit, and even offered to babysit, which is how Adrian and I scored a date night. I've felt calmer since we've been here, and spending our days on the beach has been good for my battered soul.

"Xavier is never going to want to go home," Adrian says as he drives my mom's car to the restaurant where he made reservations.

"We need to get him a sandbox in the spring."

"I was thinking the same thing. Can you imagine the mess he'll make with that?"

"It'll be adorable, like everything he does."

"Yeah, it will." He glances over at me. "I'm proud of you for not crying when you left Willow."

"I wanted to wail, but she's comfortable with my mom."

"Nia is dying to babysit when we're ready."

"We'll take her up on that sometime soon. As much as I love our babies, it's nice to get a few minutes to ourselves."

"For sure, and we need to do that more often now that

Willow is taking a bottle once in a while. Not that there's any substitute for Mommy's boobies, because there isn't."

I snort with laughter. "You're *such* a boob man."

"Guilty as charged, but I'm a *Wynter's boobs* man, to be specific."

"Thank you for clarifying."

"Not any boobs will do. I'm very particular."

I reach for his hand and curl my fingers around his. "Thanks for putting up with me this week. I know I was a lot."

"Nah, you were hurting. I don't hold that against you."

"Iris said Taylor gave a eulogy. I can't believe she could do it. I could barely breathe at Jaden's funeral, let alone speak."

"Same for me with Sadie's. Nia said a few words on my behalf, but there was no way I could've done it."

"You were in shock. What's my excuse? Jaden was sick for years by the time he died."

"It's still shocking when it actually happens."

"Yeah, I guess. How do you think Taylor is doing overall?"

"Iris said she's holding up as well as could be expected."

"I was glad to hear they're going ahead with the wedding with Taylor's blessing." I look over at him. "I was dreading hearing they'd decided to postpone it."

"I know. Me, too. It's good news that they're going ahead, and we've got Friendsgiving to look forward to this week as well."

"Life goes on."

"That it does."

We arrive at the oceanfront seafood restaurant my mother and Lou recommended and valet park the car.

"Fancy schmancy," he says as he ushers me inside with a hand on my lower back.

We're shown to a table by a window with a view of the beach and the setting sun.

"We received a phone call from your stepfather, Lou," the

hostess says. "He wants you to enjoy all the bells and whistles on him."

"Oh my gosh, that's so nice."

She hands me a note. "He asked me to give you that."

"Thank you."

"What does it say?" Adrian asks.

"'Wynter and Adrian, please enjoy tonight as my treat and know how much I love having kids, big ones and little ones, in my life for the first time. You guys are such a gift to me, and I hope you have the best time tonight. Love, Lou.'"

I'm in tears as I finish.

"Aw," Adrian says, "that's so sweet. Look at you... You've got a daddy."

I mop up my tears with the cloth napkin. "So it seems. He's the best."

"Sure is."

"But you chose the restaurant and made the plan, so thank you for bringing me to this beautiful place."

"I'm glad you like it. I wanted you to have a nice time tonight. I gotta take care of my missus and keep her happy."

"I'm mostly happy. You know that, right?"

"I do, because I am, too. 'Mostly happy' is a good way to put it."

"Always with someone missing."

"Right."

"Do you think we'll always feel their absence as much as we do now?"

"Maybe. In a way, I sort of hope so. I don't want to lose Sadie any more than I already have, if that makes sense."

"It makes all the sense. I feel the same way about Jaden. I want to keep him close even as we move forward with our new life together."

"I have to think they'd approve of us. Heck, maybe they're even hanging out together in the afterlife."

"Wouldn't that be something?"

"For sure, as long as they aren't watching us *too* closely."

He's very good at making me laugh, even when we're talking about things that should make us cry.

"If they were, Jaden would've had you killed a long time ago."

"Sadie would've stabbed you. She wasn't having it with other women ogling her man, and you ogle me a lot."

"Yikes. I need to be more careful about that."

"Don't you dare. Ogle all you want, baby."

"People who haven't been through what we have would think we were awful for talking this way."

"People who haven't been through what we have shouldn't express opinions about something they know nothing about—and hopefully never will."

"Very true. They can fuck off."

I adore his sexy grin and how it unfolds across his gorgeous face, lighting up his eyes when he's truly amused like he is now. "I love when you hold back."

"When do I ever do that?"

"Um, never?" He reaches for my hand across the table. "I'm glad to see you smiling again. It hurts me to see you hurting."

"I had the wind knocked out of me for a few days there, but I'm better now. Getting away has helped. Iris giving us permission to skip the services helped. But I really hope Taylor comes back to the group."

"I do, too. And I get why it hit you so hard. It did for me, too. It's an awful reminder that there're simply no guarantees ever."

"I hate that system. I want to overhaul it and find a better way."

"Let me know how that goes." He plays with my fingers like he always does, his touch sending a shiver of awareness down my spine. "You know, I was thinking... Going forward... We don't need to stay involved in the Wild Widows at the same level we are now. It might be better for us to be less engrossed in the lives and stories of other widows."

"I would so miss not seeing them all every week anymore."

"We can still see them socially, but we don't have to remain on the front lines of widow central if it no longer serves our best interests."

"I suppose that's true, but I feel the need to continue paying forward what was given so generously to me at a time when I had zero hope that the future could be anything other than grim and depressing."

"Which is fair, but maybe we dial it back a bit. We don't have to attend every meeting and hear every terrible tale of loss and grief. I'm not sure it's a good idea to dwell in that space indefinitely, you know?"

Nodding, I take back my hand to grab a piece of bread. "It's something to think about, for sure. Just so you know... I think I'd need a twelve-step program to wean myself off regular doses of Iris and Gage and all their wisdom."

"They'd still be there for us if we aren't active members of the group. You know that."

"They say I'm their proudest accomplishment."

"You were a feral tiger when you first joined," he says, grinning, "and look at you now."

"Now I'm a domesticated house cat with two kittens. Meow."

He fans his face. "You're making me hot."

I sputter with laughter. "Oh my God. Relax, will you?"

"I'm on a date with my best girl. I'm not planning to relax for hours and hours."

Rolling my eyes, I say, "Thanks for the warning."

"Love you forever, wife."

"Love you longer cuz I'm so much younger, husband."

Smiling, he raises his glass in a toast to me. "Well played, love."

Kinsley

On Tuesday, I meet Luke for lunch in Georgetown, near his office. He has forty-five minutes between patients, so I get to the restaurant early and secure a table for us so we can make the most of every minute.

I'm as nervous as I can recall being since I lost Rory, which makes me feel foolish as a grown woman, a mother and a professional. My internal narrator has been working overtime as I debated every detail of this outing, from what to wear to how to do my hair to whether I'd put on too much makeup to what time I should leave the house. I ended up wearing jeans and a cute sweater and wore my hair up in a twist.

By the time I see Luke come through the door, I'm exhausted from the mental energy I've expended to get this far.

I wave to him, and when he spots me, his warm smile settles my nerves.

He's wearing a light blue dress shirt with a navy blue tie and has an ID on a lanyard that he's tucked into the pocket of his shirt. Even from a distance, I'm struck by how incredibly handsome he is with tousled dark blond hair and golden brown eyes. As he makes his way toward me, I notice female heads turning to take in the splendor.

Shut up, Kinsley. Just shut the hell up.

Still smiling, he sits across from me and exhales as if he's completed a race to get there. "Everything ran late this morning. Naturally, that happens when I have an important lunch to get to."

Our lunch is *important.*

You're shutting up, Kinsley. Remember?

"Well, I'm glad you were able to make it."

"I was gonna get here one way or the other."

Do I still have to shut up when he says stuff like that? Yes!

"How was the traffic?" he asks.

"Not terrible, but it's midday."

"True. It's a beast going home every night, but that's my decompression time between one full-time job and the other. I don't complain about the traffic."

As I imagine what his days must be like juggling so many competing demands, my heart goes out to him. "It's got to be a lot."

"It is, but the kids are always so happy to see me at the end of the day. They make it all worth it."

I want to ask who takes care of him while he's taking care of countless patients and four motherless children, but I've been told to shut up, so I hold that thought. For now, anyway.

A waitress comes by with glasses of ice water and menus. "Can I get you anything else to drink?"

"I'll have unsweetened tea, please."

"Same," he says. "Thank you."

She smiles at him, because she's only human. He doesn't notice. "Coming right up."

"What looks good to you?" he asks as he peruses the menu.

"Probably a salad."

"I'm getting a Reuben with french fries that you'll help me eat."

"If I must," I say with a laugh.

"You must." He takes a sip of water. "So tell me more about Kinsley. We've talked about the bad stuff, so tell me something good."

"Hmmm, well, I work part time while my kids are in school, doing marketing for two local nonprofits."

"Have you been in that field a long time?"

"Since I graduated from college."

"Where'd you go?"

"The University of Vermont."

"Oh, I love it up there. Burlington is such a great city."

"One of my favorite places ever, except for in the winter."

"So cold it hurts to breathe."

"Yes, exactly. What took you up there?"

"My in-laws have a place on Lake Champlain," he says. "My father-in-law is originally from Vermont."

"Ah, I see. Do you spend much time there?"

"Only in the summer. I can't do winter in Vermont with four little kids on my own. Too much equipment required."

"That's true. It's a lot to travel alone with kids. I can barely handle my two, let alone four."

"I'm sure you're a pro by now."

"It gets easier as they get older."

"That's a fact. Tell me more about your kids."

We're interrupted when the waitress comes to take our order. "Coming right up," she says with another smile for Luke. Honestly... To his credit, he has no reaction to the pretty young woman.

"You were going to tell me about your kids. I know I met them at Iris's, but there was a gaggle that night."

"We're a crowd when we all get together. My son, Christian, is eight, and my daughter, Maisy, is six. They're in third grade and kindergarten."

"I need pictures."

I call up a recent photo of my babies on my phone and hand it over to him.

He takes a long look at them before smiling as he hands the phone back to me. "I remember them now. They're adorable."

"They're good kids. I'm lucky."

"My Clarissa talked about Maisy after that night. She said she's very nice."

"Aw, that's great to hear."

"So between us, we have six kids, eight and under. In reality, we should never speak to each other again."

I laugh at the statement and the grimace that accompanies it. "We really shouldn't." *Please don't agree with that. Please don't agree with that. Shut up, Kinsley.*

"Except this is kind of fun."

I hope I'm not blushing, because that would make me mad. "Yes, it is."

"Are you going to the wedding this weekend?"

"I'm looking forward to it, and so are my kids."

"I accepted their kind invite, but I'm not sure if taking four kids to a wedding by myself is the best idea I've ever had."

I'm thrilled to know he'll be there. *Oh, Kinsley...* "All the kids are going. Yours will fit right into the madness."

"In that case, I feel better about inflicting my crew on such a special occasion."

"Gage and Iris wanted their kids' friends there because it's a big day for them, too."

"Sure is. After reading Gage's amazing posts, I'm so happy for him—and Iris and the kids, too. They deserve their happy ending."

"They really do, but we all do after what we've been through."

"Have you dated at all?" he asks.

"A little. Nothing special. It's rough out there."

"It sure is. One of my friends has tried to get me to do online dating, but the thought of it is revolting."

"You'd be very popular on the sites." The words are out of my mouth before I recall that I was supposed to be shutting up.

His left brow goes up, and naturally, it's a good look on him. "You think so?"

"Uh, yeah. They'd snap you up so fast you wouldn't know what hit you." *Great time for diarrhea of the mouth, Kinsley.*

"Until they find out I have four little kids and no mommy."

"Nah, that'd be catnip to them. They'd all want to save you and your babies."

His curled lip indicates his thoughts on that. "Ew."

I can't stop laughing at the face he makes. "Don't tell me you haven't heard from any of the PTA mommies yet."

"A few have reached out to ask if they can help with anything."

"I'll tell you what they want to help you with…"

His gorgeous eyes go wide. "No way."

"Luke, are you serious? They want to be the ones to keep the poor widower's bed warm." *Take an Imodium, Kinsley. Stat. You're talking about his* bed, *for crying out loud.*

He gives me a curious glance. "Have the daddies hit on you?"

"Two of them, both married to women I know."

"Come on."

"True story, and at the holiday hullabaloo, no less."

"What the hell is that?"

"It's an event at school where the kids get to shop for their parents and other people on their list. I was working the bake sale table when one of them asked if I needed any help around the house, and he was talking about *my* plumbing, not the house's."

"Stop it!" He roars with laughter. "You've got to be kidding me."

"I wish I was."

"What'd the other one say?"

"Apparently, he comes through my neighborhood around midday 'on his route' and could stop by if I need anything."

"What route is he on?"

"I have no idea, and I don't want to know."

"Unbelievable."

"Is it, though?"

"I guess not."

"People hear about a lonely widow and see opportunity. They think we're so desperate for any attention we can get that their stupid come-on lines will actually work. And the worst part is they always say something nice at first, like how much they enjoyed Rory and how sad they are that he's gone."

"Ruthless." He shakes his head with dismay. Then his eyes go wide again. "Oh my God, I just remembered… One of the ones who called made sure to mention that she'd worked on a committee with Bella and thought the world of her. She was so sad to hear she'd passed."

"She was *so* sad until she realized you're now single and in need of what she has to offer."

"Wow, I didn't see that at the time."

"Stick with us veterans. We'll show you the ropes, although please know that sometimes they're simply offering help and nothing else. It's just that it can be hard to tell the difference."

"I'm fine without the ropes."

When he seems to realize there are a lot of ways that statement could be interpreted, he loses it laughing and takes me down with him.

"Metaphorically speaking," he adds when the laughter passes.

"Too funny. I knew what you meant."

"Just making sure, and for what it's worth, I've seen a lot of the sincerity along with the weirdness."

Our lunch is served, and he pushes the fries my way like the devil he is. We discover we both like them with ketchup *and* vinegar.

"Bella thought vinegar was disgusting."

"Rory hated the combination. He'd say, 'One or the other, Kins. One or the other.'"

"That's the stuff I've missed the most," he says. "The things that were unique to us, the language only we spoke, the inside jokes, the *Seinfeld* quotes."

I lean in a little closer. "'I'll tell you what... There's fifty bucks in it for you if you do it.'"

He stares at me, looking a bit stunned. "You speak *Seinfeld*."

"Fluently."

"Wow. We might require a second date to fully process this discovery."

Hearing this was an official date makes me giddy, and I refuse to shut up about it. "I'd be down with that."

"Let's make it happen. Soon."

Twenty-Five

Iris

Holiday-wedding madness begins on Tuesday afternoon, with the much-anticipated arrival of Mimi and Stan from Florida. The kids are out of their minds with excitement to see the couple who've become extra grandparents to them since Gage joined our family.

Our relationship with the parents of my future husband's late wife is one of the true blessings in this strange widow life. And of course they come with Thanksgiving gifts for the kids, who are delighted to discover that's a thing.

Mimi hugs me like we've known each other for decades rather than a year. "Oh, my sweet girl, I've been wanting to hug you for days now. I'm so very sorry about your dear friend's loss."

I immediately tear up at her kind condolences. "Thank you. It's been a lot, to say the least. But I'm glad you're here, and we can start shopping and cooking."

"I have good news on that front." Mimi is positively beaming with excitement. "With Gage's blessing, Stan and I arranged everything, and dinner will be delivered on Thursday morning."

"What? Oh my God. For real?"

"Yes, ma'am. I hope this comes as good news. We figured we could sacrifice some of the family recipes for this one year to make it easy on ourselves after a rough couple of weeks and with the wedding this weekend."

I hug her tightly. "You figured absolutely right. Thank you so much. I really don't have to do anything?"

"Not one thing, except it might be fun to make some pies with the kids."

"Let's do that. For sure."

Eleanor and Carter arrive on Tuesday night, and the house is filled with the happy noise of kids playing, laughing and screaming the way they do when they're excited.

On Wednesday, with the kids out of school for the holiday, we spend the day baking, making an absolute disastrous mess of the kitchen and decompressing from the strain of the last two weeks.

Everything is better when Mimi and Stan are here, and I enjoy catching up with Eleanor, who's become such a great friend despite the circumstances that brought us together.

"I was so sorry to hear about your friend's husband," she says as we enjoy a late afternoon glass of wine before the Wild Widows meeting tonight. I'm looking forward to seeing everyone and to hearing their updates. I especially want to know how the rest of Wynter and Adrian's time away was.

"Thank you. It was a rough loss."

"I'll make myself scarce when your friends arrive."

"Oh, please don't. Despite what brought us together, we're a good time had by all. I want you to meet them."

"I'd love to."

I'm so glad that Wynter and Adrian are the first to arrive. I immediately notice the new freckles on her nose from being in the sun, as well as the smile on her cute face, which is a huge relief. "How was the trip?" I ask as I hug them both and note they're each carrying large tote bags.

"It was outstanding," Adrian says. "Just what we needed."

"I'm so glad you guys did that. Self-care for the win." I gesture to the bags. "What's all that?"

"We'll tell you when the others arrive," Wynter says with a mysterious smile.

"Hmmm. Why do I feel like something's afoot?"

Wynter shrugs. "That's just your suspicious nature working overtime."

Eleanor laughs and then coughs, as if she's trying to hide it.

"It's okay," I tell her. "You can't not laugh when Wynter is around."

I introduce her to them and then to Roni and Derek when they arrive, each of them holding a handle on a large cooler.

"What the hell is happening?"

"Stuff," Roni says. "None of your business."

Joy comes in with yet another huge bag and a cooler slung over her shoulder, followed by Kinsley bearing a bag and Naomi with an actual box.

"Someone better start talking right now," I say with pretend outrage. Whatever they're up to, I'm well aware that it's all for me, and I'm incredibly moved.

"Where's Gage?" Kinsley asks with a nervous glance toward the living room.

"So this was his doing, then, huh?"

"I can neither confirm nor deny any form of advance plotting," Joy says.

"Don't go all defense attorney on me, missy."

"I represent neither side."

The others laugh when I stick my tongue out at her.

Christy, Lexi, Brielle, Angela and Luke arrive next, bringing a whole host of new aromas that're beginning to add up to one conclusion: Thanksgiving dinner.

"You guys..." I peek into the bag that Brielle deposits on the counter and see a huge pan of stuffing. "What've you done?"

"We took over Turkey Day, so you don't have to do anything."

"But Mimi said they ordered it."

"I lied," Mimi says with a giggle from the doorway to the garage where she, Stan and the four kids are waiting to join the party. They were supposed to be taking my kids and Carter out to dinner while we had our meeting.

"We drove around the block, Mom," Tyler says with a peal of laughter that brings joy to my heart as he comes in to hug me.

The man who planned this surprise comes strolling into the kitchen, right out of the shower, and my heart skips a beat at the sight of him. I still love him, even when he plots behind my back.

"You and I need to talk, mister," I say to him while the others gather around to enjoy the show.

"Did anyone bring popcorn?" Derek asks as he munches on one of the carrot sticks I put out with celery and ranch dip.

"I didn't think of that!" Roni says. "Next time we plot with Gage against Iris, there needs to be popcorn."

"I'll make a note," Joy says.

"Welcome to Friendsgiving." Gage puts his arm around me and kisses the top of my head. "We thought you had enough on your plate—"

"Metaphor intended," Wynter says.

Everyone laughs at her comment.

"That we decided to take Thanksgiving dinner off your to-do list," Gage says.

I smile up at him. "You're very pleased with yourself."

"I am indeed. I smell a feast!"

"We came in hot," Joy says. "Hotter than usual."

"Thank you, guys. Thank you so very, very much."

"We're all incredibly thankful for you, Iris, never more so than in the last two weeks," Roni says.

"Love you all."

"Love you more," Joy says.

As they begin loading platters of turkey and massive portions of side dishes onto my counter, I'm overcome with love for these incredible friends—and for the man I get to marry in three days.

Angela

IT'S BLACK FRIDAY, and I'm going out for dinner with Brad tonight with no kids in tow. The excitement level is through the roof all day as I count down to a few hours alone with Brad with no one expecting anything from either of us. Mostly, I'm looking forward to the time alone with him, which has me feeling guilty as hell.

How can I be excited about going out with a guy who isn't Spencer?

I take a call from my sister Sam, surprised to hear from her after spending the day together yesterday at the White House. "Hey, what's up?"

"That's what I was calling to ask you."

"What do you mean?"

"You were quiet yesterday. It had to be so hard getting through Thanksgiving without Spence, so I just wanted to make sure you're okay."

"It was a great day, surrounded by all our favorite people. I'm fine."

"You'd tell me if you weren't, wouldn't you?"

"Maybe. Maybe not."

"Come on, Ang. It's me. Please tell me you'd come to me if you need anything."

"You're the busiest person any of us knows, Sam."

Her deep sigh comes through the line loud and clear. "I am never too busy for you or your kids. Ever."

"Thank you for the reminder. There is one thing I've been meaning to mention to you…"

"What?"

"I… Um… Well…"

"This oughta be good," she says with a snort of laughter.

"There might be a new guy."

"What? Since when? Who? Does Tracy know?"

I start to laugh and can't stop. Once a detective, always a detective.

"Quit your laughing and start spilling the deets, woman."

I decide to have a little fun with her, since fun has been in short supply around here lately. "It's someone you know."

"Do I need to come over there and beat this out of you?"

"As if you could."

"I could so kick your ass, but I'd never do that to a single mom."

"Whatever you say, killer."

"*Who's the guy?*"

"Brad Albright."

"*The paramedic whose wife was also killed by the fentanyl?*"

I hold the phone away from my ear. "Must you screech?"

"I'm not screeching, but holy shitballs, Ang. How long has this been going on?"

"We've been friends since you introduced us. We're going out by ourselves for the first time tonight."

"This is *huge*. He's a great guy, and he totally gets what you've been through."

"Yes, he does, and he has a lot of the same feelings about it that I do."

"I love this for you. As I recall, he's also very handsome."

"I guess. I haven't noticed."

"Stop, you're not that widowed."

I laugh hard at how she says that. "Relax, will you? It's just dinner. Don't make it into a federal case."

"Too late. Everything's federal at the White House."

I've forgotten how amazing it is to laugh at stupid shit. It's been a minute since that happened as easily as it has lately. "Well played, FLOTUS."

"It's gotta be good for something. Most important question of all—does Tracy know about this?"

"Maybe?"

"No way! That's so unfair. Why does she get to know things before me?"

"Because she babysits for me on the regular."

"I would, too, if it means having the inside scoop."

"That's the only reason?"

"Well, of course I enjoy every second with my niece and nephews, too."

"Of course."

"I'd love to babysit for you any time so you can get your groove on with that sexy firefighter."

"Too soon, Sam. Much too soon."

"Talk to me in a few weeks, when the tension is all tense and stuff."

"I'm ending this call—and this sisterhood."

"As if you could ever get rid of me."

"I'd like to right now."

"All kidding aside, have the best time, call me tomorrow and tell me everything. Take notes so you don't forget any of the good stuff."

"Bye, Sam." I'm cracking up as I hit the red button to get rid of her.

I'm sure she's already calling Tracy to get more information.

While Jack is at a playdate with a friend from school and my little ones are napping, I take a shower and spend extra time blow-drying and straightening my hair. Then I stand in my closet, taking a visual inventory, looking for something I never wore with Spence, a criterion that narrows the choices to a few random items.

I pick the sweater Sam gave me for my birthday, which

would make her happy to know she's going on the date with me. The thought of her actually going with me makes me laugh as I pull on a newer pair of jeans that fit me again now that I've lost most of the weight I gained with Josh and then go into the bathroom to put on makeup.

Ella comes to find me while I'm in there and does a double take when she sees me a little dressed up and made up, too. "Mommy so pretty."

"Aw, thank you, baby. How was your nap?"

"Good."

I bend to pick her up for a snuggle.

"Mommy smell good."

"Thank you."

I probably ought to put more effort into my appearance, so she doesn't grow up to think my regular messy look is the goal.

"I miss Daddy."

Ugh, I wasn't prepared for that. She hasn't mentioned him in a while, which makes me sad.

"I do, too, honey."

"Daddy come home soon."

I'm gutted. "He would if he could."

The single tear that slides down her sweet face is my undoing. I shouldn't be going anywhere, let alone on a date after losing the father of my children. I'm deeply torn by what I want to do and what I probably ought to do.

Then I catch a glimpse of my reflection in the mirror and see that I look more like my old self than I have since that terrible morning at Camp David. I need this night out. I need it badly.

After kissing away Ella's tear, I ask her if she wants to talk about it.

She shakes her head, so I carry her downstairs and set her up with *Paw Patrol*. Then I go into the kitchen to slice an apple and put a little peanut butter in a bowl for dipping. I sit next to her on the sofa while she watches her favorite show and munches on her favorite snack. I'm fairly certain that I've succeeded in rebooting her mainframe away from painful memories, which is a relief, even if the guilt is ever present.

I've come to accept that guilt is a permanent part of my life now. No matter what I'm doing or who I'm doing it with, I'm always thinking of the person who's gone and never coming back. I'll ache forever for my precious babies, who'll grow up without the daddy who loved them more than life itself. And I'll ache for Spence, who tried so hard to get better so he could be the husband and father he once was.

Tracy comes in a short time later and smiles when she sees me done up for my big night out. "You look beautiful, but then again, you always do, even when you don't try. Bitch."

Laughing, I say, "Big sisters are good for my ego, and little sisters are a pain in my ass."

"Ah, yes, I got an earful this afternoon about keeping secrets and such. I told her it wasn't my news to share."

"Did that pacify her?"

"Hardly. We're talking about the bloodhound, after all."

"True," I say with another laugh. "So Ella had a daddy moment after her nap that's got me wondering if I ought to be leaving."

"Yes, you ought to be leaving. She'll be fine with Auntie Tracy. I brought paper dolls for her."

"Oh, she'll love that. I haven't thought about them in an age."

"Remember how much we used to love them?"

"So much. You're the best. Thank you for everything you do for us."

"I love you all, and you'd better not replace me with Sam as your favorite babysitter."

"I'd never do that, but I might need to toss her a bone to keep her happy."

"I'll allow an occasional bone."

"Gee, thanks. Josh will be hungry when he wakes up."

"I've got it covered. Go on and have a great time. Don't worry about anything here. Mike is bringing dinner over later."

"Aunt and uncle of the year."

"Tell that to the ones at the White House."

"Let's keep it between us."

I leave her laughing as she tosses something to me that I catch in the air, so it won't hit me. When I realize it's a condom, I let out a scream. "*What the hell, Trace?*"

"Your face, though." She's bent double with laughter. "You can never be too safe."

I throw it back at her. "Where'd you even get that?"

"I'll never tell."

"It's probably old and moldy from your pre-Mike days."

"I'll have you know it's brand-new, and there're more where that came from." She comes to me, tucks the "thing" into my purse and kisses my cheek. "When you're ready."

"Buzz off. I'm nowhere near ready for that."

"Yes, you are, and it's okay if you want to."

"Bye, Tracy."

"Bye, Ang. Don't be a prude."

I let the door slam in her face. She deserves it. Ugh, way to put that in my head when I had to build myself up to get through dinner. Hell, I had to build myself up to walk out the door. As I stand at the curb waiting for Brad, I hope none of my neighbors see me getting into his truck and make a thing of it. Thanks to my sister's high profile—and mine by proximity—as well as the huge coverage that followed Spencer's death, me going on a date might be newsworthy.

I can't think about that, or I'll turn right back around and forget the whole thing.

Twenty-Six

Angela

Thankfully, Brad's truck comes around the corner before I can talk myself out of going. His kids are spending tonight and tomorrow night with his in-laws. I asked him to be my plus one to Iris and Gage's wedding, and we've chosen not to take our kids so we can have some adult time. Our kids aren't close to Iris's. Not yet, anyway, so there is no good reason to take them, even though they're invited.

How lucky am I that my sister was able to babysit two nights in a row? She says she has no life, but I'm sure she'd cancel plans to make it possible for me to go out and have fun. There's no one in this world quite like my Tracy, and yes, she was mine long before I had to share her with Sam.

"What's so funny?" Brad asks as I attempt to climb into his huge black pickup truck.

He extends a hand to help me in.

"I was thinking about how I was forced to share my older sister with my younger sister and how she was mine first."

"That sounds like my family. We all wanted a piece of my

oldest sister, Carla, and she used to tell us there was plenty to go around."

"Sounds like us. Sam and I would tug-o-war for Tracy, and she was so patient with us. She still is. She's our go-to person for all the things."

"I love that you have that kind of support from her."

"And Sam. It's a different kind of support from her, but it's just as important."

"I love how you refer to the first lady as Sam."

"What else should I call her?"

"I don't know. It's just funny."

"She's my sister, and not for nothing, but she'd hate for us to add to the hoopla that surrounds her and Nick."

"The president."

"My brother-in-law."

He laughs. "It's insane."

"How do you think we feel? We had Thanksgiving at the White House yesterday."

"That's so cool."

"It's become kind of routine to us in the last year, as strange as that may sound. We're there so often that it's just Sam and Nick's house."

"The most famous house in the world."

"How did the drop-off go with the kids?"

"It was fine. They're excited to have Grandma and Grandpa's full attention for a couple of days. And my in-laws have lots of plans for them. They had a whole agenda written down."

"They'll have a great time."

"I feel bad that I'm absolutely elated for a couple of kid-free days."

"Don't feel bad. I'd worry about you if you weren't excited to have the break."

"When you're all they have, you shouldn't be glad to be rid of them for a minute."

"You're not all they have, and any single parent will tell you to enjoy every minute of every break you get."

"Thank you for absolving me of my guilt."

"Can you do the same for me? Ella had a sad daddy moment after her nap that had me feeling guilty about going out."

"Ouch. Did you think about canceling?"

"For a second. Or two."

"I'm glad you didn't."

"I am, too."

After a long silence, he says, "This is weird, right?"

"Very. I never thought I'd be on a first date again."

"Me either. I was relieved to be done with all that."

"Oh God, same. Dating was the worst!"

"Tell me your worst dating horror story."

"I have so many tied for last place, but the ultimate had to be my ex-boyfriend Johnny. We were together about three years, and I was starting to think we were headed for marriage when he told me, and I quote, 'I'm not done sowing my wild oats yet.'"

Brad gasped. "He actually said that?"

"Those very words. It's funny now, but at the time... God, I was devastated. I thought we were solid, and the worst part is I'd gone back to him after meeting Spencer, which was a huge mistake. I was so glad to get a second chance with Spence a year or so later. Ironically, I reconnected with him at the same party where Sam met Nick."

"I'm sorry Johnny treated you that way."

"It was a long time ago now and barely registers on the heartbreak-o-meter after more recent events."

"He's a nothingburger in the grand scheme of things."

"For sure, but at the time... I was crushed."

"I can imagine. What a crappy thing for him to say. Why not just be like, 'I'm not in the same place you are regarding the future, and I think some time apart might benefit me.' Or something an actual adult would say?"

"That would've been nice. I'm a big believer in people being allowed to end relationships that aren't working for them, but to say it like that was just cruel after we'd spent years together."

"Sure was. What became of him?"

"I have no idea. I never hear anything about him, which is fine with me. What about you? What was your biggest disaster?"

"I dated my sister's best friend, and it ended badly. Took my sister a long time to forgive me for that."

"Define 'badly'…"

"I told her that I felt our relationship had run its course, and that didn't go over well. I tried to be as nice about it as I possibly could, but she wasn't having it. I was immediately the villain because I wanted different things."

"Did your sister forgive you?"

"Not entirely. She was mad at me for a long time, and I started to hold a grudge against her for giving me shit about breaking up with someone in the nicest way I could."

"Are they still friends?"

"Yes, but not like they used to be, which is also my fault, apparently."

"It's all so messy."

"I swear I was totally upstanding with her. No wild-oats bullshit. Later, I found out she'd been collecting bride maga-zines because she thought we were getting married. I was twenty-one and in no way ready for any of that."

"Yikes."

"Right? I'm so glad I waited until I was twenty-nine to get married. I would've messed it up if I'd done it earlier."

"You also hadn't met the right person."

"That's true, too."

"How'd you meet Mary Alice?"

"She's the sister of one of my firefighter friends, and let me tell you, I was hesitant to go down that road again. I made him swear to me that if I decided to end things with her, it wasn't going to be a deal breaker between us. He said as long as I was upstanding in all my dealings with her, we'd be fine."

"And you believed him?"

"I did. We were tight. He knew I was a good guy who wouldn't be an asshole to his sister, and besides, he saw that I really liked her after we met at a fire department picnic."

"So your good friend became your brother-in-law."

"He did. He was best man at the wedding."

"That's a great story. Are you still close?"

"More so than ever after losing her. He and his wife have really stepped up for me and the kids. They're my best friends."

"I'm so glad you have them."

"And many others I'd be lost without. I feel extraordinarily blessed that way. I've heard that a lot of widows and widowers feel abandoned after the first months pass and real life sets in. My people have remained faithful."

"Most of mine have, too."

"Who've you lost?"

"A couple of mom friends who came in hot at first and then faded into the ether after a while. I'd only known them a couple of years, since our kids were in kindergarten, but I'd kind of hoped we'd go the distance together."

"Why do you think they dropped out?"

"They don't know what to say to me. I'm living their worst nightmare, and being around me is a reminder that it can happen to them, too. That's my theory, anyway."

"Lame."

"Very, but from what I've read, it's a common experience for widows."

"It's still lame."

"No one wants to associate with tragedy and sudden death. It's too real for them."

"Poor babies. How do they cope?"

"It's hard for them, Brad. Be nice."

He laughs. "People are so messed up."

"They really are, but we're killing the widow game."

"Hell yes, we are. The one thing I never wanted to be successful at."

"Same. Can we put it on a résumé? 'I'm an excellent widow and single mother.'"

"I'd give you the job."

He surprises me when he reaches for my hand as if it's something he's done a million times before. "Is this okay?"

I nod and smile as I note his hand feels different than Spencer's did. Brad's is more calloused from hard work. In addition to his role with the fire department, he does carpentry and home renovation projects on the side. He's continued to take a few of those jobs since Mary Alice died.

"Did you finish the project at your friend's house?"

"Yep. All done. New everything in their main bathroom."

"Are there photos?"

"Of course. I post them to Facebook, which is how I get more work. I'll show you when we get to the restaurant."

"Which do you like better? The renovation or the fire department?"

"I like them both for different reasons. With the fire department, I like the camaraderie with the people I work with and how you never know what's waiting for you on any call. There's a level of excitement to it you don't get with any other job. I also dig the health insurance and retirement plan. With the reno, I like setting my own schedule and picking projects that appeal to me."

"Is there a way you could go part time with the fire department and focus more time on the reno?"

"I've been thinking about that. I'd be crazy to give up the retirement and health benefits at this point, but maybe working two shifts a week instead of four would make more sense with everything else."

"Would they go for it?"

"They already offered me a reduced schedule if needed."

"That's good of them."

"Well, it's easier to do that than lose me and have to start all over training someone new."

"Still, it's nice to have options."

"It is, but my biggest challenge will be managing my kids when I go back to work full time. Daphne is in school during the day, and Drake is in daycare, but if I have to work overnight shifts on occasion, that becomes more complicated. The grandparents will help, but it'll be a juggling act."

"I can help, too. They're welcome to stay with us any time you need help."

"That's nice of you to offer, but you have your hands full enough without adding them."

"The kids entertain each other. It works out great. I'd love to watch them any time you have to work overnight."

"Well, thanks. That'd solve a rather pressing concern as I contemplate going back to work. The grandparents are enjoying their occasional travels, and I'd never want to clip their wings by saddling them with regular kid duties."

"I've got you covered."

We cross the 14th Street Bridge from the District into Northern Virginia. "Where're you taking me, anyway?"

"A place I know in Arlington, hopefully far enough off the grid that no one will bother you there."

"Thank you for thinking of that. I still can't believe people recognize me because of my sister. The fundraiser was such a blessing, but that and Spencer's death also raised my profile, which I so didn't want."

"They must feel bad about that part of it."

"They do, but it's not their fault. I'm so proud of them both."

"They seem like an incredible couple."

"Oh, they are. Super devoted to their family, each other and their work."

"Mary Alice had a girl crush on your sister. She said she was a badass."

"She is, but don't tell her I said that. It'll go straight to her fat head."

He gives my hand a squeeze that sets off a riot of sensation throughout my body. It's been such a long time since I've been touched by a man that I'm totally overreacting to innocent handholding.

"Your secrets are safe with me."

"That's good to know, and likewise."

He takes a right into a parking lot. "This is the place. It's nothing fancy, but the food is good, and people tend to mind their own business. I've seen congresspeople and other DC types in here, and no one makes a thing of it."

"Sounds perfect. Thanks for thinking about the public aspect."

"Let me help you out so you don't break an ankle."

He comes around the truck to give me a hand out.

"That's a big drop."

"Mary Alice hated this thing and refused to ride in it." He tucks my hand into his arm and glances my way. "Is it okay to tell you that? I'm not sure what the rules of dating as a widow are."

"Mention of late spouses is allowed and encouraged. I don't understand why anyone would be jealous or threatened by someone who's dead."

"Exactly. How stupid is that?"

"It's nice to know I'm hanging out with someone who's capable of all the things that come with a serious relationship, you know?"

"Definitely an advantage to dating someone who hasn't experienced what we have."

He holds the door to the restaurant for me and ushers me in

ahead of him into a cozy space with almost every table occupied and a crowd at the bar. "I have a reservation for two," he tells the hostess. "Brad Albright."

"Right this way," she says, smiling as she leads us to a quiet table in the back corner.

On the way, I notice a woman looking at me, but I keep moving, hoping she doesn't recognize me.

"I saw that lady looking at you," he says when we're seated. "Do you feel okay about staying?"

"I'm not sure she knows who I am. I hope she doesn't. And yes, I'm fine with staying. This is nice."

"Glad you like it. I haven't been here in ages, since before..."

"Is it hard to come back?"

"Not like I thought it would be. I debated bringing you somewhere I'd been with Mary Alice, but I knew it was more private than a lot of other places we could've gone."

"It's totally fine. You did good. Thank you for thinking of the privacy factor."

"Brad? I thought that was you! Welcome back."

He's startled by the appearance of a pretty young woman with dark blonde hair in a ponytail and a friendly smile. She glances at me and does a double take when she realizes I'm not Mary Alice.

"Oh, um..."

"Hey, Callie. How are you?"

She's so rattled to see him with someone other than his wife that she can barely function. "I, um, I'm good."

"Did you hear that my wife died last year?"

"I didn't. Oh my goodness. I'm so sorry. She was a lovely person."

"Yes, she was. Callie, this is my friend Angela. Angela, Callie and her husband are the restaurant owners."

"It's nice to meet you," I say.

"Yes, you, too." She's obviously undone by the news of

Mary Alice's passing. Her attention returns to Brad. "Are you... You're doing okay?"

"As well as can be expected. Single parenthood is a big adjustment."

"I'm sure it is. Well, I'll let you enjoy your dinner. It's nice to see you."

"You, too."

"Sorry," he says. "That was awkward. I figured everyone knew by now."

"No need to be sorry."

"I shouldn't have brought you to a place where they knew her."

"It's no big deal. Really. It's bound to happen to both of us."

While I honestly believe that's true, the encounter with Callie has changed the entire vibe of the evening—and not for the better.

Twenty-Seven

Brad

What was I thinking, bringing her here where people knew Mary Alice and would naturally ask about her when they saw me with another woman? Honestly, it never occurred to me that there were people who knew us who haven't heard she died. Thanks to Angela's proximity to the president and first lady, it was a big story when their brother-in-law died of fentanyl poisoning. I assume the entire world knows about what happened to all the victims, but why would they pay that kind of attention?

What was a nuclear bomb in my life barely registered to others.

I'm out of sorts after Callie's shock at seeing me with someone who isn't Mary Alice, as if I'm cheating on my wife or something. Or maybe she thinks it's too soon for me to be out with someone else.

"Do you want to go?" Angela asks quietly.

I realize I've been in a heck of a brood for quite a few minutes.

"No, I'm sorry. That was just..."

"I know. I get it. What're you thinking?"

"Did she think I was cheating on my wife at a place we used to go together? Is she appalled that I'm already out with someone new? And why do I care what she thinks?"

"From everything I've read and heard, dating again is the most fraught of all the terribly fraught young widow challenges. Everyone has opinions, and they feel free to share them with someone who's so tender and raw that the words lacerate deeply."

I'm nodding from the first use of the word *fraught*. It's all so fraught with peril and heartache and sadness and hope. "Don't they know... We'd give anything to go back to who and what we were the day before? That we'd give anything to not have lost the person we loved the most?"

"All they see is someone who used to be married venturing out with someone new. They see blood in the water."

"They need to get a life and stay out of mine."

"Point of order... Callie didn't do anything wrong. She was just surprised because she hadn't heard about Mary Alice."

"I wonder how that's possible with all the publicity the story got."

"Thanks to my connection to the first couple."

"And because the fentanyl topic is one that gets a lot of attention, especially in a situation like ours."

"Yes, that, too."

"It's astonishing to me that someone who knew us didn't know she died. It never occurred to me that some people hadn't heard."

A waitress comes to the table, apologizes for the wait, and recites the list of specials and takes our drink order.

Angela asks for a glass of Chardonnay, while I have a draft beer.

"Brad."

I glance at her.

"You haven't done anything wrong. You're doing everything you can to get through the worst tragedy of your life, and you shouldn't feel guilty."

"Do you? Feel guilty at all, being here with me?"

"Only in the sense that changing my mindset from married to single is taking more time than I thought it would. But despite that, I'm single and free to do what I want with whomever I want. As are you."

"I'm trying to imagine what it would be like to be out with someone who didn't understand what this is like."

"It would be even harder than this is."

The waitress returns with our drinks and takes our dinner order. I order enchiladas, while Angela requests the fish tacos.

"You know what the good news is?" she asks after taking a sip of her wine.

"There's good news?"

"Always. And the good news is, you loved Mary Alice so much that it pains you to be moving on without her. I'd be concerned if that wasn't the case, you know?"

"I get that and same goes. Hearing you talk about Spencer has helped me get to know you."

She holds up her glass for a toast. "Enough of the hard stuff. We're supposed to be having fun, so let's get going with that."

I touch my glass to hers. "I'll drink to fun."

"To fun."

Angela

AFTER THE ROUGH START, we manage to salvage our evening. Even though we're relieved to have the break from our kids, we end up talking about them and sharing funny stories about things they've said and done.

I laughed as hard as I have in months when he told me about Drake bringing him the first poop he did in the potty, carrying it like a badge of honor.

On the way home, he reaches for my hand again.

"This was fun," he says. "Thanks for helping me through the rough spot."

"No problem, and it was fun. It's nice to get a break from all the things."

"I don't know how you do it with three, including a baby."

"Luckily, he's an angel, and he's made it easy on his single mom."

"Still. Three's a lot."

"So is two. Hell, one is a lot."

"You know what else is a lot? Five. Five is a *lot a lot*."

I laugh at the way he says that. "Sure is, but we're a long way from having five kids together, so let's slow our roll, pal."

"I'm just saying... If we were to go the distance, there're five kids waiting for us at the finish line. Is that off-putting for you?"

"Not at all, but you're the one who would be getting three more, so I should be asking you that."

"I'm not put off. I already love your kids."

"Likewise, but this is a heavy topic for a first date between two widows and single parents."

"Yes, it is, but because we're widowed single parents, it's probably never too soon for any topic. Lotta people involved in this friendship of ours. If, say, one of us had an aversion to the idea of raising someone else's kids, that might be a good thing to learn at the outset versus a few months down the road when everyone is more heavily invested. See what I mean?"

"I have no such aversion."

"Nor do I." He glances my way, grinning. "Good to know, right?"

"Indeed." He's so cute when he's pleased with himself.

My phone rings with a call from Tracy that puts me on high alert, as she'd never call me unless something was wrong. "Hey."

"So... a friend just texted me a picture of you with Brad tonight. She said she saw it on social media with a caption about how quickly you got over your dead husband."

I'm going to be sick.

"What?" Brad asks. "What's wrong?"

I put my phone on speaker. "C-can you say that again, Trace?"

After she repeats it, he says, "Oh my God," and pulls over into the breakdown lane on 395 North.

I open the door, desperate for air as I deeply regret the fish tacos. "What do we do, Trace? Tell me what to do."

"I called Sam, and she's got Lilia and Roni on it. They'll put out a statement that the violation of your privacy is egregious in light of your tragic loss and anyone throwing shade at a widow ought to be ashamed of themselves. Something to that effect. Also, she feels sick that this happened because you're related to her."

"It's not her fault that people can't mind their own freaking business."

When Brad hands me a tissue, I realize I'm crying, which makes me even angrier. I was having such a nice time.

"Are you okay with them putting out a statement?" Tracy asks.

"Yeah, it's fine. Well, it's not fine, but someone's gotta say it. May as well be her."

"She's very upset. I'm sure you'll hear from her when she calms down."

"We're almost home."

"See you when you get here, and sorry to have to call you with this nonsense."

"Thanks for the heads-up. My phone is vibrating nonstop, which means everyone I know is texting me."

"Ignore it all for now. It'll keep."

"Yeah, okay. I will. Be home soon."

After we end the call, I stare straight ahead into the odd fluorescent light that makes it look like daytime on the interstate that cuts through the District.

"I'm sorry that happened," Brad says. "We should've stayed in."

"No, we shouldn't have had to worry about such a thing. People need to mind their own freaking business."

"That's true, but still... We gave them the opportunity."

"We didn't do anything wrong! We had dinner, for crying out loud. Since when are widows not allowed to have dinner with a member of the opposite sex?"

"You said sex."

Laughter explodes from my chest. I laugh so hard, I see stars. I'm literally crying from laughing, which is much better than crying from heartbreak. "Ahhh," I say after a long siege of hilarity. "Thank you for that. I needed it."

"You're beautiful all the time, but when you laugh... Wow."

"Aw, thanks. You haven't seen much of my laughter side. Used to be a lot of that once upon a time. It's good to know I still can."

"Let's do more of that and less of the sad shit, okay?"

I look over at him and smile as I nod.

He crooks a finger to bring me closer and leans across the center console to kiss me—and I let him. It's a good kiss, soft, sweet and full of the promise of things to come. And when we pull back from each other, he's smiling. "Our first kiss was on the side of the road on 395."

"Maybe we should post a sign to mark the spot."

"I won't forget it."

"Neither will I."

Iris

THE FUROR that explodes around Angela and her friend Brad is horrific and disgusting. Social media is on fire, and the whole world suddenly has an opinion about what constitutes "too soon" for a widow to begin a new relationship. The Wild

Widows are in an uproar over it. Even Taylor has texted to ask if Angela is okay and if she can do anything to help.

Angela is most definitely not okay, but she's keeping her head down, taking care of her kids and trying to mostly ignore the online dissection of her life and choices. From what she's told me, Brad is doing the same. Her sister's White House communications team has been outstanding with devastating take-downs of people who have opinions on a topic they're lucky to know nothing about.

Some have gone so far as to suggest Angela should return the money raised by the GoFundMe since she was able to move on so quickly after the loss of her husband. And how is more than eighteen months considered "quickly"?

It's disgusting and heartbreaking for all of us who understand what she's been through and how taking that first step forward is such a big deal, only to have a nightmare unfold as a result.

She told me last night she's still planning to attend the wedding and won't let nasty people dictate how she lives her life. However, she won't be bringing Brad, as she'd originally planned. That hurts my heart for both of them. I hope they can hold on to the friendship they were forming when all hell broke loose.

Gage comes into our room, where I'm curled up on the chaise, answering the multitude of texts that've come in over the last few hours as the Wild Widows went to battle for Angela— and themselves by extension. I'm so proud of the comments they've left on some of the nastier posts about how lucky those people are to not have any clue what Angela and Brad have been through. Our team is doing good work out there, and I couldn't be prouder of them.

I'm staying behind the scenes so I won't let this situation take over my life at a time when I should be focused on Gage, the kids and our wedding later today. My hair and makeup team is coming in hot in an hour, but until then, I'm trying to relax and decompress while Mimi and Stan have Eleanor and the four kids out to lunch. Naturally, Mimi has bonded with Eleanor and declared Carter to be her fourth adopted grandchild. I couldn't love her more.

"How's it going in command central?" Gage asks when he sits at the foot of the chaise. We debated spending last night and today apart out of superstition and decided to hell with that. We wanted to spend this day like we do all the others—together.

"Pretty good, all things considered."

"And you're staying offline and out of the fray?"

"I am but still getting a few reports here and there."

"No reports allowed. This is your day, and the others are taking good care of Angela and Brad."

"Yes, they sure are. I'm so proud of them."

"Me, too. We've raised them well."

I laugh and hold out a hand to him. "We've helped to give them the tools they need to fight back in a situation like this, and that's why what we do with the Wild Widows is so important and necessary."

"Does that mean you've decided to stay fully involved?"

"I have, and it's because I want to, not because I feel I have to. Imagine Angela facing something like this without the support of our group."

"I can't."

"Exactly. We can't let these sweet, wounded people fend for themselves in this unforgiving world."

"No, we really can't," he says, "and this situation with Angela and Brad has made me see that, too. Imagine if this had happened to us when we were first together and didn't have the amazing support of the widows to prop us up. We might never have gotten to this day."

"Oh, we would've gotten here one way or the other, but having their support definitely helped."

"Would you have crawled naked into bed with me with a

justice of the peace waiting at the bedside to entrap me into marriage?"

"If that's what it took, but mad props for your vivid imagination."

As he settles into my embrace, I run my fingers through his hair, which he had cut shorter than usual for the wedding. I like it longer and unruly, the way it usually is, but the haircut makes him look almost boyish, which is adorable. "You've inspired my vivid imagination with your shenanigans."

"Whatever could you be referring to?"

"Gee, I wonder. Hey, babe?"

"Yes, dear?"

"I want you to know... I've had two other best days of my life when I married Natasha and had the girls, and I expect today to be the third one. In some ways, this one is even bigger than the other two because, for a long time, I never imagined I'd have anything like what I do with you and the kids. Thank you for that."

"Oh, Gage, my love... Thank you for *everything*. You not only overcame your fears of more loss to take me on, but you've become so important to the kids. They love you even more than I do, which I wouldn't have thought possible."

"How lucky are we in the great aftermath of disaster?"

"Luckier than most and smart enough to know it."

He kisses the back of my left hand, on which I wear his ring. "What do you say we make it official?"

"I say yes to everything."

"That makes you the best wife in history."

"I can't wait to be your wife."

"I can't wait either."

Twenty-Eight

Taylor

I'm determined to attend Iris's wedding even though I feel like a beached whale and even my favorite maternity dresses are tight on me. Kate has come over from next door to help me get ready and is curling my hair in long spirals while I try to sit still.

Eliza comes in to check on my progress and lets out a happy-sounding gasp. "Mommy! You look so pretty!"

"Auntie Kate is a magician."

"Your mom is naturally gorgeous. I'm just helping her pull it all together."

"And Auntie Kate is a fiction writer now, too."

Kate laughs while Eliza's little brows knit with confusion.

I reach out to her and bring her in close to me while Kate sees to the finishing touches.

"Did you decide on a movie for us to watch tonight?" Kate asks.

She generously offered to stay with the kids so I can attend the wedding. My parents and sisters left yesterday, after promising to be back soon for another visit. In some ways, I'm relieved to have the house to ourselves after an endless parade of people for the last two weeks, but the quiet is also a reminder of the one person who'll never again come strolling through the door.

I miss him fiercely. I long for him every minute of every day and deep into every sleepless night.

I force my thoughts away from him for right now, so I won't ruin the makeup Kate carefully applied to hide the dark circles under my eyes.

The baby is a constant reminder of the man I loved with all my heart and soul. Our little one is always on the move, like his daddy was, and I'll be surprised if I get through the next week without him making his appearance.

Christy and Trey are my dates to the wedding, and they'll be arriving to pick me up in about twenty minutes.

While Kate takes Eliza downstairs to supervise dinner for her and Miles, I put finishing touches on my outfit and check myself in the full-length mirror that Will installed for me on the back of our bedroom door. I decide I look as good as I can under the circumstances.

I'm worried about taking attention away from the bride and groom, but when I told Iris that, she said to stop being silly and get my ass to the wedding—if I felt up to it. No pressure, of course. I love her so much. I want to be there for her the way she and Gage have been there for me since the second I called her with the news of Will's accident.

His foreman, Bryan, has been doing his best to keep things running smoothly without Will, but it's been a struggle for him to manage the job sites and the business. It's become clear to me that I'm going to have to step in to help at some point, but not until after the baby is born. Bryan has assured me he can handle it for a while and has promised to ask for help if he needs it.

The business is highly successful, so I'd be crazy not to do what I can to save it and keep it running, but the thought of that is just another thing that makes me want to crawl into bed and pull the covers over my head indefinitely.

Since that's not an option, it looks like I'll be getting into the construction business.

In an interesting development, my new Wild Widows friend Lexi's fiancé, Tom, has offered to help if I need it, as he, too, is in the construction business and apparently met Will in the past. I thanked them both and told them I'll definitely need all the help I can get as I figure out how to keep Will's business running without him.

Add that to the list of things I never expected to have to deal with in my life. The list gets longer all the time.

With one last check in the mirror, I decide I'm presentable. I grab my purse and the dressy winter coat that won't button over my belly and head for the stairs, determined to have a good time tonight.

All my problems will still be there in the morning, and soon enough, I'll have three kids to care for on my own. I may as well try to have some fun while I can.

Iris

BEFORE I LEAVE the house to marry Gage, I decide to spend a few minutes with Mike. I haven't done that in a while. Finding out about his affair with Eleanor and the child that resulted changed how I feel about him forever. That said, he was my first love, my husband, the father of my children, and I still wish he hadn't died so tragically.

I won't lie. It's rough to find out after your husband is dead that he had a secret life that didn't involve you and your children—and to understand that we probably wouldn't have gone the distance had he lived. Many of my widow friends have no doubt whatsoever that the person they lost was the love of their life. That's not true for me. Not anymore.

However, I wanted a minute with him, the good memories and the overwhelming love I once felt for him before I pledge my heart and future to Gage.

I sit behind the desk in the office where Mike did the paperwork for his aviation business and hold a framed photo of him with the kids. "Well, Michael, I wanted you to hear it from me, which is more than you did for me, incidentally. But never mind about that. I'm getting married today. I think you'd like Gage, and I know you'd appreciate everything he does for the kids. They adore their Daddy Gage, but they still remember you and miss you and will always love you. As will I.

"Despite everything, I love you. I miss you. And I think of you every day. I hope wherever you are, you can see that we're doing okay and that there's joy in our lives. It didn't happen overnight... That's for sure. But we've done it, and I hope you're proud of us."

After I return the photo to the desk, I take one last look at the life I used to live before I step forward into the new one with Gage.

He and Tyler left earlier with Stan to meet his father and brother at the country club where we're holding the wedding. I found out Gage is a member when he suggested we have it there. I've teased him mercilessly about being a country clubber. He rolls his eyes and says it was good for business when he was still running his company and how he's never gotten around to quitting.

That's coming in handy today because it's a beautiful venue for a wedding.

I drive Mimi, Sophia and Laney to the club around noon to start preparing for the four o'clock ceremony.

Hours later, when we've been primped to within an inch of our lives, I can't believe the miracle that's taken place with my hair and makeup.

Sophia and Laney are adorable in the white dresses they chose to be my flower girls. The stylist did elaborate updos for both of them, with flowers tucked into their hair and lipstick that makes them feel so grown up. I can't wait for Gage to see them. They're delirious with excitement as we count down to the final moments before the ceremony begins.

Roni and Derek will be our only attendants, and I love the idea of four widows standing together as Gage and I pledge our love and our lives to each other. At some point over the last couple of years, they've become our closest friends. We didn't consider asking anyone else.

I'm sure my stepsister and Gage's brother expected to resume the roles they had in our first weddings, but we wanted people who represented the journey we both undertook to get from disaster to this day.

Tyler will escort me down the aisle and serve as our ring bearer. He's with Gage and Derek until the last minute.

"You look stunning, Iris, but then again, you always do," Roni says when she gives me the final once-over. She's wearing a lovely lilac silk gown, with her hair up in an elaborate style to match mine and the girls'.

"Aw, shucks, in this old thing?"

My white silk dress is simple and unadorned, leaving my shoulders bare. It has a short train with flowers embroidered at the hem. I didn't want a veil, so my mother suggested the diamond tiara my grandmother wore to marry my grandfather. I'm thrilled to have achieved my goal of looking bridal but not overdone for my second time around. "Haha. Whatever you say. You'll stop his heart in that sexy dress."

"Well, I hope not. I'm ready to leave widowhood behind."

"The heart stopping will be in a good way in this case."

"You look beautiful, too."

"Thanks to your hair and makeup magicians."

"They do good work." I reach for her hand and hold on tight. "How're you doing?" She's been fighting the good fight on behalf of Angela and Brad since the blowup over their date, and I can see the toll it's taken on her so soon after Taylor's loss knocked the wind out of us.

"I'm okay but seething with outrage that it was necessary to go to war."

"Right there with you, friend. How's Angela doing?"

"Better than I'd be if I were her," Roni says.

"And Brad?"

"It's been tough. Apparently, he has a sister-in-law who 'can't believe he's already dating again' and hasn't held back with him in person and online."

"Someone needs to bitch-slap her."

"No kidding. And poor Sam is out of her mind that it's happening in the first place."

I shake my head with disappointment in people. "No good deed goes unpunished."

"I said that to her yesterday. The GoFundMe was such a huge success, but now they're paying the price for all the exposure it gave to Angela and her story—and Brad's by extension."

"It's revolting. The whole thing. They did nothing wrong, and I hope the uproar won't be a setback for them."

"We're trying to keep that from happening by fighting back against the haters, but it's an uphill battle," Roni says with a sigh.

"And Mary Alice's sister... Ugh."

"It's probably her grief for her sister talking, but she really needs to shut up."

"Seriously."

"Anyway..." Roni makes a visible attempt to rally. "Enough about all of that. Today is about happy, joyful things and two people who deserve everything wonderful."

"I don't know about that."

"I do, and everyone else agrees. You deserve the best of everything, and we can't wait to celebrate you guys. Your victory is one for all of us."

"Thank you for being by my side today and always."

"Love you both so much."

"Likewise."

Gage

TYLER IS BOUNCING off the walls with excitement as Derek and I try to keep him contained for another few minutes. My dad and brother have gone to join my mother, sister-in-law and the other extended family members who've come from all over to be with me today.

"How soon until I walk Mommy down the aisle?" Tyler asks for the hundredth time in the last hour.

"Ten more minutes," I tell him.

"He's not going to make it," Derek says with a laugh.

Thankfully, the club's wedding coordinator comes a few minutes later to collect Tyler seconds before he spontaneously combusts.

"See you out there, hotshot," I tell him as I adjust his bow tie and straighten his hair one last time. "Love you."

He throws himself at me in a spontaneous hug. "I love you, too. Thanks for marrying us. We're a lot."

I laugh. "You're just right. Take good care of your mommy for me."

"I will."

He runs for the door but gives me a look over his shoulder that says everything about the bond we've formed.

I give him a thumbs-up that earns me a big grin before he disappears through the door.

"Phew," I say to Derek. "I thought he was gonna blow."

"I know. Remember when we had that kind of energy?"

"I'm not sure I ever did."

Derek comes closer to give me a last once-over. "You look good."

"Thanks for standing up for me."

"I'm incredibly honored that you asked me, and Roni is, too."

"It's funny when you think about who stood there the first time and how different life is now. How different everything is."

"For sure. A whole new cast of characters in the after, with some of the original peeps hanging in there for the long haul."

"Not as many as you thought, though."

"The ones who matter are the ones who stay."

"Yes, that exactly."

"Those are your words. You wrote that in one of your posts, about how tragedy separates you from the people who aren't meant to stay."

"Did I? Well, that's rather profound of me."

He smiles. "You can't know how much your words have meant to me over the years as I rebuilt my life. Any time I thought I couldn't keep going, I'd fall into the Gage Collier rabbit hole and reemerge with the feeling that if you could do it, so could I."

"That means a lot to me. Thank you for saying so."

"It's true for so many people. You took an unimaginable tragedy and turned it into such a gift to others suffering through loss."

"It's how I survived, by talking about it. I'm so glad it helps you and others."

The wedding coordinator returns to give us the signal that it's time.

My heart gives a happy, joyful lift. I can't wait to see Iris and the girls.

Derek hugs me. "I'll see you out there."

"Be right there."

Iris suggested that we ask Mimi and Stan to walk me in as a bridge between the past and future. They've been so instrumental in getting me through the worst time in my life. They're a big part of the reason I survived and am so ready for this next step with Iris and the kids.

When they come into the room, they're smiling and tearful and as overwhelmed as I've felt all day.

"You look so handsome," Mimi says, her hand over her heart.

"Thank you for agreeing to do this."

"Oh, my love... We're so honored to be part of your big day and to represent Natasha and the girls."

"They're smiling down on us today," Stan says gruffly. "I have no doubt about that. They'd love Iris and the kids as much as we do."

"I want you to know... Your love and support have made all this possible. You never wavered. You welcomed Iris and her kids like they were family to you from minute one. You never made me feel like I was doing something wrong by moving on with my life. Those are the most incredible gifts you ever could've given me, and they've made all the difference."

Mimi wipes a tear from her eye. "We've loved you like a son for as long as we've known you, and we always will."

We have a three-way group hug and emerge sniffing and laughing.

"Let's get out there before they start without us," Stan says.

We make our way to the back of the big room where the ceremony will be held. After Iris chose the flowers she wanted to decorate the space, I secretly called the florist and doubled the order, knowing how much she loves flowers of any kind. The scent is overpowering, and she'll love it.

"It's so beautiful," Mimi whispers as she hooks her hand through my left arm while Stan takes the right one.

I catch my mother's eye and see that she's wiping away tears. They loved the idea of Mimi and Stan escorting me and fully understand the symbolism. I've been lucky to be so well supported by all the most important people in my life. Not all my widow friends have been so fortunate.

Iris and I chose Sting's song "Brand New Day" to be played as the wedding party comes in, and as I hear the first notes, I'm filled with the emotion of the moment and everything the song represents to us.

As we make our way up the long aisle to where Derek stands waiting for me, I take in the glowing, excited faces of our Wild Widows, many of them with their new partners, and other friends and family who mean so much to me and Iris.

Taylor stands at the end of one aisle, smiling at me as I approach. I'm so glad she's here, and Iris will be, too.

At the front of the room, I hug Mimi and then Stan. "Thank you."

"Love you so much," she whispers.

"Love you more."

"All the best to you and Iris, son," Stan says when he shakes my hand.

I'm too choked up to do anything but nod.

Our program identified them to our guests as Natasha's parents and Ivy and Hazel's grandparents. When I turn to face them, there's not a dry eye in the room.

I hope my girls are close by today and know that I still love them with my whole heart and soul, even as I prepare to marry Iris and the kids.

When Sophia and Laney come to the doorway, wearing pretty white dresses with their hair up and lips tinged with color, I'm immediately in tears. They're so damned cute as they make their way toward me, dropping rose petals from the baskets they're carrying, smiling as big as I've ever seen and delighted with everything about this.

All their grandparents are mopping up tears as the little angels come toward me.

I kneel to hug them both and whisper how much I love being their Daddy Gage.

We hold on to one another for a long time as our guests sniffle right along with us. I hope the videographer is getting this so Iris can see it later.

I finally release them, and they go to their assigned seats to wait for Roni as she makes her way down the aisle, smiling to me and Derek as she hugs the girls.

Next, Iris and Tyler appear in the doorway, and my heart aches with love for the woman who's made this new life possible and the son I never had before Tyler.

They're so adorable as Tyler escorts his mother down the aisle. His effort to take the occasion seriously is hilarious, as anyone who knows him can tell he's barely holding it together.

As they arrive at the front, I kneel to hug him. "You did such a great job, buddy. I'm so proud of you."

"Thank you."

"I love you."

"I love you, too."

He takes his mother's hand and turns it over to me, as we rehearsed yesterday.

Finally, I'm left with my bride, who's so beautiful and sexy and perfect, she takes my breath away. I'm so thankful for the night she crawled into my bed and changed both our lives.

Our forever starts right now.

Iris

He's so handsome and emotional and all the things I love about him as he takes my hand with a big smile. The wedding planner told me how he knelt to hug the girls, and I can't wait to see that on the video.

He takes my hand from Tyler and tucks it into his arm as we turn to take the final step toward what we hope will be a long, happy, loving chapter two.

We asked Joy to preside over our ceremony, because who else would we have asked? We never considered anyone else.

"Friends and family," she says, "on behalf of Iris, Gage, Tyler, Sophia and Laney, we thank you for joining us today as we join this family in matrimony. That means marriage," she adds for the sake of the kids.

They giggle.

"Those of us who've been in the front row as this extraordinary couple fell in love can attest that there're no two people in the world who deserve this happy new beginning more than they and their children do."

That leads to a huge round of applause.

"I thought y'all might agree with me. Iris and Gage, you've given of yourself to so many others on this crazy ride we're on as widows. Your selflessness and compassion are the thing of legend among our crew, and we thank you for setting the tone and the example of faith, hope, optimism and love that we all aspire to follow. We love you and your children with all our hearts and are honored to bear witness to your love as you pledge the rest of your lives to each other. What do you say? Are you ready?"

"We are," we say together.

"Then let's get down to business. Gage?"

He turns to me, takes my hands and looks at me with love, the way he always does. "Iris... my love, my best friend, my coconspirator, my everything... When we first met, I was engulfed in darkness so bleak I thought I might never find my way back to the light. But thanks to you and our Wild Widows and all the people who've stood by me through these last few years, I'm able to take this momentous step with you and our kids. Thank you for helping to lead me back to the light, for showing me how much joy there can be in the after and for allowing me to be Daddy Gage to the precious children you had with Mike. Every day with you is a new adventure, full of laughter and love, Legos, spaghetti, Cool Ranch Doritos and all the things that make a life worth living."

I love that he chose a favorite thing of each of the kids to include.

Roni hands me a tissue that I use to wipe away my tears before they make a mess of me.

"I, Gage Collier, take you, Iris Levington, to be my wife. I take Tyler, Sophia and Laney to be my precious children. Being your Daddy Gage is one of the great honors of my life. I promise to love, honor and adore you all for the rest of my life and to handle all math homework until Laney graduates from college."

That gets a big laugh, especially from the people who know me best and understand what a big deal that is.

I'm laughing and crying and smiling so big as he gazes into my eyes with all the considerable love in his heart. How lucky we are to be loved by him.

"I, Iris Levington, take you, Gage Collier, to be my husband and Daddy Gage to our children. I thank you for all the things you already are to us and all the things you'll become as we usher our children to adulthood together. I promise to love and honor you, to make you laugh every day and to forever honor the memory of Natasha, Ivy and Hazel. I love you so much, and I always will."

"Tyler," Joy says, "can we have the rings?"

"Oh, um..."

I gasp as I look over to find him laughing with glee at having faked us out.

He hands the rings over to Joy as I give him a playful look that makes him laugh again.

Joy drops four rings into Gage's hand.

He turns toward the girls and Tyler and signals for them to come to him. He gets down on one knee to present a gold ring to each child. "I can't officially become your Daddy Gage without a ring. I love you, and I'm here for you for as long as you need me."

The three of them hug him as I give up the fight to contain my tears.

When he returns to me, I go up on tiptoes to kiss him.

"We're not there yet," Joy says, sparking laughter among the flood of tears.

"Oh, we're so there," I reply.

Gage smiles as he puts the platinum diamond band we chose together on my finger and kisses the back of my hand. "With this ring, I thee wed."

Then I put the matching ring on him as I gaze up at him looking down at me. "With this ring, I thee wed."

"By the power vested in me by the Commonwealth of Virginia and the internet, I'm honored and delighted to declare you husband, wife, mother and father. You may now kiss the bride, Gage."

He wraps his arms around me and plants a sizzler on me that has our guests cheering for us.

We emerge from the kiss smiling, happy and married.

"Let's party," he says as he turns to lead me and the kids down the aisle toward the room where the reception will be held.

Kinsley

I'M an emotional wreck after the ceremony and struggling to contain my tears.

Luke hands me a tissue, since I've used up all of mine.

When Gage gave the kids rings, I was done for.

Luke reached for my hand at that pivotal moment, and I was surprised by how natural it felt to hold on to him.

My two kids are sitting to my left, and his four are to his right.

We take up an entire row, which is something we'll probably laugh about later.

He's called me every night since our lunch. On Thanksgiving night, we talked for three hours before he said he had to sleep, or he'd be steamrolled by the kids in the morning. But he made sure to add that he had no desire to end the call.

I've stopped telling myself to shut up, because I'm enjoying this thing with him so, so much, more than I've enjoyed just about anything since Rory died.

And as far as I can tell, he's enjoying it, too.

To make everything even better, our kids get along great and were so happy to see one another again when we met in the parking lot to walk in together. They hugged like old friends seeing each other for the first time in years. It was adorable, and we were both moved by their excitement.

When he put his hand on my lower back to usher me through the door to the country club, I nearly came unglued. I'm such a dork. I don't remember being like this in the past, but there's just something about him that does it for me—and every other single woman in the room.

But he doesn't pay anyone else an ounce of attention as he focuses on me and the kids. I like that about him. I like that he's oblivious to the fact that other women find him attractive. He's respectful when he's with me and doesn't make me feel like I'm in some sort of competition for him.

This girl ain't playing that game, so I'm thankful to not have to. Did I mention he's wearing a gorgeous gray suit that was clearly made to order and fits him like a dream? He's paired it with a lavender dress shirt and purple tie. Did I tell him purple is my favorite color? I think maybe I did... His kids are beautifully attired in dresses and suits. I want to ask if he does the girls' hair himself, but I'm fairly certain he must. Who else would do it?

The reception is set up as several long tables, and we'll be sitting with our Wild Widows, including Christy, Trey, Joy, Bernie, Roni, Derek, Naomi, Brielle, Lexi, Tom, Hallie, Robin, Angela, Wynter, Adrian and Taylor.

I'm so glad Taylor came, and despite everything, she smiles a lot as we talk and tease and do what we do, which Iris told us is what Taylor would want. Iris sent a text last night asking us to be ourselves with Taylor and not tone down the revelry because of her. *She needs some lighthearted fun, and you guys are the best at that,* Iris said.

So that's what we do, while the kids have their own large table in the middle of the room, where the parents can keep an eye on them. I love the way Iris and Gage have incorporated so many kids into their big day and made it easy for their parents to enjoy themselves with the kids in full view.

The bride and groom are outside taking photos with their children and their families, as well as Roni and Derek, while the rest of us enjoy appetizers and drinks.

"You did an amazing job, Joy," Brielle says.

Adrian raises his glass in a toast to Joy. "Hear, hear."

"Mama Joy for the win," Naomi adds.

"Awww, y'all are too sweet," Joy says, smiling. "What an honor to marry our fearless leaders."

When Luke's youngest daughter, Phoebe, tugs on his pant leg, he bends to talk to her. Then he says to me, "Nature calls. Be right back."

"You want me to take her?"

"Nah, I've got it, but thanks."

He gives me a warm smile that makes my skin tingle with awareness before he walks away.

"Start talking," Naomi says the minute he's out of earshot.

"Holy house on fire," Brielle says. "Have you been holding out on us, Kins?"

"Relax, people. We're friends. Nothing to see here."

"Then why do I have singe marks on my arm?" asks Joy, who is standing next to me.

They crack me up. "Oh, hush."

Maisy comes to me, holding hands with Luke's older daughter, Clarissa.

"Where'd my dad go?" Clarissa asks.

"He took Phoebe to the restroom."

"Oh, okay. I was wondering where she was, too."

"Let's go dance," Maisy says.

They take off for the dance floor.

When I return my attention to my friends, they're looking at me with intrigued expressions.

"Knock it off," I tell them.

"Speaking of knocking, don't let him knock you up," Wynter says. "Six kids is already a lot. Seven is almost a baseball team."

While the others laugh their stupid asses off, I glare at Wynter. "Thanks for the advice."

"I'm here all night," she says, sending them into new fits of laughter.

"Is it always like this with you guys?" Taylor asks as she wipes up laughter tears.

"Pretty much," Brielle says. "Except when something shitty happens. Then we're not quite as irreverent."

"You have to watch out for Wynter, though," Naomi says with an affectionate glance toward our youngest member. "She's the problem."

"Whatever," Wynter says disdainfully. "I'm the comic relief around here."

"That you are, love," Adrian says with a grin.

While the others fill Taylor in on some of Wynter's more outrageous moments, I turn to Angela, who's standing next to me, vibrating with tension. Her arms are crossed, as if that alone can protect her. "How're you doing?"

"Never been better."

"We're glad you came."

"I almost didn't."

"We would've missed you."

"I feel like everyone is looking at me."

"No one is looking at you, and if they do, we'll poke their eyes out."

She laughs. "I need to hire you guys to go everywhere with me."

"We'd do it for free. What's happened to you and Brad is outrageous and offensive."

"Thank you for your support. It's meant a lot to me."

"How's he holding up?"

"It's been rough for both of us, but having his sister-in-law spouting off and questioning his loyalty to his late wife has been brutal."

"I took great pleasure in telling her to shut her mouth and

pray she'll never be the one mourning a lost spouse while trying to put her life back together."

"That was well said."

"Tell me you're not letting the haters win."

"We're trying to stay focused on the truth and what matters. Despite that, it's taken a toll on our new friendship. I'm hoping we'll work through it, but I'm not sure."

She looks so dejected. My heart goes out to her. "I'm sorry to hear that."

"I am, too. I was enjoying the time with him. He understands where I'm at and how I feel like no one else in my life can. There's comfort in that, you know?"

Before I can answer, Luke returns from the restroom mission with Phoebe. "Hey, Angela. I've been thinking about you and your friend this week. People freaking suck."

"That's a fact," she says. "I'm getting a drink since I'm going home with Roni and Derek and don't have to drive."

"Make it a double," I tell her. "You deserve it."

She smiles. "Yes, I do."

After she walks away, I turn my attention to Luke. "What a dreadful situation."

"It's horrible. People need to mind their own damned business."

"Wouldn't that be nice?"

The band leader asks us to take our seats so we can greet the wedding party. Those of us with children in attendance supervise getting them to seats and remind them of their manners before returning to our table nearby.

"They're so excited to sit with the other kids," Luke said. "Hopefully, Phoebe can hold it together. I put Beckham in charge of her."

"I'm sure they'll be fine."

"I worry that I rely on him too much. He's only eight, but he loves being the big brother and is very protective of the others."

As he says that, Beckham leans over to listen to something his brother, Nolan, is telling him before picking up the napkin Phoebe dropped on the floor.

I pat Luke's arm. "Exhale. They'll be fine. And if they're not, we're right here."

"True. Thanks for the reminder." He takes a drink of water and makes a visible effort to relax. I already know he doesn't drink at all if he's driving his kids, so he'll be sticking to water. I'm allowing myself one glass of wine early in the evening before I have to drive the kids home.

"Ladies and gentlemen, please join me in welcoming our wedding party. First up, put your hands together for all the parents of the bride and groom!"

We clap for Gage's parents, Iris's mother and stepfather and for Mimi and Stan, all of whom are beaming as they come into the reception room. I absolutely love that Gage included Natasha's parents in this group.

"And now for our matron of honor and best man, Roni Connolly and Derek Kavanaugh!"

The Wild Widows hoot and holler for our friends, who are smiling as they head for the seats we saved for them.

"Next up, let's welcome Tyler, Sophia and Laney Levington!"

They're greeted with a huge ovation that delights them. Tyler leads the way, holding hands with his younger sisters. They're absolutely adorable.

Iris's mother shows them to their seats at the kids' table.

"And now, for the moment we've all been waiting for, let's have a huge welcome for our bride and groom, Gage and Iris, Mr. Collier and Mrs. Levington-Collier!"

The newly married couple are positively beaming with happiness as they come in holding hands and waving to their guests. They go right into their first dance as husband and wife.

As the band launches into "Your Song" by Elton John, Luke goes stiff next to me.

"What's wrong?"

"Our fucking song," he whispers. "Mine and Bella's."

Under the table, I reach for his hand and hold on tight. "You want to go get some air?"

"I can't leave the kids."

"I'll ask Brielle to keep an eye on them."

"Yeah, okay."

I lean over to whisper to Brielle. "Luke is triggered by the song. We're going to get some air. Will you keep an eye on the kids?"

"I got you covered. Go ahead."

"Thanks."

I release his hand but give his arm a tug. "Come on."

The kids are watching the bride and groom and don't notice when we sneak out of the room.

We step into the foyer, and Luke takes deep breaths of the chilly air in the unheated space. "I'm sorry. I wasn't expecting that."

"No need to apologize, and of course you weren't."

"Stuff like that... When it comes out of nowhere, it's always a gut punch."

"Sure is. I was in the car last week, and Rory's favorite song came on. I hadn't heard it in a while, and it hit me hard. A million memories all at once."

"That's exactly it. What song was his favorite?"

"'Southern Cross' by Crosby, Stills and Nash."

"That's a great one. I sang 'Your Song' to Bella at karaoke when we were first dating. It was our song from then on."

"You can sing?"

"When did I say that?"

I laugh. "I see how it is."

"I made a mess of it, but she loved how I got up there and gave it my all."

"I'll bet she did."

When tears fill his eyes, he shakes his head. "So fucking

crazy how a few notes of a song can undo an otherwise pretty good day."

"Widowhood is a minefield of memories waiting to come for us with no warning."

"That it is." He makes a visible effort to shake off the melancholy. "I think I forgot to tell you how beautiful you look tonight."

Whoa, didn't see that coming. "Thank you." I'll never admit to having gone all out, with a hair appointment this morning and a new dress purchased with him in mind that leaves one shoulder bare and clings to all the right places.

"I should've said that the first time I thought it, which was in the parking lot when we first arrived."

Smiling, I put my hand on his bicep. "Are you going to be okay?"

"I'm better than I was. Thanks for getting me out of there."

"Any time." A shiver runs through me from the chilly air in the foyer.

He removes his suit coat and drapes it over me, enveloping me in a rich, male scent that makes me want to wallow in it. Would it be weird to sniff his jacket? *Shut up, Kinsley.*

"Thank you."

He looks over my shoulder, toward the room where the festivities are proceeding without us. "I should get back. The kids..."

"Are fine. If they need you, Brielle will find us. Take another minute, Luke."

He inhales a deep breath and lets it out slowly. "This is the stuff you can't understand until it happens to you. The people coming for Angela and Brad... They're so lucky they don't know what it's like."

"And they don't even know how lucky they are."

"Most of them will never know." He reaches for my hand and links our fingers. "Not like we do."

My heart skips a crazy beat from the way he looks at me.

"This, with us... It feels good, doesn't it?"

I nod as I try not to completely lose my shit. "It does."

"Will you dance with me tonight, Kinsley?" he asks with a shy grin that's so adorable, I can't take it.

"Yes, Luke, I'll dance with you."

Thirty

Gage

I'm loving every minute of this day, from Iris's sexy dress to the kids in their fancy party clothes to my extended family and the friends from all eras of my life, those who stayed close after I lost Nat and the girls, who've traveled to celebrate with us. Many of them met Iris for the first time tonight.

The best part is that after it's over, I get to spend every day for the rest of my life with Iris and the kids, who are mine now, too.

We have an appointment with Joy the week after next to sign the adoption paperwork. They'll keep their father's last name, but I'll be their legal parent. Iris will hyphenate her last names until the kids are adults, so she has their name—and mine. I can't wait until the adoption is official and we have something else to celebrate in this new life of ours.

I also can't wait to surprise Iris with the plans I made for our honeymoon, but that's not for a few more hours. In the meantime, I plan to fully enjoy every minute of this party that was so many years in the making.

For a long time after Nat and the girls died, I couldn't see past the deep fog of unbearable grief to picture the life I have today. Iris and her sweet kids have given me a beautiful second act that I'll never take for granted, knowing all too well how quickly things can change.

The bandleader calls Roni and Derek to the stage. "Let's hear it for our matron of honor and best man, who are, I'm told, engaged to be married as well!"

After a warm round of applause for our attendants, Derek steps up to the microphone. "Thank you all for being here today to celebrate Gage and Iris as well as Tyler, Sophia and Laney. Let's hear it for the new family!"

As our guests cheer for us, the kids come to sit with us—or, more accurately, to sit on *top* of us. We gather them in and hold them close. Tyler has lost his bow tie, and his shirt is untucked. Laney's hair has broken loose from the multitude of pins that were holding it in place. Sophia looks as if she'd rather be home and in bed by now, which is on-brand for her.

I love them madly.

"Many of you know Iris and Gage from childhood, college, work, parenthood, neighborhoods, etc. Roni and I know them as the leaders of a group called the Wild Widows, which Iris and her friends Christy and Taylor, who are here tonight, formed years ago to support young widows. Why, you might ask, do young widows need extra support? That's a great question and one most people don't have to think much about. If you've never had to ponder the subject, consider yourself lucky. Roni and I are both widows, as are our friends over there... Raise your hands, people."

The Wild Widows stand and give a wave as the other guests warmly applaud them. I love that Derek has called them out for special attention.

"Unlike the more common older widows, young widows face the daunting reality of having most of their lives ahead of them when they lose their spouse, decades to fill with something other than what they thought they'd have. We face judgment from people who know nothing about what it's like to confront this daunting challenge. We're so thankful to have each other to walk through this experience together and to have days like today to remind us that even after the worst thing has happened, there's so much more left to look forward to. This is true even as we continue to honor those we've lost, including Iris's husband, Mike, and Gage's wife, Natasha, as well as his daughters, Ivy and Hazel, who are always with Iris and Gage in everything they do and always will be."

He steps aside and turns the microphone over to Roni.

"If you know Iris and Gage well enough to attend their wedding, then you also know how loving and giving they are to the people in their lives," she says. "We've been 'lucky' to share this chapter of our story with them, to learn from them, to grow with them, to laugh with them—a lot more often than you'd expect for widows—and to love them with all our hearts. I'm a writer and communicator, and yet, I lack the proper words to articulate what these two people have meant to so many of us, so I'll just say this... No one deserves happily ever after more than they do."

"Raise your glasses to Gage, Iris, Tyler, Sophia and Laney," Derek says. "To a lifetime of love and happiness."

Iris and I are in tears as we work around the kids to applaud our friends and their heartfelt toast.

"Why are people doing that to their glasses?" Tyler asks as the crowd taps silverware against crystal.

"They want us to kiss," I tell him.

"Ew, I'm outta here." He scurries off, creating an opening for me to lean across the girls to kiss my wife.

Iris and I share a smile that says it all.

Angela

DINNER IS a choice of filet mignon, lobster tail or chicken Marsala. I chose the filet, and while it's tender and perfectly cooked, it might as well be made of charcoal. It's been impossible to enjoy anything since the shit hit the fan last night.

I came so close to bailing out on the wedding, but in the end, I couldn't do that to Iris and Gage, who've been such an enormous source of support to me during the hardest time in my life. Though I'm surrounded by friends, I feel other people looking at me, either because they recognize me or they're trying to figure out how they know me.

I want to scream in their faces, *I'm the first lady's sister, the widowed one who dared to have dinner with a male friend eighteen months after her husband died—and the whole world showed up to deride me for it. That's how you know me.*

I'm not used to being the subject of this rabid level of attention, the kind my sister and brother-in-law deal with every day. It would make me insane to have people talking about me this way all the time.

"Is your meal satisfactory, ma'am?" one of the waiters asks when he notices I've barely touched my plate.

"It's delicious, but I'm not feeling well."

"Would you like me to box it up for you?"

"That would be great. Thank you."

"No problem."

"Are you all right, Angela?" Brielle asks.

"I'm having a tough time keeping my game face on. I might sneak out, but I feel terrible leaving so soon."

"Iris and Gage would want you to do whatever you need to. If anyone understands, they sure do, and the rest of us do, too. I give you so much credit for hanging in there."

"Just barely hanging in."

"I know we're not fans of trite sayings around here, but this too *will* pass. People will move on to something else in no time."

She's right, and I agree with her, but unfortunately, the

damage is done. It's caused a rupture in my relationship with Brad that's yet another painful loss. "Can't happen fast enough for me."

The waiter returns with my take-home box.

"Thank you so much."

"I hope you feel better," he says.

"Me, too." To Brielle, I say, "Please tell Iris and Gage…" I'm surprised by the knot of emotion that lodges in my throat. "Tell them I love them, and I'm so happy for them."

"I will. Check in tomorrow? Let me know how you're doing?"

Nodding, I give her a quick hug. "Thanks for the support, not just today, but always."

"We're always here for you. You're stuck with us."

Tears fill my eyes. She's so sweet and lovely, with her dark hair cut into a cute bob. "Thank you."

"How are you getting home?"

I was supposed to go with Roni and Derek. "I'll get an Uber. Will you let Roni know?"

"Yep. Be safe."

The others are occupied watching the cutting of the cake, so I'm able to scoot out without making a fuss, which is a huge relief.

When I reach for my phone to summon an Uber, I find a text from Brad. *How's the wedding?*

It was lovely, but I'm heading out. Not in the mood…

You want to come over? Kids are in bed.

Other than a few texts commiserating about "the situation," that's the first overture he's made toward me since we kissed on 395 last night, right before we learned the full extent of the nightmare unfolding online. I'm not sure I want to go running back to him after he's gone silent on me all day. But I want to understand why he pulled away when things got hard.

After a long pause spent staring at the screen, I arrange for the Uber to take me to his house.

Yes, I reply to him, *we need to talk. I'll be there in forty minutes.*

He sends two thumbs-up.

I hope I don't regret this.

Iris

TODAY HAS BEEN RIGHT out of a dream come true, from the rings Gage gave the kids to their delight in dressing up in their fancy clothes to his heartfelt vows and all the people who came from far and wide to share in this moment with us.

We debated endlessly about hiring a DJ or a band. I'd wanted the DJ, but he'd advocated for the band he'd heard so much about from people at the club. They've pulled out all the stops, with everything from Big Band to Bruno Mars and Lady Gaga and everything in between, with a horn section that's to die for. Our guests have been dancing nonstop for hours.

"You were right about the band," I tell him as we dance to a slow version of "The Way You Look Tonight."

"I'm right about most things."

"Oh jeez. I walked straight into that one."

His low chuckle makes me smile.

"They're awesome."

"Yes, they are." He pulls back to look down at me. "Are you happy, love?"

"So happy it doesn't seem real."

"It's real, and it's the first day of the rest of our lives. I'm so glad I get to spend the rest of my life with you."

"And I'm glad I get to spend mine with you, the only guy who could put up with me and my crazy kids and my Wild Widows."

"I love all your craziness, as you know."

I snuggle into his embrace, steeped in the peace that's been so hard-won for both of us.

"Are you ready to get to the wedding night?"

"So soon?"

"It's almost ten, and your mom is about to take the kids home."

We booked the band only until ten because we had so many little ones coming and figured the party would end on the earlier side.

"It went by way too fast."

"But we've had the time of our lives."

I smile at his mention of the song we chose to end the festivities. "We sure did."

Gage gives the band leader a signal to go ahead and wrap things up with one final song.

"Ladies and gentlemen, grab your dance partners and make your way to the dance floor for one last spin as we wish Gage and Iris all the best of everything in their new lives together."

They send us off with a rousing rendition of "(I've Had) The Time of My Life" that has all our guests dancing, even the kids.

Luke and Kinsley have danced together all night, often surrounded by six little ones. They make for a gorgeous couple, and my sweet friend is obviously smitten. As far as I know, she's hardly dated since losing Rory four years ago, so it's a thrill to see her possibly moving into a new relationship with such a lovely guy. Gage and I think the world of Luke, whom we met through Tyler. He's in school with Luke's son Beckham.

Lexi and Tom, Adrian and Wynter, Christy and Trey, Joy and Bernie, Roni and Derek, Luke and Kinsley, Hallie and Robin, Brielle, Naomi and Taylor moving slowly due to her pregnancy—all of them are dancing and smiling and having the time of their lives, or so it seems.

I'm looking directly at Taylor, which is how I see her grimace as she stops moving and looks down at the puddle on the floor.

Oh shit!

I tap on Gage's shoulder. "Taylor's water just broke."

"Oh my God. Okay, what do we do?"

"Let me check with her."

Taylor is surrounded by Wild Widows, so I have to nudge my way in.

"What can we do?"

"I, uh, I need to get to the hospital, I guess."

"We'll take her," Brielle says on behalf of herself and Naomi.

"We'll go, too," Christy and Joy say at the same time.

"No need," Brielle replies. "Go have fun with your dates. The single ladies have got this."

"Is that okay, Tay?" I ask her, since she hardly knows them.

"More than fine. I'll call my mom and sisters when I get there. And my neighbor Kate, who's with the kids."

I give her a tight hug. "Love you so much. I can't wait to meet your little guy."

As I pull back from her, I notice her chin is quivering. The only person she wants with her is the one she'll never see again.

"You've got this." I wait until she looks directly at me. "You. Have. Got. This."

She nods.

"Love you."

"Love you, too. Such a great wedding."

"Thanks for being here. Meant so much to me." I release her into the care of Brielle and Naomi, who'll stay with her until her family arrives.

"Is she okay?" Gage asks.

The band has said good night, and the waitstaff has begun cleaning up. The party's over.

"I think she will be, but it's just so fucking sad."

"Yes, it is, but she's in good hands, and we need to continue our celebration while she brings another little one for us to love and spoil into the world."

"You're right." I have to force my mind off Taylor's

impending labor so I can keep the focus on my new husband. "When are you going to tell me where we're going tonight?"

"When we get there."

He's been mysterious about the plans for after the wedding, telling me only to pack for chilly weather and some sightseeing.

My mom and stepfather are staying with the kids this week so we can take a little honeymoon. That seems like a silly word to describe the trip following a second wedding for two widows, but as Gage said, what else should we call it?

He's planned the whole thing, and I let him because I had more than enough to handle leading up to the wedding. I've left lists on top of lists for my mom to keep the kids on their schedule this week, and as we say good night to them and tell them we'll see them next weekend, I expect tears and pleas for us not to go.

But instead, they tell us they love us and to have a good time on our trip.

Laney makes me promise to FaceTime with her every day.

I glance at my mother, who's standing with Mimi and Stan, all of them looking pleased with themselves.

"What's going on, you guys?"

"Mimi and Stan agreed to spend this week with us, and the kids are thrilled to have a surplus of grandparents to manipulate while you're gone," Mom tells me.

"Oh, I love that. So much excitement, no time for tears."

"We were hoping it would play out that way," Mimi says as she hugs us both. "Have the best time ever. We've got your babies."

"Love you so much," Gage says gruffly.

"Love you more," Mimi says.

They leave with the kids a few minutes later, and we say our goodbyes to the rest of our guests, until only the Wild Widows are remaining as the cleanup continues around us.

Derek produces a bottle of champagne and a stack of plastic glasses. He pops the cork as Roni hands out the glasses.

When we each have one, he raises his in a toast to us. "To Iris and Gage, our fearless leaders, we love you both so much, and we're so happy to share your well-deserved chapter two with you. Here's to decades of love and happiness."

"I'll drink to that," Roni says as the others concur.

"Thank you for this," Gage says to his best man. "Thank you for everything. You guys like to give us all the credit, but I know Iris would agree when I say *you* put *us* back together and made today possible. Love you all."

We part with hugs and promises to send pictures from wherever we end up.

Gage leads me outside to where a chauffeured Bentley awaits.

"What the what..."

"Nothing but the best for my wife." He gestures to the back door with a flourish. "Shall we?"

"Yes, please."

Inside the luxurious car is another bottle of chilled champagne that he opens and pours for us.

"To my wife."

"To my husband."

We touch glasses and share a kiss before we each take a sip of bubbly. I'm so caught up in him that I forget to try to figure out where the car is taking us until we come to a stop half an hour later.

"Where are we?"

"Reagan National," he says of the DC-area airport. "Come with me, my love."

I'm giddy with excitement and buzzed on champagne as I follow him out of the car to realize we're on a tarmac. A red carpet has been laid out, leading to a private jet. "*What* is happening, Mr. Collier?" He sold his company for a bundle, but he never flaunts his wealth or does crazy things like this. I suppose once in a while is okay, right?

I want to giggle at the direction my thoughts have taken. Yes, it's more than okay.

He guides me toward the stairs. "Right this way, Mrs. Collier."

In a million years, I never expected a private jet, but I probably should have. My husband doesn't do anything halfway.

He has his hands on my waist as he follows me up the stairs. "I wanted you all to myself tonight, so I decided to splurge."

I take in the luxurious accommodations. "Holy moly."

We're met by a steward with more champagne. "Welcome aboard, Mr. and Mrs. Collier, and congratulations."

"Thank you! This is so exciting!"

Gage chuckles at my enthusiasm as he helps me into my seat and buckles me in for takeoff.

"Now will you tell me where we're going?"

He reaches into his suit coat and pulls something from the inside pocket that he hands to me.

I'm stunned speechless when I see the Eiffel Tower on a tourist brochure for Paris. I turn to him, mouth hanging open. "*Paris?* We're going to *Paris?*"

"No objections?" he asks, smiling.

I throw myself at him as best I can while buckled into my seat. "Best surprise ever. I can't believe this is my life, that you're my life and you did this and... I love you. I just love you so much."

"Love you, too, babe. And my only goal in life is to make you and our kids happy."

"Goal achieved times ten million today."

His sexy grin is one of my favorite things. "My work here is just getting started."

As we taxi for takeoff for *Paris*, I hold on tight to his hand. "I can't wait to see what's next."

"Neither can I."

Iris

We're in bed on the plane, an hour from landing in Paris, when I receive a text from Taylor with a photo of her and her newborn son. Her smile is big, but her puffy eyes tell the true story of how devastation is coexisting with elation.

Say hello to Deacon William Lonergan, seven pounds, twelve ounces, nineteen inches. Mom and baby are both doing well, all things considered. Hope you have the best time on your trip and come by when you get home to meet Deacon. Thank you for everything these last few weeks. I'll never have the words to tell you how much you both mean to me and the kids. Much love!

He's beautiful! OMG, well done, Momma, and we love his name! Can't wait to meet him!!! So much love to you and the kids.

There's more I want to say, but it'll keep for another time. I share the photo and text with Gage, who smiles as he reads it. "What a cutie he is."

"I see Will in him. Do you?"

"That was my first thought."

"Joy and sadness all at once."

"For sure." He takes my phone from me and puts it on the bedside table. "Come here."

"I'm here."

"Closer."

Laughing, I close the single inch between us as he cups my backside to pull me in. "Better?"

"Almost perfect." He kisses me for the thousandth time since we took off and adjourned to the bedroom in the back of the plane to continue our celebration in private.

"What would make it better?"

Effortlessly, or so it seems to me, he moves me so I'm on top of him, legs spread over his erection. "Now we're talking."

"You're insatiable, Mr. Collier." We've already consummated our marriage twice, catching a nap in between.

"Because my wife is so sexy, I can't resist her."

"We'll be dead on arrival in Paris—*I still can't believe we're going to Paris*—if we don't get a little sleep."

"We'll sleep later." With his hands on my hips, he guides me as I take him in, wincing from a pinch of soreness from our earlier rounds.

"Are you okay?"

Smiling, I nod as I slowly take him to the hilt. He loves it this way, and I endeavor to drag out the pleasure as long as possible, the way he always does to me.

I grasp his hands and anchor them over his head as I take him on a slow, torturous ride.

"Is this the kind of wife you're going to be?" he asks between gasps.

Laughing, I go even slower, provoking a groan of protest.

Only when the pilot comes on to announce our initial descent into Paris do I decide to move things along, so we'll be ready for landing.

I leave him panting and sweating in the aftermath of explosive desire. I'm laid out on top of him, happily trapped by his arms around me as we come down from the high—literally as the plane begins to descend.

"Thank you," he says softly.

"For taking mercy on you?"

"For that and every single other thing. All of it, from the minute you intentionally seduced me at the beach—"

"Wait just a second! I will not be maligned this way!"

He smiles and kisses me. "For all of it. Thank you for giving me a reason to go on when I wasn't sure I could."

"Same to you, love. Thank you for taking on me and my three kids and all the insanity that comes with us."

"Thank you for making me fall in love with you, even when I tried to avoid it."

"We already had you firmly in our trap. There was no getting away from us."

He squeezes me tightly. "Now you've really got me."

"And I'm never letting you go."

WANT to find out what happened after Angela and Brad's kiss on 395? Watch for SOMEONE TO SAVE, coming in 2027!

Ahhhh, this book had me by the throat from the first page to the last! Although I hated what happened to her husband, I loved giving Taylor a story after she'd exited stage left when she remarried. I loved the way Iris, Gage and all the Wild Widows stepped up for her and how her loss forced them to confront some of their demons. It was fun to write new scenes for each of them and to advance all their stories within the larger context of Taylor's tragedy.

To end with Iris and Gage's wedding felt like the best way to leave the widows on an uplifting note until we see them again next year in Angela's story, SOMEONE TO SAVE. I'm also intrigued by Kinsley and Luke. I can't wait to see what happens with them and to help Taylor write her chapter three, if that's how her story unfolds. We'll see.

Join the SOMEONE TO REMEMBER Reader Group at *facebook.com/groups/someonetoremember* to talk about this book with spoilers permitted, and the Wild Widows Series Group (no spoilers please) at *facebook.com/groups/thewildwidowsseries* and the Wild Widows Grief Support Group at *facebook.com/groups/wwsupportgroup1/*.

I LOVE MY WILD WIDOWS! They're truly one of my favorite casts of characters, and I hope to spend many more years with them.

Thank you to my editors, Linda Ingmanson and Joyce Lamb, as well as my beta readers Anne Woodall, Kara Conrad and Tracey Suppo. Thanks to my continuity queen, Gwen Neff, and to the Wild Widows Series beta readers: Amy, Karina, Gina, Jennifer and Marianne.

To the team that supports me every day, I couldn't do this without you: Julie Cupp, Lisa Cafferty, Jean Mello, Nikki Haley and Ashley Lopez, as well as my family, Dan, Emily and Jake.

Thank you most of all to the readers who show up for every new book with so much love and enthusiasm. I appreciate you all more than you'll ever know!

Much love,

Marie

Contemporary Romances Available from Marie Force

The Wild Widows Series—a Fatal Series Spin-Off

Book 1: Someone Like You *(Roni & Derek)*

Book 2: Someone to Hold *(Iris & Gage)*

Book 3: Someone to Love *(Wynter & Adrian)*

Book 4: Someone to Watch Over Me *(Lexi & Tom)*

Book 5: Someone to Remember *(All Cast)*

Book 6: Someone to Save *(2027)*

The Gansett Island Series*

Book 1: Maid for Love *(Mac & Maddie)*

Book 2: Fool for Love *(Joe & Janey)*

Book 3: Ready for Love *(Luke & Sydney)*

Book 4: Falling for Love *(Grant & Stephanie)*

Book 5: Hoping for Love *(Evan & Grace)*

Book 6: Season for Love *(Owen & Laura)*

Book 7: Longing for Love *(Blaine & Tiffany)*

Book 8: Waiting for Love *(Adam & Abby)*

Book 9: Time for Love *(David & Daisy)*

Book 10: Meant for Love *(Jenny & Alex)*

Book 10.5: Chance for Love, *A Gansett Island Novella (Jared & Lizzie)*

Book 11: Gansett After Dark *(Owen & Laura)*

Book 12: Kisses After Dark *(Shane & Katie)*

Book 13: Love After Dark *(Paul & Hope)*

Book 14: Celebration After Dark *(Big Mac & Linda)*

Book 15: Desire After Dark *(Slim & Erin)*

Book 16: Light After Dark *(Mallory & Quinn)*

Book 17: Victoria & Shannon (Episode 1)

Book 18: Kevin & Chelsea (Episode 2)

A Gansett Island Christmas Novella *(Appears in Mine After Dark)*

Book 19: Mine After Dark *(Riley & Nikki)*

Book 20: Yours After Dark *(Finn & Chloe)*

Book 21: Trouble After Dark *(Deacon & Julia)*

Book 22: Rescue After Dark *(Mason & Jordan)*

Book 23: Blackout After Dark *(Full Cast)*

Book 24: Temptation After Dark *(Gigi & Cooper)*

Book 25: Resilience After Dark *(Jace & Cindy)*

Book 26: Hurricane After Dark *(Full Cast)*

Book 27: Renewal After Dark *(Duke & McKenzie)*

Book 28: Delivery After Dark *(Full Cast)*

Gansett Island Compendium, Volume 1, Books 1-14

Gansett Island Compendium, Volume 2, Books 15-28

Downeast

Dan & Kara: A Downeast Prequel

Homecoming: A Downeast Novel

The Quantum Series

Book 1: Virtuous *(Flynn & Natalie)*

Book 2: Valorous *(Flynn & Natalie)*

Book 3: Victorious *(Flynn & Natalie)*

Book 4: Rapturous *(Addie & Hayden)*

Book 5: Ravenous *(Jasper & Ellie)*

Book 6: Delirious *(Kristian & Aileen)*

Book 7: Outrageous *(Emmett & Leah)*

Book 8: Famous *(Marlowe & Sebastian)*

Book 9: Illustrious *(Max & Stella)*

Book 10: Momentous *(Olivia's story, coming 2026)*

Remington Family Law Series—A Quantum Series Spin-Off

Book 1: Acrimonious

Book 2: Contentious *(Sept. 2026)*

Book 3: Ferocious *(2027)*

The Miami Nights Series*

Book 1: How Much I Feel *(Carmen & Jason)*

Book 2: How Much I Care *(Maria & Austin)*

Book 3: How Much I Love *(Dee's story)*

Nochebuena, A Miami Nights Novella

Book 4: How Much I Want *(Nico & Sofia)*

Book 5: How Much I Need *(Milo & Gianna)*

The Green Mountain Series*

Book 1: All You Need Is Love *(Will & Cameron)*

Book 2: I Want to Hold Your Hand *(Nolan & Hannah)*

Book 3: I Saw Her Standing There *(Colton & Lucy)*

Book 4: And I Love Her *(Hunter & Megan)*

Novella: You'll Be Mine *(Will & Cam's Wedding)*

Book 5: It's Only Love *(Gavin & Ella)*

Book 6: Ain't She Sweet *(Tyler & Charlotte)*

The Butler, Vermont Series*

(Continuation of Green Mountain)

Book 1: Every Little Thing *(Grayson & Emma)*

Book 2: Can't Buy Me Love *(Mary & Patrick)*

Book 3: Here Comes the Sun (*Wade & Mia*)

Book 4: Till There Was You *(Lucas & Dani)*

Book 5: All My Loving *(Landon & Amanda)*

Book 6: Let It Be *(Lincoln & Molly)*

Book 7: Come Together *(Noah & Brianna)*

Book 8: Here, There & Everywhere *(Izzy & Cabot)*

Book 9: The Long and Winding Road *(Max & Lexi)*

The Treading Water Series*

Book 1: Treading Water *(Jack & Andy)*

Book 2: Marking Time *(Clare & Aidan)*

Book 3: Starting Over *(Brandon & Daphne)*

Book 4: Coming Home *(Reid & Kate)*

Book 5: Finding Forever *(Maggie & Brayden)*

Single Titles

In the Air Tonight

Five Years Gone

One Year Home

Sex Machine

Sex God

Georgia on My Mind

True North

The Fall

The Wreck

Love at First Flight

Everyone Loves a Hero

Line of Scrimmage

Romantic Suspense Novels Available from Marie Force

The First Family Series
Book 1: State of Affairs

Book 2: State of Grace

Book 3: State of the Union

Book 4: State of Shock

Book 5: State of Denial

Book 6: State of Bliss

Book 7: State of Suspense

Book 8: State of Alert

Book 9: State of Retribution

Book 10: State of Preservation

Book 11: State of Unrest

Book 12: State of Mind *(2026)*

Read Sam and Nick's earlier stories in the Fatal Series!

The Fatal Series*
One Night With You, *A Fatal Series Prequel Novella*

Book 1: Fatal Affair

Book 2: Fatal Justice

Book 3: Fatal Consequences

Book 3.5: Fatal Destiny, *the Wedding Novella*

Book 4: Fatal Flaw

Book 5: Fatal Deception

Book 6: Fatal Mistake

Book 7: Fatal Jeopardy

Book 8: Fatal Scandal

Book 9: Fatal Frenzy

Book 10: Fatal Identity

Book 11: Fatal Threat

Book 12: Fatal Chaos

Book 13: Fatal Invasion

Book 14: Fatal Reckoning

Book 15: Fatal Accusation

Book 16: Fatal Fraud

Fatal Series Compendium

Historical Romance Available from Marie Force

*The Gilded Series**
Book 1: Duchess by Deception
Book 2: Deceived by Desire

** Completed Series*

Marie Force is the *New York Times* best-selling author of 120 contemporary romance, romantic suspense and erotic romance novels. Her series include Remington Family Law, Fatal, First Family, Gansett Island, Butler Vermont, Quantum, Treading Water, Miami  Nights and Wild Widows. She has also written 12 single titles.

Her books have sold more than 15 million copies worldwide, have been translated into more than a dozen languages and have appeared on the *New York Times* bestseller list more than 30 times. She is also a *USA Today* and #1 *Wall Street Journal* bestseller, as well as a Spiegel bestseller in Germany.

Her goals in life are simple—to spend as much time as possible with her adult children, to keep writing books for as long as she possibly can and to never be on a flight that makes the news.

Join Marie's mailing list on her website at *marieforce.com* for news about new books and upcoming appearances in your area. Follow her on Facebook, at *www.Facebook.com/MarieForce Author* and Instagram *@marieforceauthor*. Contact Marie at *marie@marieforce.com*.